Lonely for the Future

JAMES T. FARRELL

Lonely for the Future

DOUBLEDAY & COMPANY, INC.

GARDEN CITY, NEW YORK

1966

*All of the characters in this book
are fictitious, and any resemblance
to actual persons, living or dead,
is purely coincidental.*

To My Friend Felix Kolodziej

Chapter One

George Raymond was on time, arriving to pick up Eddie Ryan at seven-thirty. It was the evening of the last Sunday in March, 1927. Eddie had suggested that they go to the Bohemian Forum which was located in the basement of the Kent Hotel, about a half block south of 57th Street on Cottage Grove Avenue.

George Raymond was twenty-two, a year younger than Eddie, but taller.

He and Eddie had first met in the fall of 1919, when they both wore short pants. It was an afternoon in November. Eddie had missed out in seeing the other kids around 58th Street and South Park Avenue. The kids at St. Michael's with whom he used to go around were giving him the ditch because of Robbie Waterman whose family was very rich. Robbie was supposed to be a fighter but he wasn't in Eddie's class. Once they had boxed with the gloves that Eddie's uncle, Dick Dunne, had bought him. Eddie had made Robbie quit in less than two minutes with a left jab to the right side of his stomach. If Robbie hadn't bent over, Eddie would have followed with a right to the jaw.

Robbie wouldn't let Eddie play in his backyard and that's where the bunch had gone. It wasn't his bunch any more.

On the afternoon that he'd met George, Eddie had run into Herbie Goldman who lived next door to him. Herbie's old man ran the grocery store on 58th Street between Calumet Avenue and the El station. They were walking in Washington Park with no particular aim in mind. Some kids were playing touch football on the withering grass. Eddie and Herbie walked across their field of play.

Suddenly a tall kid in an oxford gray suit yelled to them to get off the field. Eddie didn't like being ordered around; they weren't interrupting the play. He was no slouch with his fists and he wasn't going to let some strange kid give him orders. Eddie continued across the grass with a lack of concern. Herbie followed him.

The strange kid rushed up to Eddie and Herbie and asked what the hell they thought they were trying to pull, and to get off the knot of ground where he and the others were playing.

"Herbie," Eddie said, ignoring him, "didn't somebody tell us that Washington Park ain't private?"

"Yeh, something like that. I heard it said but I forget where or who it was who told me."

"You weren't told wrong, Herbie," Eddie said.

The other kids crowded around them. Eddie noticed a number of familiar faces, among them Charles Raymond who had been a couple of years behind him at St. Michael's. He and Charles had often walked home from school together.

Eddie, in his display of cold disregard for the strange kid, was enjoying himself.

"Who do you think you are?" the kid asked in anger.

"Me, myself, and I."

Eddie faced him. He was a bit taller but Eddie was not

afraid of him. He missed noticing the resemblance of features between Charles Raymond and this strange kid.

Suddenly, Eddie looked at Charles:

"Come on, Charles, let's you and I clean up this bunch."

The strange kid who had been growing angrier by the minute almost laughed. Charles Raymond smiled, "He's my brother. George."

The other kids smiled.

The tension was broken.

The strange kid opened up with a friendly smile:

"I'm George Raymond. You're a friend of my kid brother?"

"I'm Eddie Ryan."

George Raymond and Eddie Ryan shook hands. Eddie and Herbie got out of their way. They never had a fist fight.

II

George and Eddie became friendly, very friendly, but not friends. Eddie sensed that George liked him. He guessed, too, that if they had had a fight on that afternoon in the park, that he, Eddie, would not have had an easy time of it. He found out that George Raymond could fight, but not by having a fight with him.

He saw George from time to time. George was not well known around 58th Street. The Raymond family hadn't lived in the neighborhood very long. They came from Kickapoo, downstate in Illinois. They had lived first at 53rd and Prairie Avenue. George, the second oldest son, had gone to Immaculate Conception, the parochial school that Eddie had first attended. Then the Raymonds had moved to 57th Street and Prairie Avenue. But since he had already started at Immaculate Conception, George

continued to go there. His younger brother Charles went
to St. Michael's where he was two classes behind Eddie.
The two older Raymond children, Roger and Camille, had
run away from home. Roger had joined the Navy shortly
after the American declaration of war against Imperial
Germany in April, 1917. It was soon after Roger's enlist-
ment that the Raymonds had moved to Chicago. They
had been in Chicago less than three weeks when Camille,
the beautiful and beautifully plump, dark auburn-haired
daughter, had eloped with a thirty-year-old man, Roy Sidney. Roy was Jewish, beginning to get bald, and ran a
rather successful direct-by-mail advertising agency in the
Chicago Loop.

Eddie Ryan had heard this much about the Raymonds,
but he and the other kids in the neighborhood had little
curiosity or interest in family matters of the kids they
knew.

Eddie was still ashamed that his father was a working
man and went to work in workman's clothes, carrying his
lunch wrapped in newspaper.

A few times on Saturday mornings, Eddie took walks in
Washington Park with George and Charles. George usually
talked about Kickapoo, and he would tell about growing
up there, to the age of twelve. It was different for a kid
there than it was here in a city like Chicago, he'd say. He
could go hiking in the woods there, and there was fishing.
He used to fish a lot in the Catawba River. He had caught
a helluva lot of fish out of that river.

Eddie said that his Uncle Dick had taken him the summer before to the Silver Michigan Farm at Silver, Michigan, which was a little one-horse town. The Farm was on
the shores of Silver Lake. It wasn't much of a lake if you
compared it with Lake Michigan, but it was a big enough
lake, and was good fishing. He had gone fishing with his
Uncle Dick; one of them had always gotten some fish,

every day. Eddie had caught a bass that weighed over a pound. Of course they had caught bullheads and some of them had weighed more.

Bullhead or catfish were easy to catch, probably the easiest fish there were to catch, George Raymond had said.

Eddie Ryan said that he didn't know about that. He asked what about perch; he and his Uncle Dick had caught a lot of them in Silver Lake.

Yes, perch were easy fishing.

"And they're good eating, too," Eddie Ryan had said.

So is trout, George Raymond threw in, he used to catch plenty of them.

Eddie had never eaten trout. He liked fish, though, except for the bones. His Uncle Larry said that he was a lazy eater.

"What the hell!" George Raymond had said. He, too, would be a lazy eater, in fact, a lazy anything except, maybe, a lazy fighter. You couldn't be a lazy fighter and win.

They used to walk around the Washington Park lagoon. Listening to George talk about Kickapoo, Eddie got to wishing that he had grown up in a place like that. He remembered Tom Sawyer and Huck Finn.

It was autumn. The leaden skies were a gloomy sign of the approaching winter.

Eddie's life centered more and more around high school. George Raymond had already started working. He got a job paying fifty dollars a week with the telephone company, but Eddie never did learn exactly what George did to get this big salary. It was more than his father made. George had left home and was living in a rented room with a new buddy, Patsy O'Leary, who hailed from a Valley State farm.

George Raymond had begun to wear long pants. Most of the other kids Eddie's age, and even of George's age, were wearing them. Some of the fellows had become cake-eaters and were wearing bell bottoms.

Eddie was one of the last kids his age in the neighborhood to start wearing long pants. In the spring of 1920, his Uncle Dick gave him a suit which more or less fit him, and he wore it to Sunday Mass.

III

Eddie was slower than most of the other guys around 58th Street, the "punks" as the older fellows called them. George Raymond wasn't. He was one of the most daredevil; and would take almost any dare. One day he jumped into the muddy lagoon with a new tan summer suit on. Wet and muddy, he went to a party.

Whenever Eddie and George bumped into each other, they would be friendly. If Eddie had nothing to say, George could manage the conversation. He would cite some of his escapades, or he would make them up. He didn't have one line, he had many—as many lines as he needed, it seemed, with a few additional ones to spare. George Raymond was a "gee" with a line. Of course these lines were reserved for broads and he was admired for his technique in putting them over with the babes, the bims.

Then there were a couple of years during which George Raymond and Eddie Ryan had little contact with each other.

In the ways of the world—sex, dates, booze, pickups, high times, crap shooting, pool, parties, and poker—George Raymond was advancing by strides.

Eddie Ryan wasn't. He was shy and did not have dates. He didn't drink, he didn't smoke, he didn't gamble. He didn't run around with a bunch or go to the poolroom near

the 58th Street El station. He imagined that he loved
Gertrude Dawson still, as he had from the time they had
been at St. Michael's grammar school together. He daydreamed of her. He daydreamed of other girls too, but not
nearly as much as he did of Gertrude Dawson. He did well
in his studies and he was excited about sports. He hoped
that Gertrude Dawson would hear of him. He wanted to be
an athletic hero, or some kind of a hero, so that she would
hear of him. He envisioned his future through athletic
dreams, mainly of baseball. Sometimes he enjoyed himself
as a world's champion prize fighter.

Eddie spent a lot of time alone. He read sports pages,
magazines, and a few books. He read a serial in *The
Saturday Evening Post*, "The Drums of Jeopardy," by a
writer named Marquand, and he really liked it. He could
hardly wait for the weekly installments. He read Western
stories, some of them about a character named Hopalong
Cassidy. He read Burt L. Standish's books about Lefty
Locke and big league baseball, and stories by Sax Roh-
mer, Octavus Roy Cohen, and by a lot of other writers. He
remembered most of the names of the writers just the
same as he remembered nearly everything.

Eddie Ryan was considered a good kid, and an innocent
one who had not lost his cherry yet. Some of the other fellows talked bunk, pretending that they had lost theirs when
they hadn't.

George Raymond lost his cherry at seventeen. It was
with a pickup in Washington Park. He and the pickup
had walked around the lagoon to the wooded island and
George had put the blocks to her on a bench. She had no
idea that it was his first time and he didn't tell her. George
didn't think that it was as hot as it had been cracked up to
be—not the gash that he had picked up. She had seemed
to like it, plenty. Her name was Rosalind but she had said
about six times, maybe ten:

—Call me Rosy.

After this conquest, George felt that he now knew what he had known with commanding knowledge. That was when you gave it to a broad, you gave it to her hard and right until she moaned. Then she was under your power. Why she'd even be your slave if you wanted to make her one.

Power, more than pleasure, or pleasure from power—this was the feeling George Raymond had after it had happened.

The Washington Park boathouse was one of the places where the young fellows from the neighborhood often gathered. George Raymond found enough listeners to hear tell of how he had laid Rosy.

George's success raised hopes among the boys that they would be able to pick up Rosy or a girl like Rosy and take her over on the wooded island.

IV

All of this was during the first years of the 1920s.

These were happy years for George Raymond. He felt his oats by the bagfuls. He began to be much charmed with and by himself, and the sound of his own voice enchanted him, and sometimes amused him.

Even though he had lived in the neighborhood for just a few years and was a newcomer, he forged ahead as one of the leading spirits among the fellows of his own age. He was admired more than he was liked; but he had no great need to be liked. It was enough that he was noticed, and a little feared.

Many guys who thought that they were pals were merely accomplices in adolescence. Most of them were grammar school graduates and were already working. A few, like

Frankie Flannagan, had gone to high school for a year. Almost all of them could have gone to high school if they had wanted to.

George Raymond was considered smarter than the rest of them. There was more to his position than a quicker wit and a better mind, George Raymond used his mind, a lot. He could turn a simple act—like a group of fellows going to see a Mary Pickford movie—into intrigue. He found enjoyment in such intrigue and in manipulating and using the others. It tickled him; it was amusing. Also, it gave him a feeling of power.

All of this helped to make George Raymond important. He felt the need of being important. He was a Raymond, the Raymond of the Raymonds. He half-smiled when he thought like this because he didn't think he ought to carry anything too far. He didn't want to be a joke. And it was in part a fake, the idea of being a Raymond, as though the Raymonds had a coat of arms and were of nobility born. He probably did have remote and forgotten ancestors from the days when knighthood was in flower. He liked to say that wherever George Raymond was, knighthood was still in bloom and flower. Sometimes he'd chuckle at his own speculations, call them ruminations about knighthood and the phenomenon of being a Raymond.

George had started using words in such a manner—the phenomenon of being a Raymond. Few of the other fellows around the neighborhood, or the Greek's poolroom, where he circulated, would use such words or talk as he talked.

He felt superior to the other fellows and he would not apologize to them for anything that he did, let alone for the way he thought. He accepted his all-around superiority, and this included his idea of his fighting power. George Raymond did not dwell upon this; he merely took it for granted. It was a fact.

George did not know fear. He was fearless in the same way that he assumed his own superiority. It was something that was, and that was without alternative.

He was inclined to have his own way, and much of his energy went into seeing that he got it. When he did get it, he would often, not always, think that he had put something over on the other fellows.

George Raymond was fascinated by himself and his growing up, but he had some curiosity about the world as well. There had been surprises for him in his development, and in the easy way that he managed to shift to Chicago from Kickapoo, a small town of no account by Chicago standards, the kind of town described as a place where they take in the sidewalks at night, where nine o'clock is midnight.

This humor was as coarse and crass as a coon's ass down on the farm. It tickled him; and city slickers, some of them were, who pulled off this stale humor. Not even a jackass would haw-haw or hee-haw at such humor.

At first, when he was a kid, he would get sore. He had a quick temper, sometimes a violently quick temper. Soon, there were not too many of these jokes sprung on him. By the time he was in long pants, there were very few who remembered that George Raymond had come from Kickapoo.

Fighting was really George Raymond's speed. From time to time, strangers from other neighborhoods would wander out of bounds and attract notice in one way or another that got them a good clouting from George's bunch and other neighborhood kids.

George Raymond got the idea from these episodes of forming a group called The Smiling Sluggers. It was informal; there were no meetings, no by-laws, and no dues. He was the leader of the group. He took more pride in the name that he had thought up than in what The Smiling

Sluggers did, for they didn't do much fighting or slugging after they had taken on the name. But they got a kick out of talking about themselves, collectively, under their new name, "The Smiling Sluggers."

V

The early 1920s were good years for George Raymond and for many of the other young fellows. It was the Jazz Age. The appeal of jazz music and the sensuousness associated with it was a weekly, a bi-weekly, a tri-weekly, or nightly pleasure. The cake-eaters and flappers danced—close together—tightly pressed against one another in the abdominal regions. To George Raymond and the other fellows, this was called "socking it in" or "rubbing it in." Many of the fellows took to picking up girls in Washington Park or at movies or public dance halls or any place they could find them. This was called gash-hunting. They would brag about how much gash they got.

Dancing was the thing to do on a date. Girls in their teens became more free in their associations with young fellows than their mothers had been; far more than their grandmothers had been. Dates were unchaperoned. There was fun, or the hope of fun.

There was boozing. This was in violation of the law; and a fellow could feel that he was as lawless as men used to be in the Wild West, which had been enlivened in memory by moving pictures going back to Bronco Billy and in films featuring William S. Hart.

Not many years before, the fellows had played Cowboys and Indians. They had heard about and read about Buffalo Bill, Jesse James, and the James brothers, too. They had grown up on stories of men, real men, who had lived in adventurous times. These had been seed beds of ideas and notions and hopes of being a hero.

And there was sports, and the heroes of sports. Fighters, baseball players, football players, wrestlers, basketball players, and track men. These were another source of hope, ambition, or pseudo ambition.

You had to have what it takes to be an athlete and to become a hero. Few of the fellows believed that they had what it takes, except in their daydreams. But who could tell? Didn't the underdog win many times when he didn't have the chance of a snowball in Hell, or a whore in Heaven? If the right kind of a chance came along, dreams could come true.

The fellows of George Raymond's age had almost gotten the right kind of a chance. There had been the War. They had played War and they had dreamed War; but they had still been kids on November 11, 1918, when the War had ended. If the War had gone on long enough, they could have gotten into it by joining the colors. When the War was safely over, there was a certain disappointment in many of them. They might have become heroes. They might have captured a German machine-gun nest, single-handed, and nabbed a whole slew of Heinies, yelling "Kamerad," and who knows but that they could have pulled off the feat of capturing the Kaiser, Kaiser Bill.

These thoughts were only no-account ones and they couldn't come true.

Nonetheless, they left a residue of disappointment, a kind of anger and frustration.

It was easy sometimes to think that you could have gone through shots and shells, through mud holes and the hell of death, and not even be scratched; and you could have killed Germans like they were so many flies to fall dead on the floor. The Germans who were killed in their imaginations had no reality as persons, as men. They were no different than the tribe of Indians that they had imagined killing when they were kids with nothing to do, and were walking around pretending to be cowboys. *Pop, bing, bang, bam,* and another Redskin bit the dust.

The aching for heroism varied from one fellow to the next, but it was in most of those who were about the same age as George Raymond and Eddie Ryan. And George Raymond acted as though he were quieting this ache.

He fancied, rather than daydreamed, as he himself liked to phrase it. He didn't indulge in daydreams or pipe-dreams; for him, it was fancying, seeing vividly whatever he wanted to happen.

George Raymond was far less moody than Eddie Ryan. George was one of the most quick-tempered young fellows in the neighborhood. Eddie sometimes thought that he was, but he wasn't. He was patient and had already developed quite a degree of stoicism. With this stoicism and patience, there came moodiness. George was far too quick-tempered to be moody. If George got sore, he was likely to boil up, and then tee off on some guy. After smacking the guy in the puss, he'd cool off.

Anger was more effective than moodiness in the Raymond household, which was taut with temperament. In the past, George's flaring disposition had been influenced by the behavior of his sister. Hers was a more fiery, more melodramatic temperament. And, Camille Raymond, being female, could carry on with tears and sobs. A fellow couldn't. Neither Camille nor Roger would give George his way, no matter how he cut up or had tantrums. They didn't care if he burned up his brain with hot-headedness. They would give it back to him, especially Camille, even though she was more prone to line up with George against Roger than with Roger against George.

He had often heard his father, G. N. Raymond, say that

the honey of charm worked better than the vinegar of anger. And his mother, Suzanne Raymond, used to say that a smile charms and wins, but a growl annoys and loses.

George was beginning to discover this for himself. He smiled. He charmed. Even at home, his temper tantrums became less frequent. This was while the family still lived in Kickapoo, Illinois.

George was his mother's favorite. She was a small woman, but strong, with dark hair and intense, dark eyes. His father was a big man, a bit fleshy, and getting bald. The handsomeness of his youth seemed to be fading away into his big-boned features. He was a reserved, quiet man with a dignified appearance. He was also gentle; but there were times when his three sons and his daughter would be, like that poet said, "too much with him."

G. N. Raymond was a strict man and his quiet self-reserve made him seem even more strict than he was. He gave the impression of being a "strong, silent man."

Suzanne, his wife, knew him well. He was as honest as the day was long. He was true, true blue. Physically, he was strong, very strong; but this was not what was meant by a "strong, silent man." She knew this better than anyone else in the world. She knew what her G.N. was like.

This meant that she knew that G. N. Raymond would always concede to her; and his greatest source of strength was her, Suzanne Raymond. But she built up the idea of her husband as a strong, silent man—especially among their children.

All four of her children were bright and intelligent; temperamental and sensitive. They were not easily fooled, certainly not her son, George. They knew; and they would always go to her, not to their father.

Mrs. Raymond did not mind the flareups in their happy home. That is, she didn't mind them until she did mind them, and then the noise and confusion and the shouts would become too much. Whenever it got to this point, she would complain of a headache, of weakness, or of vertigo. Sometimes she would hint that she was afraid that she might be having a heart attack.

In these moments when she seemed so weak, Suzanne Raymond triumphed as the mistress of her own home, and a big home it was in Kickapoo.

And it wasn't all pretending. Sometimes when her children argued with each other and started to shout, she really did feel weak and really did believe that she could have a heart attack. She soon learned that by pretending to feel a weak spell coming on, she could have peace and quiet. She was proud of herself, proud that she had found a way to manage her temperamental children.

It was George who first spotted the twinkle in her dark eyes during one of her attacks. He didn't let on, not even when she was pretending to be on the verge of something horrible, all because of their scrapping; and he knew she was no more on the verge of anything than any of them were.

Mother thought that her little game was a secret; but he knew. And two people knowing a secret made it no secret.

Charles Raymond, who was two years younger than George, was always out of luck one way or the other. He was the baby, the kid, the kid brother, the baby brother. He could yell and he did yell. Likely as not the whole family would tell him to pipe down, to freeze his tongue, to be quiet.

Despite the Raymond shows, which they called their fights and squabbles, they were going along happy enough in Kickapoo.

Then it was 1917, and the United States of America declared war on Imperial Germany.

One morning, Roger was not at the breakfast table. It

was a school day and he should have been there. He was in
high school, a student at St. Hilary's, which was a boarding school as well as a day school, and took in pupils from
grammar school through the fourth year of college.

Mrs. Raymond asked about Roger. Mr. Raymond looked
at the empty place.

"What in the deuce does he think he's doing, playing a
game of some kind on us?" Mr. Raymond asked. Then he
paused. He sat up straight and waited in silence for Roger
to come down and take his place at the table. Roger did
not appear. Mrs. Raymond called out to him to come to
breakfast now. As his mother did this, George Raymond
guessed what had happened.

In another moment or so, Charles shot away from the
table to look for his brother. George got up and sauntered
out of the room.

Camille, his mother and father—all followed George out
of the dining room. There were a few seconds of suspense,
almost fear. Suddenly Charles yelled excitedly from
Roger's room up on the second floor.

"Mother! Father! Mother!"

They all hurried to the stairs. Charles was tearing out
of Roger's room, running toward the stairway.

"Slow down. You aren't going to a fire."

Charles sprang down the stairs so fast that he lost his
balance and plunged face forward to the bottom.

George, seeing how excited Charles had been when he
came out of Roger's room, had anticipated what might
happen. He tried to reach the bottom of the stairway in
time to catch Charles, or at least break the fall if he should
fall.

"Father! Mother!" Charles yelled again. He had a slip
of white paper in his hand. Before he could tell them anything, he plunged forward, and landed head-first at the bottom of the stairs. George didn't reach him in time.

They all heard the thud when his face hit the wooden floor. He let out a shriek the instant it happened.

Mrs. Raymond was stunned. Then, she sprang forward, her arms outstretched, and bent down to her youngest child. Charles was bleeding. The note had fallen to the floor but no one picked it up. They were all concerned about Charles. Mrs. Raymond gently sponged his face and checked for broken bones. There didn't seem to be any, although he had a bloody nose and a large lump on his forehead. However, Charles was frightened and his face was pale. Mrs. Raymond said that maybe if he would lie down, he could sleep. She promised to sit with him a while.

Her husband hovered helplessly nearby.

George walked over and picked up the note that had fallen from Charles' hand. It was from Roger. He wrote that he had left home to join the armed forces because America was at war. George handed the note to his father. Mr. Raymond read the note but he said nothing to George who stood, waiting, to hear what his old man would say, how he would take it. But Mr. Raymond said nothing. His lips quivered for an instant.

George told Camille, and she burst out: "Good for Roger!"

George smiled. He approved, but with envy. If there was going to be a hero in the Raymond family, he wanted it to be him, George Raymond, not Roger. His time would come; he was just a kid twelve years old; but kids grow up, and he, more than any of the others, would be The Raymond.

Mr. Raymond waited until his wife was free. He said something to her, quietly, and they went upstairs to their bedroom. They talked behind the closed door in lowered voices. It had become a habit for them to speak in almost a whisper when they discussed adult matters and what they believed pertained privately to them.

G.N. was proud that his oldest son was brave and ready
to fight for his country, and for the country of their ancestors. But he was shaken, and he shadowed back in his own
reserve because he didn't want Suzanne to know this. Even
after years of marriage, he was shy, just as he had been
when he was a young fellow.

He was caught unaware, and he was under the strain
of contradictory feelings. In the main, he was proud of
Roger, but he was worried, too. Suppose his son was killed.
He was hurt that Roger hadn't consulted him; a son should
talk such matters over with his father. His oldest son had
ignored him, had not even come to him for a word, and
on such a matter. He felt hurt.

"He didn't tell us, he didn't say a word. He could have
said something."

"But, G.N., darling, he was probably afraid that we'd
try to stop him."

"But he should have known it would be all right. I'm an
American, it's my country, too."

"I'd have tried to talk some sense into his head," Suzanne had said with spirited firmness.

"I was young once myself."

With a teasing, affectionate smile, Suzanne Raymond
had said, "I know you were, dear man."

G.N. did not blush but he imagined that he was blush-
ing. Suzanne Raymond remarked that Roger would write
to them, she was certain that he would.

"We'll pray to God to protect him," Suzanne said with a
touch of sorrow.

Mr. Raymond was afraid that she would break into tears.

They knelt by their testered bed, and with clasped hands,
they looked to a picture of Jesus when young, like a boy,
and they prayed for the safety of their firstborn, Roger
Raymond, who had run away from home to fight in de-

fense of his country in war. They prayed to God and to the Virgin Mary.

Then they came out of the room and went downstairs. Camille and George had started to get ready for school.

"I'll forego that extra cup of coffee, Suzanne. I have to be off."

"Yes, dear."

"Children, hurry up or you'll be late for school."

There were quick movements upstairs.

G.N. left the kitchen and started upstairs again. He needed to put on a stiff white collar and tie, and put on his cuff links. His shoes squeaked on the stairs.

Mrs. Raymond set to her day's work. She began by clearing the table of dishes to be washed. She paused a moment to look out the window.

Oh, such a bright, sunny April day. Spring.

VI

Shortly after Roger had run away from home, the Raymonds moved to Chicago. Roger had joined the Navy and was stationed at the Great Lakes Training Station near Chicago.

The family had not yet become accustomed to Roger's absence when, on her seventeenth birthday, Camille eloped with Roy Sidney. This caused even more excitement, commotion, and resentment than Roger's flight. Camille was a girl. G.N. was upset; he felt himself flouted, ignored, and disregarded like an old fogey.

And she had eloped with a Jew, a Jew almost fifteen years her senior. This Sidney made more money than G.N., who was trying to recoup as a Chicago real estate man.

Camille's desertion was a painful repudiation of him. That was what G.N. felt. He suffered visibly, but mostly in silence. Alone with Suzanne, he would tell her something of how he felt.

—They can't wait to leave us. Is there something wrong with us? Are we poison?

—They're young, and they have our temperaments.

—You told your father. You didn't run off, or sneak off to do anything.

—Thank God that she married him. She's a girl. At least they're married.

—I hope so.

—She said so in her telegram.

—To a Jew.

—I know, but he's not poor; he'll be able to take care of her comfortably.

—So can we.

—I agree with you, G.N., darling, but I try to look at the bright side if there is a bright side.

Suzanne didn't speak for a moment.

—I'm her mother and she didn't come to me or say a word to me.

—And I'm her father.

They both seemed to be out of words but not out of thoughts, nor of feelings.

—She had a good home, G.N. said.

It sounded like a lament.

—Yes, answered Suzanne in a low voice, almost a whisper.

G.N. could see that Suzanne was nearly crushed, as he was. All of those years of work, all of their ups and downs, their struggles and worries, what for? Two of their four children had run away. The thought was disheartening and Suzanne's sadness added to this.

G.N. sighed. There was a bottom to disheartenment. It was called Despair. He was near despair.

It was through resolution that he snapped his mind up.

A sadness of broken hopes, broken sentiments, broken feelings remained; but he refused to allow himself to become despaired.

—All we can do is hope for the best.

G.N. and Suzanne were in their nineteenth year of marriage; and they had devoted many of these years to hoping.

Now they were hoping in Chicago.

VII

G. N. Raymond had saved up about four hundred dollars and Suzanne had a dowry of a thousand dollars. They rented a large wooden house with extra rooms for the children who were to come. Suzanne fixed it up, bringing some of her family furniture and picking out new pieces at Kane's Furniture Store on Fox Street, the main street in Kickapoo.

They were a handsome, healthy-looking couple. Wherever they went, they were greeted by smiles, good wishes and neighborly warmth. Everyone said that there couldn't be two young people more suited to one another. This marriage just went to prove that love and happiness could be real things, true things, when the right young people could find it.

G.N. was told that he couldn't have found a better girl if he'd looked far and wide, all the way to St. Louis and Chicago and points beyond. He was a lucky young fellow, yes he was.

G.N. believed this. Their first days after the honeymoon in Chicago were wonderful. There was an intensity of passion that seemed both fierce and tender, calm and violent. There were moments when they wondered in bewilderment how people could ever be unhappy if they were in love and married.

Suzanne's family believed that she was too good for G.N.

He should be grateful for what he got and should go on to prove that he was worthy of his good fortune. Suzanne could easily have done better, and G.N. and all the Raymonds may as well be apprised of the fact. Not that there was anything wrong with G. N. Raymond himself, not at all, there was no objection to him, especially since Suzanne loved him, with all of the soul of a pure and lovely girl of such fine ancestry. But the Raymonds, generally, were a horse of another color, that's all one meant, and goodness, yes, one certainly wished the two young people happiness and success, and lots and lots of it.

G.N. and Suzanne had both graduated from parochial grammar school. G.N. had gone to work at fifteen with his father who had a carriage place with a blacksmith shop next door. G.N. had learned to keep books and do many other things but he didn't want to spend his entire life doing these. He wanted to strike out on his own and let his brother stay on in the family business.

For a while, he had tinkered about, hoping to invent something and become known all over America; but this had come to nothing.

G.N. was big for his age and often described as being strong as an ox. A couple of his friends said that he ought to become a prize fighter or a wrestler. G.N. daydreamed of this and would sometimes imagine himself becoming the boxing champion of the world. When Jim Corbett knocked out John L. Sullivan in New Orleans, G.N.'s dreams were spurred. He read about "Gentleman Jim" and the fight in the newspapers. He was thrilled by Corbett's victory, a victory of brains over brawn. He was growing up strong and he'd have plenty of brawn. He had no doubt about this but he was an advocate of brains over brawn; and if he had both brains and brawn, why couldn't he do what Corbett had done? There could be other champions of the world besides the Irish. He would uphold the honor of his French ancestry.

Imagine him getting off the train, driving home in a carriage after winning the World Championship, and being met by the town band, and Suzanne waiting for him with love, tenderness and admiration in her eyes. He would give her the champion's belt right there at the station, in front of the whole world, while the band was playing.

Being quite gentle, G.N. did not pick fights; and because of his strength and his size, there were few who would have dared to start a fight with him. And if he didn't fight, how could he become a great pugilist? He didn't know how to go about a career which would enable him to knock the block off "Gentleman Jim" Corbett; and a little later, to solar plexus the stuffing out of Ruby Bob Fitzsimmons instead of bothering to trim Corbett, since Fitzsimmons had already done that and had become the heavyweight Champion of the World.

If he went to St. Louis, or better still, to Chicago, he could find a way to be taught and gradually to get started on a pugilistic career. He had the urge to try out, to do some learning for himself. He wanted to fight, not out of meanness or the desire to hurt some other fellow, but for education. Call it education or practice, he'd have to get some in before he could be anywhere near perfect. And, G.N. reasoned, a world champion should be somewhere close to perfect. He did some practicing in the barn and in his room, though not nearly enough to attain his ideal of perfection of form. When he shadow-boxed, he became impatient with practice. He'd slug the air for a few minutes and quit.

One Sunday afternoon, after he had stopped shadow-boxing, G.N. decided that he must either get real practice or quit altogether, as far as thinking about a future in pugilism was concerned.

There were other careers.

On that particular afternoon, he went to see Suzanne. He was in a fretting mood. They took a walk. He tried not to fret, but he did, nevertheless. He felt big and awkward beside Suzanne, who was so dainty and small beside him. Gad she was beautiful, by golly she was, the most beautiful girl in town. He must seem clumsy as an ox or a hippopotamus beside her. He didn't quite feel like that, not exactly, but he felt damned awkward. This awkwardness was not just because of his physical size; it was in the mind, as people often said everything was in the mind, or many things were, if not everything. He felt oafish, and unworthy of Suzanne. He had to make himself worthy of her by doing something big and outstanding. He had to make his name important enough in the world so that she'd be proud of it when he gave it to her at the altar of St. Boniface's wooden church.

They walked down by the river. The beauty of the day, and of the river and trees and sky, and the beauty of Suzanne was the beauty of the world. This gave him the feeling of a dream full of electricity that almost made him tingle. He was afraid that he was being foolish, so foolish that he might be a damned fool. These thoughts and feelings were like poetry. They were the everyday feelings of someone who should be a moody man. Did anyone in Kickapoo talk the way he had just been thinking? A big fellow like him should be strong and be able to chew his tobacco with the best of them instead of thinking of the beautiful sunshine falling on the running water of the river.

"You're very silent today," Suzanne teased.

"Yes," he said, just above a mumble.

He hoped that she'd think of him as one who was growing up to be a strong, silent man.

"I know, George, you aren't the biggest talker in town."

"Some of them that are big talkers will never be big in any other way, that's my humble opinion."

"You don't have to be a big talker to tell me if you like my new dress, George."

The blood rushed to his head. He could have fallen on his tail in front of her and the whole town and he wouldn't have felt any more ridiculous.

"You're the prettiest girl in town," G.N. said, in shy confusion.

He'd wanted to say "most beautiful" not "prettiest"; and "in the world" rather than "in town." The right words resisted coming out; he couldn't speak them; he intended to use them but left them as mere good intentions paving his inner feeling of love.

"Is that all you can tell me, George?"

G.N. wished that he could say something.

"I guess I'm too silent," he said.

"Silence is not the most flattering compliment a girl can receive in a new Sunday dress."

"No, but silence is golden."

"Don't keep too much gold to yourself, George," she tossed back at him and the sound of her voice was as teasing as her eyes.

"I was fancying myself a strong, silent man," he confessed with a brief suggestion of a smile.

"You should be strong, but sometimes with broken silence."

"You're so beautiful, Suzanne."

"I'm beautiful if you think so."

"Think so! Why . . ."

He paused in a struggle for words.

Suzanne was carried away with bubbling, singing laughter which so infected G.N. that he was soon bent over in chortling laughter himself, which released all of his solemn shyness.

They gazed at one another with tears in their eyes from their laughing. She seemed to grow toward him and into his arms and they kissed with long, loving, and hungry passion under an oak tree, while the wind shook the broad old branches as though in hurried playfulness. Suzanne was awakened in every nerve with his lips on hers, his tongue in her mouth, his arms almost crushing her, and his big, strong body tense and hard against her. She was wild with all of the life of the world in her body and in her; and she was weak with a heat like the sun burning in her with a fire of pain. She was nothing but pulsations and passion and gasping breath and fluttering.

"Oh, George!" Suzanne said.

They walked home on that Sunday afternoon as silent as the stretching shadows. They understood their silence as little as they did the shadows. After such clinging and hungering kisses, after all of her was in his arms and her mouth had been open to his tongue, and after she had held him and the pressure of all his strength, and had all but abandoned herself to him, he saw himself as less awkward, less like any other young fellow in town.

The irrepressible beam on his face was the outward glow of a newly awakened strength within him. He walked with more than himself, he walked with love. They were young and their passion for each other seemed to them the hunger of the world.

They were married soon after that Sunday afternoon, for Suzanne could no more have remained a virgin than the dark night could have held back the morning.

George Norman still looked for a fight but found none. He was so full of the conquering of his conquered heart that he had no more need to practice, or to do anything but to be with Suzanne. He could beat his weight in wild cats all the livelong day.

G.N. fretted, though, even in the happiness of his marriage. He wanted to get to the top of the heap. He sought a road for fast travel toward fame and fortune. He wanted to be a big man and a rich one; and he wanted this all the more once he was married. Instead of settling down with marriage, he began to grow dissatisfied with himself. A new century was coming. He was going to be a man of that new century, a man of the twentieth century. Or was he? The twentieth century wouldn't come and fall into his lap, nor would it be a Santa Claus coming down the chimney to leave him gifts.

He tried to keep his ambitions at bay, or even put them out of his mind. The future need not be a cause for worry. Gradually, he and Suzanne could become more prosperous, saving here and there, and in time, they could be well enough off to be among the leading citizens of town.

He had serious responsibilities to meet and he had become a man; he must act like one.

And there he was, back again, pitching horseshoes which he did a few evenings a week. He liked the game and he was good; one of the best around his neck of the woods. Pitching horseshoes took his mind off his dissatisfactions and his ideas of becoming a big man.

There were times that G.N. was convinced that his life was a rich one, and there was no young man more fortunate than he was. Then he'd worry; he wanted to rip up stakes and make a fresh, clean start.

He knew he ought to talk it over with Suzanne but he didn't; he wanted her to think that he was a man capable of big things because he could take strong and bold action.

Sometimes Suzanne would tell him that he was quiet, and he would smile with a kind of shyness that she loved, and her dark eyes would twinkle in her pretty and intelligent face. She'd tease him and he'd become confused in embarrassment and pleasure. G.N. liked her teasing.

Suzanne did get a confession out of G.N.—he admitted

that he was worried. He ought to be advancing more in life and making more money and a name for himself—it would all be for her. For this, Suzanne gave him laughing forgiveness. She loved him, as he was, and she was as happy as she could be, just the way they were. She didn't know how she could be happier and he was a goose, a silly goose, and a great big boy, and she loved him, loved him dearly, more dearly than anyone in the world.

G.N. accepted her affectionate words, almost as absolution, but he was not released from worry about their future. With such faith in him, such loving tenderness for him, shouldn't he strive all the harder? He'd ask himself questions like this. He must be able to lay as much of the world as he could at her feet. It was his duty, his debt of honor, to be a success in life, or at least to make the utmost try, not to spare himself in the battle.

G.N. tried. He tried many things. Shortly after his talk with Suzanne, he thought that, maybe, he could get his first start as a salesman. That would provide him with experience, and through experience, he could learn more of psychology. He'd meet different types of men, in different towns and cities. He'd see more of the world, and match wits with successful businessmen, because his theory was that selling was a game, a matching of wits. There was money to be made in selling.

Since marrying Suzanne, he had given plenty of thought to his chances of success in different possible lines. Selling was the most promising of any that he could figure out, unless he tried prize fighting or wrestling. And these would constitute a risk. The chances weren't nearly as good as in selling if you figured it right. He didn't have much education but he was as intelligent as the next one and he read a newspaper every day, sometimes a paper from Chicago, or St. Louis, or Springfield, the state capital. He had an idea of what was going on in the world, a better idea than

many of the others in town had, even the older men. And
he read magazines, too, and sometimes a book. He looked
at advertisements and he thought about products and styles
and watched for news or signs of anything new. You never
could tell when and where you'd hit upon something that
was your opportunity for fame and fortune. And he was
beginning to feel, more and more, that he was about to
hit upon G. N. Raymond's little key to all of that.

VIII

One spring night as Suzanne and G.N. sat on the porch,
Suzanne told him that she was going to have a baby. She
was bright with happiness. G.N. wanted to react as he
should, to match her joy with his own. But he couldn't.
He wasn't accustomed to quick and joyful responses and
expressions. He wasn't a young man who could meet surprises and change with fluency of expression. All he said
was:

"Good."

Suzanne knew her husband's traits. She understood; and
more than tolerated his reserve and formal dignity. She
enjoyed them. She knew that he was as decent as decency
itself, and kind, loving, tender, and responsible. He would
give his life for her if he were called upon to do so. She
knew this.

But the announcement of their first baby was a big
event.

"Good," he said again; it was all he could say. However,
it was not all that he meant, or felt. What he felt was
submerged and he had but inklings of it. The notion of
strength and silence had started to take with him.

Suzanne knew this about her young husband and she
was affectionately amused by it. She was the conqueror of

his reserve. She, and she alone, could crush this reserve and release the wild strength of his passion. She was the mistress of his body and his soul and she knew this fact well. Sex was no casual experience, no purely physiological function for Suzanne. It was the expression, the ecstasy, and the realization of love. It was a sacrifice of herself and a joy so intense that she would sometimes think that she was dying, and wanting to die, just like that. Theirs was a union blessed by God and made sacred. And its end and purpose was God's end; and for the first time, she was going to serve God's purpose. She was going to give birth to a human being with a soul. She was exalted with happiness, and she was afraid. She wanted him to say more, but she didn't know what she wanted him to say. She wanted him to say more than the moon could say if the moon had tongue, more than the sun, the spring, trees, more than the bubbling river, more than she knew.

Suzanne waited a second or two, filling up with pain and anger. G.N. said no more, and her pain found outlet in tears. Since they had been married, almost two years earlier, they had not had a serious quarrel. On one or two occasions when Suzanne had become temperamental or cross, G.N. had conceded to her wishes.

Suzanne wanted to get mad at G.N. but she didn't know why except that he was a man and she was a woman. She never had gotten mad the way she wanted to, and she knew that now she was going to get furious and that she would cry. She had to, to let go, for reasons she didn't even know. She was a woman, a woman who was going to have her first baby, and she had to feel something different from what she had ever felt before in her whole life.

She remembered all that she had heard of men, of going down into the valley of the shadow of death, of the agony of women giving birth, of men not understanding a woman and woman's lot, of the helplessness of men when a woman's great hour came and the pain tore her insides apart, and the shadow of death hovered over her bed of agony and blood. All this became like a sudden store of feeling within her and she could not control herself. She did not feel real anger or hatred against G.N.; she loved him, and he was good and kind, strong and tender, and gave her happiness. She was angry with all she had heard, and her feelings surprised her as much as they surprised poor G.N.

Suzanne broke into sobs and told G.N. that he was mean and cold and had no feeling. She was voicing all of the years of her growing up, her innocence, her girlhood, and all of her ideas of being a woman. The storm of womanhood broke within her and she let loose a cloudburst of tears. Her storm was like pelting rain, lightning and thunder. She was shaking inside.

G.N. sat in mute astonishment. His lips quivered. He was as dumfounded and helpless as he would be if the world ended. In his stunned condition, it was the same as if the world had ended.

He turned to speak but he was mute. His lips trembled. He wanted to reach out his hand to touch and caress her. He didn't; he couldn't.

Suzanne was weeping somewhat convulsively, catching her breath and emitting sobs which sounded acute with anguish.

"Suzanne," G.N. said very softly.

"Oh, I could die, I could . . ."

"You won't die," G.N. told her very quickly and very, very tenderly.

She rose and rushed into the house, leaving the echo of a broken-hearted wail behind her.

G.N. sat for a moment, gathering his thoughts. He regained his calmness but it was a melancholy calm. He feared that he might be whistling in the dark; he might have lost what was most precious to him. He couldn't lose it. He couldn't. He heard Suzanne's sobs inside and he heard the chirping of the crickets and grasshoppers. For a moment more, he sat.

Then he rose and went in to Suzanne. She had flung herself on the bed, waiting for him to come and comfort her. She felt foolish. She was ashamed of herself, more than she had ever been in her whole life. She cried, more quietly now. She was waiting for her dear G.N.

And he came.

They made up and they knew how much they loved one another and it was a love mixed with reverence.

And when the child was born, he was named Roger.

And G.N. was melancholy for a youth that was gone, a wind blown across a prairie, a shadow that had swept over a field. Years had slid into a darkened well, and his strength had, little by little, been lost, his youth—gone, like the hair on his head. But the memory of youth didn't blow away as did youth itself. And the memory had the tincture of sadness.

And for G.N. those best years had gone by without his achieving all the victories that he had been so determined to win.

G.N. had tried many things. He had sold six or seven products, from insurance to bicycles. He had gone into real estate. He had even tried prize fighting and had won five fights before being knocked out in Moline, Illinois. He had been sheriff for one term. He had tried acting; and for a short time, running a grocery store.

Three more children had come. Camille, George, and Charles.

And it was after Roger had run away from home to join the colors that G.N. and Suzanne moved from Kickapoo to Chicago with their three other children.

IX

Camille's elopement just a few weeks after their move to Chicago saddened her parents. It was as though their two oldest children had struck them with blows right square at the heart.

But one must go on. So said Suzanne Raymond many times, just as her mother before her in Kickapoo had said many times. They would just have to accept the fact that both their children had committed perfectly natural and not unprecedented acts. They could have done what they did differently, but then their children weren't children any more. They had taken on the prerogatives of adults. They were living grown-up lives; Roger as a sailor, Camille as a wife. Both had found places in life before their eighteenth birthdays.

—If only he wasn't a Jew, G.N. would comment.

—Jew or not, he's her legal husband and he has a pile of money. Maybe he's a good Jew.

Suzanne was on the telephone with her daughter the minute that Camille had returned from her honeymoon in California.

Camille lived on Lincoln Park West. It was a good address and Camille's husband must be paying a pretty penny in rent. Suzanne didn't tell G.N. right away that she had spoken with Camille; but he knew from the way that she talked that she must have found out something and that things were all right.

—But it would be better if he were a Gentile.

Suzanne wished this but she would leave well enough alone, or in this case, bad enough.

As time wore on, Suzanne Raymond forgot her disappointment. She still had George, and he was her favorite.

And then there was Charles, and G.N. himself, who was only a grown-up boy—so she had her three boys.

In the fall of 1917, not too long after he'd finished boot training, Roger stopped writing for a while. They didn't know where he was. Every time the doorbell rang, Suzanne dreaded to answer it, it could be a notice about Roger. Oh, it was an awful feeling. She wouldn't think of telling poor G.N. But it wasn't necessary to tell G.N. He had similar feelings, and he wouldn't think of telling Suzanne. He would hope for the best.

She prayed to God that He wouldn't allow anything to happen to her son.

Thank heavens, she did have her family. And that George, what a real boy he was. He could charm the birds right out of the trees, that one could. She'd even take small change out of G.N.'s pocket and give it to George. It wasn't exactly stealing, after all, he was her husband. He'd probably give it to her if she asked him, but she knew that he thought she was spoiling George.

—Good old mother, thought George.

X

They heard from Roger. He had been transferred to Norfolk, Virginia.

And then, Camille became pregnant.

In due time, she had a healthy seven and a half pound baby, whom they named Wayne. G.N. was a smiling grandfather. It was Suzanne who first thought of baptism. She spoke to Camille and told her that G.N. was adamant about this. He did become adamant later when Suzanne brought it to his mind. Roy Sidney didn't care. It didn't matter to him. So the baby was baptized at the Holy Name Cathedral.

When the war ended, a burden was removed from the hearts of Suzanne and G.N. Roger was out of danger of being killed by the Germans. He had seen no action.

Roger wanted, at least, to see the world. Instead of going home, he signed up to ship out on a freighter going to Liverpool.

The months were passing along, and the Raymond family settled down in a smaller apartment at 57th and Prairie.

It was shortly after this that Eddie Ryan met George Raymond in the park playing touch football, when they almost had a fight.

Chapter Two

I

It was just a few minutes before eight on that Sunday night in March, 1927 when Eddie Ryan and George Raymond entered the 58th Street entrance of Washington Park on their way to the Bohemian Forum.

The sky was vast over the park. The night seemed bigger and brighter than it had a moment ago. The park was a place of shadows and silhouettes on which the moon and stars dropped falling shimmers of silvered light.

"Shadows, silhouettes and falling shimmers," Eddie said.

"And the trees black against the night."

"Yes, black against the night."

"Like philosophers and Buddhas," George observed.

They walked toward the boathouse on a path familiar to both of them. The sound of their shoes crunching gravel seemed loud in the vast still night. The park was deserted except for an occasional automobile on the driveway.

George nodded toward an open space on the right.

"That's where I fought Big Boots."

"Yeh," Eddie replied.

He had not seen the fight but he had heard about it. He didn't want to hear about it again now. He was full of the night, full of expectations, full of himself.

"Hell, I rather liked Big Boots." George gave a laugh.

"Yeh, so did I."

They fell into the silence of their own thoughts under the spell of the misty March night. The far space of the park widened their view of the sky. It was loud with stars. The world was celebrating itself with all the familiar luster of the stars and the familiar, yet never-familiar moon.

Eddie felt wanting, hungry, and yearning. All of his life was but a moment of the sky.

Would he find what he was looking for at the Bohemian Forum?

Eddie Ryan had dropped out of classes at the University of Chicago. He had decided during the week's vacation between winter and spring quarters. The decision had been coming since January; but he had made it in an instant. It was in the morning, on March 16. He was at work, Station 207, National Oil Company of Illinois, he thought in self-mockery.

He was going to be a writer or he would go to Hell on an empty stomach, like a bum. It was after he had decided that he had seen Professor Lyman who had tried weakly to convince him that he was making a mistake. He had taken Lyman's course during the last quarter. Lyman had told them all to write as much as they wanted.

Eddie had.

He had submitted hundreds of pages of manuscript to Lyman.

For the first time in his life, he was expressing his feelings and his emotions.

II

Eddie felt anger and pity for his family and he wanted to
write about them and about himself. He wanted to write
about the neighborhoods in which he had lived, about the
boys he had known. He wanted to write about everything.
He had begun to try but his efforts were immature. He
didn't write systematically. At home, he was not commu-
nicative and saw his family as people betrayed by all that
they had believed. Tragedy seemed to be impending for
them and to be hanging over their heads. The world for
him was beyond Chicago and what he had already known
and seen and lived and felt. Many times he would dream
of all the places he would see, the things he would do. He
thought of New York.

When his friend Peter Moore had told him about the
Bohemian Forum, he had hoped that he would meet people there who would be interested in books and in writing
and in ideas. When he had mentioned the Forum to
George Raymond, George had said he was "game" to go.

"It was a good idea of yours, Eddie, suggesting this joint.
The Bohemian Forum—isn't that what it's called?"

"Yeh, I thought there might be something interesting,
that's all," Eddie said.

They passed the deserted boathouse. Its lights were dim
with a pathetic dreariness. There was loneliness. The boathouse was lonely. But tonight, he, Eddie Ryan, didn't feel
lonely. He was with his friend George Raymond. They
were on their way, maybe, to some kind of adventure, some
special happening, some surprise. He didn't feel lonely but
he did have a jab, a quick thrust of loneliness. He had
been lonely many times and he would be again. The boathouse with its dim lighting reminded him of this.

Eddie stared at the stars. He strained to put his feelings into words. The effort was relieving, yet it was a failure—he couldn't capture the beauty of the night with words of equal beauty.

"Look at the trees, philosophers of the night," George Raymond said, pointing to the far-off trees with their black trunks and bare branches.

"Yeh," answered Eddie.

"Like brooding Buddhas," George said.

"Uh-huh," muttered Eddie.

"Philosophers brooding darkly, dark as the philosophy of Schopenhauer," George said.

Eddie mumbled again.

His mind was on the Bohemian Forum, on what might happen there, on what he hoped would happen there. He hoped that there would be a girl, a special girl, the wanted girl at the center of his hopes.

"Maybe you'll get material for a story at the Forum, Eddie."

"Yeh."

III

Eddie remembered the hawk-nosed prostitute at the 35th Street El station. He had written about her for Professor Lyman's course at the University.

One night, after locking up the station at eight o'clock, as usual, he couldn't stand it any longer. He felt he couldn't go on—getting up at 6:45 A.M., shaving, washing, dressing, eating the breakfast that his grandmother cooked for him, meeting Peter Moore on the sidewalk below and walking across Washington Park with him to attend his three classes on campus. They were usually eight, nine, and ten o'clock classes. Then, he'd either go back home, study a little, perhaps have a bite to eat, or else go to Harper Library on campus, or very rarely, to the campus Coffee Shop, then get to 35th and Morgan to relieve his partner, Timmy Toomey, who had been born in Dublin and had been a policeman there before he had come out to America.

He'd work at the station and study every spare moment even though his supervisors had warned him about reading on the job. At eight o'clock, he'd close up, take a 35th Street trolley car to the 35th Street elevated station. On the car, he'd read a novel. At 35th Street, he'd get on a southbound Jackson Park or Englewood local train and continue reading. He'd get off the train at 58th Street. Sometimes he'd stop in the Greek's restaurant and have coffee and pie and talk with his friend, Gus, a Greek language poet. They'd talk of Plato or Socrates, Nietzsche or Walt Whitman, modern Greece or classical Greece, Heine, Goethe, Shelley, Lord Byron, modern America, war. If he didn't stop to see Gus, he'd go straight home. In either case, he was home by nine and he'd study and drink coffee, study and drink coffee, fight sleep until finally he had to acknowledge defeat and go to bed.

But on this particular night, he could not take it. He got off the streetcar in front of the elevated station and stood, looking around. A whore propositioned him. She was about thirty, plump and small and round. Her nose was too big, giving her face a rather hawklike and almost vulturous character. She had straight, jet black hair which she wore bobbed and with bangs. She had on a blue coat with the gray fur on the collar worn and dirty, and a clean but cheap white cotton dress with red dots. Her voice was husky and coarse. She looked coarse. Her lips were too thick for the heavy dark red, almost purple, lipstick she wore. But he couldn't take it any longer. She called him honey and dear and asked him if he wanted some love.

She said it would be two dollars. He had agreed and followed her up a dirty stairway over a delicatessen. She had led him into a room lit by a dim bulb in the fixture in the center of the ceiling. A few pieces of female underclothes with the pink almost washed out of them had been flung on an old chair. The bed was unmade. A knitted quilt was crumpled over the foot. There was small disorder on a dresser in one corner. The room smelled like an unaired quilt.

There was a knock on the door.

"Just a minute, hon," she had said to Eddie.

He was confused. It was the first time that he had picked up a whore.

She went to the door and opened it. Eddie saw a brown-skinned Negro, wearing a white shirt with no tie.

He clenched his fists and waited. Should he swing or throw a football block at him, cut him down, and run? His briefcase full of books and his classroom notes were at his feet. He couldn't leave them.

She spoke in a low voice in the hall, and returned in a moment. He was merely her pimp; he didn't want to give Eddie any trouble.

"Didn't you want to give me more, dearie? I'll really love you up."

Eddie had been frightened when the Negro pimp had knocked on the door of the dim and ugly room. But now that the danger was gone, he was confused.

"Oh, dearie, don't you want a good loving up?"

Eddie looked at her. He was speechless. The ugliness of the entire scene was a shock, on his feelings more than his senses. The feeling of poetry in his yearnings for a girl, the desire and hunger for a beautiful girl, the mixture of loveliness and sex in her body, his thoughts of love which were linked with all that was green and growing in the world—all of this was violated by the shock of ugliness.

Eddie had not been looking for beauty. He had merely made a quick decision to buy two dollars' worth of glandular release, rather than to snap under the strain he felt, the strain that was but partly sexual, that had been imposed upon his body, his nerves, and his emotions as a result of his violent determination to know, to make himself distinguished and important by the development of his mind and talents. The ruthlessness with which he was treating his body because of a mind that was growing in many directions at once had been relentless. He had had to do something. He had known this when he closed the station up, crossed the street and stood in the shadows of the big factory. For months he had been getting on or off the elevated trains at the 35th Street elevated station. Every time he'd entered or left the station, he had glanced around and collected new impressions in his memory. He had done this with the prostitute. He had seen her in the same coat before and he knew that she either lived or performed her business functions or both in a room above the store.

"Dearie, gimme five dollars. Please, dearie. For five dollars, I'll take 'em off. I can't take 'em off for two dollars."

He took his wallet out. She looked at it. He had about ten dollars in it. He took out two one-dollar bills and handed them to her.

"Dearie, I'll give you good lovin'. I'll take my clothes off."

She had very few clothes to take off. Counting shoes as one piece, and stockings as one piece, and assuming that the blue coat had to be taken off free or without extra charge, the cost of "taking 'em off" was three dollars for four pieces of clothing. Impulsively, Eddie gave her three more dollars.

She took the money and went to the dresser. He put his wallet back in his black overcoat pocket.

The business transaction was very brief. Just before he left, she had asked:

"You ain't much experienced, are yuh?"

"No," he'd answered.

"I could tell," she said.

She didn't call him "dearie" afterward.

He left, paid his fare at the window inside of the station downstairs and waited for the train in the chilly air. He was still shocked. But he was ashamed. He felt shame because of the sordidness and ugliness of the entire scene, shame for his desires, shame for not having controlled them instead of having paid to give them such a purely glandular, feelingless outlet. Along with his feeling of shame, he felt hurt. He didn't then clearly understand how shame and hurt were as one. Neither he nor the hawk-nosed prostitute had acted like human beings to one another. Or at least not sufficiently as human beings.

IV

George and Eddie were walking over squashy ground beyond the lagoon. There was a play of shadows in the misty light ahead of them.

"What a night!" George exclaimed.

"Yes. The forlorn beauty of our hopes rides the night."

"I like that, Eddie, yes, I like it."

Eddie was pleased. He had wondered about the figure of speech. He tried many of his metaphors out on George.

"The forlorn beauty of our hopes—yes, I like that."

"Rides the night," Eddie added, "and it'll be a helluva lot more forlorn if there aren't some girls at the Bohemian Forum."

George laughed. "There's the Kent now."

They walked toward the run-down hotel. As they approached the entrance to the basement, they reached into their pockets for the fifty-cent admission fee. They entered a big square room. There were about forty people sitting around. Just as they found two seats in the back, the program started.

The chairman that night was Alec McGonigle. He introduced the speaker, John Mason, who delivered a flowery lecture on socialism and hope, with all the old-fashioned gestures. After his lecture, brief speeches were called for from the floor.

Eddie Ryan and George Raymond listened carefully. Suddenly, Eddie rose from his seat and challenged the speaker.

"There is no reason for man to hope that his life or that the life of people can be improved."

As a new customer and a newcomer, Eddie could speak.

He was challenged to debate with John Mason on the following Sunday evening. The subject was "Resolved That Life Is Not Worth Living." Eddie accepted the challenge.

When Alec McGonigle had seen Eddie Ryan and George Raymond walk into the Forum, he had been glad. He, John Mason, and Wilbert Wilmer were trying to develop a South Side Bohemian Forum which would be as good as the Wild Onion on the Near North Side. They hoped that it would eventually give the three of them a living. When Eddie and George had walked in, Alec had thought "two more customers."

After Eddie had spoken from the floor and had accepted the challenge to debate with John Mason on the following Sunday evening, Alec saw them as possible threats, rivals. Until now, he was the only young man around the place, the only one in his twenties who could get up and speak. There had been no one to compete with him for position and importance.

Chapter Three

I

Alec McGonigle was an only son. When he was a talkative little boy of five, his father, a bricklayer, walked out of his own hearth, said a "bedamned" to his kith and kin, and went off to California. Mrs. McGonigle, née Cooke, and christened Cecille, was a tall and lean woman. She was piously religious; to her, life was a time of trials and tribulations during which a series of duties must be performed. When John McGonigle, her lawful wedded husband, deserted her, Mrs. McGonigle had found a situation as a domestic servant. All of her feeling had then been fully centered in her faith, her belief in the true faith of God; and in her son, the only offspring of her wedded but blissless state.

Alec McGonigle was a bright and quick-witted boy. This disappearance of his father, whom he called "Papa" made him glad many times, because he was left alone with his mother whom he called "Mama."

He had liked to say "Mama." He had not liked to say "Papa." After "Papa" went away, he liked to hear his mother call him "The Little Man of the House."

But then, he was only a boy of five.

It wasn't long before Alec was more than five, and bigger, but not as big as he wished he was. He wanted to be as big as Buddy Smith, the big kid who kept saying all of the time:

—Well, any day now, I'll be wearing long jeans just like my old man.

And Alec wanted to be big, bigger than the biggest man there was, so big that he could look right at the man in the moon, or the sun, and talk to them. He wanted to become "The Big Man of the House" instead of "The Little Man of the House."

All the other kids had fathers. They hadn't gone away to California. If he got big enough to be "The Big Man of the House," he wouldn't feel the difference, so much, in himself and the other kids.

Every Sunday, Mrs. McGonigle dressed up Alec in a white sailor suit and white stockings and took him to Mass with her. He hated these mornings; kneeling and sitting beside his mother in one of the pews in the back of the church, on the left hand, the side that his mother said was the Blessed Virgin's side.

He would become bored, restless; and his mother, with stern kindness, would whisper to him:

"Don't move, Alec; you're in God's house at Mass."

When his mother talked to him that way, he felt ashamed and he would try with all his might not to move so much, not to move hardly at all. He kept wishing for it to be over, Mass. He'd wish and wish for it to be over with. Then he could get out of church, and get out of his sissy Sunday clothes.

Alec would sometimes be frightened of his mother when she was beside him in church. Because of God, she got so different. At home she often seemed sad; but in church, she seemed more sad. And Alec would feel nervous when she prayed like she did, pressing the palms of her hands together stiffly, nearly like boards, and at other times holding the black beads of her rosary so tight. Her thin and often chapped lips moved silently. All of a sudden, she would look at the priest up at the altar and her face would change. Her dull gray eyes suddenly became alive. Rather than mere piety, hers was a worship of emotional force that clutched her whole being. This was how she loved God.

Alec wished she wouldn't act that way. It made him afraid; and he didn't like to get afraid.

II

—God will punish him.

Alec had heard his mother tell this to his Uncle Pete just after his father had gone away, and he had known that they were talking about his father. They talked about his father like he had been a bad person. His mother hadn't been a bad person, but she was the one who was sad and unhappy.

Alec had to depend upon himself and was alone much of the time, once his father had walked out on them. This new responsibility made him glad much more than it made him sad. Even when he was alone, he was still "The Man of the House." And that was good.

III

The neighbors, especially the neighbor women, felt sorry for poor Mrs. McGonigle and were only too glad to give the poor woman a helpin' hand. Thus had Alec heard the sentiments of Mrs. Dorgan, the neighbor woman upstairs on the third floor.

Alec loved his mother, and needed her, but he was

ashamed of her too. The kids he played with didn't have
mothers who were talked about and called "poor." No one
ever called Mrs. Dorgan "Poor Mrs. Dorgan." Or "Poor
Mrs. Murphy." Or "Poor Mrs. Cavanaugh." Mr. Dorgan
supported Mrs. Dorgan. He went to work in an office every
day. Mr. Dorgan went to work "at business." His father
had gone to work with bricks. Mr. Dorgan went to work a
long time after his mother left the house.

—Yes, poor Mrs. McGonigle.

Playing alone one afternoon, Alec had many thoughts
like these. Just when they were making him get mad, Mrs.
Dorgan called from the back porch and asked him if he
wanted something to eat. She gave him cake and milk
which he gulped. She corrected Alec gently, and explained
that table manners were a sign of consideration. Alec was
surprised. Mrs. Dorgan hadn't spoken the way his mother
did when she told him what to do. Mrs. Dorgan talked different. She was different, she was Mrs. Dorgan, not his
mother. She had no right to tell him what to do. She had
no right. For a moment, he sulked. Mrs. Dorgan, her once
fine figure spread into an over-all plumpness of middle-
age, opened up in a smile. She kept her eyes on him, looking at him just like she was looking into his head and
knew his thoughts. She was smiling.

Alec sensed fully the neighbor woman's friendliness. He
smiled back at her.

She laughed.

And Alec laughed.

Mrs. Dorgan didn't have to go out to work the way
that his mother did. His mother cleaned house and did all
of the things Mrs. Dorgan did at home. But she did them
because she was a servant. His mother was a servant. Mrs.
Dorgan wasn't. When he grew up . . .

Alec didn't finish his thought. But he wished, and he
wished and wished, that his mother wasn't a servant.

IV

Alec started at the parish school, St. Agatha's, when he was six years old, going on seven, with three months and seven days to go.

A new burden pressed more weight on the narrow shoulders of Mrs. McGonigle. There was the tuition fee. It was one dollar, but Mrs. McGonigle could only make ends precariously meet, and every dollar was needed to give her and her precious son the breath and the bread of life, as well as to keep her head held straight and high with all of the proudness of her plain, drab and sad self. Books would have to be bought, and there would be other expenses, all small, individually, but adding together a sum that would force her to scrimp and scrape.

No matter what it cost, her son could not go to public school. No thought was needed for Mrs. McGonigle to decide on St. Agatha's parochial school for Alec. Who knows the Will of God. Couldn't it be that He had sent misfortune upon her as His means of testing her for Heaven? There was no question, no doubt about where her son would go to school. If it be the Will of God that she carry a heavier cross, then she would bend her back and bear the cross upon it.

V

It was a happy day, and fine weather, too, when Mrs. McGonigle took Alec to register for school with the sisters. She spoke with Sister Benedict, the principal, who was a sparse and tall nun with sharp features. She seemed to be sour-tempered, and Alec quickly thought that she was maybe like his mother.

Alec had gone along with his mother, mighty pleased with himself and proud, because he was going to go to school and this meant that he was starting to grow up, to get bigger. He was, too. That's what they said—Mrs. Dorgan, his mother, oh lots of people said so, said he was getting bigger.

He wanted to go to school. He couldn't wait until he got there, but he didn't know what the nuns were going to be like.

He had seen them at Mass on Sundays, and sometimes on the street. He knew that because they were nuns, they were not like his mother, but something else, different. Nuns didn't have children and they were supposed to be better than his mother or other mothers. Nuns would all go to Heaven when they died. Alec didn't like it at all that God thought that nuns were better than his mother. He didn't want the nuns to be better than her; he didn't want anybody at all to be better than his mother.

They looked funny to him in their long black dresses. They never wore anything but funny black; and he wondered if they wore nightgowns to bed like his mother did. He knew he'd better not ask his mother about this. There were lots of things he knew he could not ask his mother about. What would she say if she knew about the things he was beginning to find out about? He couldn't let on to her. It made him feel bad sometimes, not believing in the stork and knowing that babies came out of their mothers because of what the old man did to them; and thinking that God shouldn't do lots of things to people that He did. He would do things different if he was in God's place.

His mother would tell him it was a sin to have thoughts like that, thoughts against the Will of God. And she might get all holy up in the air if she knew. He couldn't let her know. He wouldn't tell her. But the thoughts came to him. He couldn't help it. They came, plop, into his head.

He couldn't tell the nuns either, especially not Sister Benedict. He didn't like her much. He didn't want her to think that he had thoughts that were sinful. He'd have to watch his step; Sister Benedict was a sourpuss nun. He'd have to watch himself. She was somebody God must like. She was here watching kids, teaching kids, boys and girls, so that they wouldn't sin.

VI

Alec learned to read quickly and was ahead of most of the boys and girls in his class. His mother said, and more than once, that she was pleased as pie with the way he was getting along. Alec was more pleased than two pies, lemon cream and apple, both kinds. Sometimes he would strut a little because he felt good enough to strut, and he'd stick his chest out and think that he was pretty smart.

And wasn't he? Didn't he prove it? Yes he proved it. That's why Sister called on him a lot.

Sister Josephine, the first-grade teacher, was a small, plump, middle-aged nun who wore gold-rimmed glasses and smiled a lot. During the first couple of months of school, she often called on Alec; and when she did, he was always able to stand up and answer the questions, and read the lesson, and this was more than a lot of the kids in his class could do. He liked being called on, so he could stand up beside his desk and give the answer to questions.

He liked school.

"I always knew it's the smart little scholar you'd be," his mother told him one night when they were eating supper.

"Sister Josephine thinks I'm smart, Mama."

"And the Lord be thanked for that, Alec."

It was himself, not the Lord, Alec thought. If God had done it, made him smart, why did God want him smarter than the other kids, and not want him to be better off? *That* was a question. And he could think of a lot more questions, too. He'd thought of a lot of them already. But he didn't want to talk to his mother about God. It made him feel . . . feel he didn't like it.

But he liked to be asked questions at school by Sister Josephine. She'd ask a question and up would go his hand, straight up, higher than his head.

"I see that you've prepared your lesson, Alec," Sister Josephine said one afternoon. "I wish some of you other boys would do the same."

On hearing these words, Alec felt like a hero and beamed with self-importance. A moment later, Sister Josephine asked who could read the day's lesson from the reader. Alec's hand was over his head before the nun had completed the question. None of the other boys followed suit. There were nineteen of them who didn't raise their hands. A few of the girls did, though.

"Alec, I'm sure you can read the lesson. I want to try some of the other boys out, dear. But now I'll call on you, girls," Sister Josephine told the class. At the same time, she glanced around the classroom, taking in all of her pupils with her quick and experienced eyes.

Alec was disappointed. Why couldn't he always be first?

"Oh, let me see now," Sister Josephine said. "Ah . . . Stone, do you . . . ?"

"Me?"

"You guessed my thought, James Stone."

The nun spoke with a touch of soft, kindly wit in her intonations. There was some laughing and snickering from the small boys and girls.

"Gee, Sister, I couldn't do it yesterday."

"Can you do better today, James?"

"My mother couldn't help me read last night and learn it."

"Well, let's give a try, James, and maybe I can help you."

"But maybe somebody else wants help more than I do, Sister."

The boys and girls laughed and sniggered more at this remark. It was funny.

Sister Josephine said that every pupil needing help would be helped by paying attention and that James Stone should go ahead and try, starting at the beginning of the lesson.

Jimmy Stone fumbled with the pages of his reader, looking for the correct pages of the day's lesson.

"Oh, there, see the page?"

Viola Talbot, a cute, snub-nosed little blond girl had whispered to Jimmy, but with a bossy air, and she had pulled the book out of his hands, and thrust her reader on him.

He took it.

"It's the right page. Don't lose it or you won't find it again," she told him, still in a bossy whisper.

"Read, Stoneface," Dickie Collins whispered.

"What's going on down there?" Sister Josephine called.

"I'm not doin' it, Sister," Jimmy said.

Alec McGonigle watched from three rows over, smiling proudly. He laughed with the others. He was smarter than Jimmy Stone.

Sister Josephine clapped her hands with a loud snap: it sounded almost like the cracking of a whip. The class knew that this was a warning signal and stiffened to attention with innocent blank expressions. There was some shuffling and rustling in the hard-backed desk seats.

"Now, James, can you read the first sentence?" asked Sister Josephine.

Jimmy Stone could read, but slowly. The way he read, Alec McGonigle could beat him. He told himself he would not be beat by Alec McGonigle.

"Jimmy, you're the stubbornest boy of the stubbornest," his mother had said to him, "that's what I want to see in my son."

"Jim, you're a chip off the old block," his father had said.

Why was he picked on and made to do this? It wasn't fair for her, Sister Josephine, to call on him this way.

"Of course a boy or girl learns to read before leaving the first grade so I'm not worried about you, James."

Blinking his eyes in bewilderment, Jimmy Stone sat down. He squeezed up his face.

—What did she mean?

Sister Josephine asked George Lawler and Pat Butcher to read. They did so, haltingly, and they made several mistakes.

Then she called on Alec.

He rattled off the lesson and sat down, proud of himself.

VII

"Teacher's pet."

"Teacher's pet."

Jimmy Stone flung the name at Alec, and Beady McGuire took it up. This was during the lunch hour period, between twelve and one o'clock. Pupils from the first to eighth grades were playing in the school yard. The boys were running, playing tag, wrestling, and tackling one another. Some of the younger girls were also running about. The older ones were playing hopscotch, or standing and sitting, chatting and giggling. It was close to one o'clock, time for the bell to summon them back to the afternoon's prison sessions of the classroom. The children played as though time were forever, or were never, and thus they could go on as they were, forever.

Three nuns stood close to the lines of boys and girls at distances that gave each about a third of the pupils to watch.

VIII

After the episode in the school yard, Alec did not raise his hand so readily when Sister Josephine asked a question. He wanted to be liked by the kids. He didn't want them picking on him, calling him "Teacher's pet" or "Show-off" McGonigle. He still liked answering questions, but many times he would let another hand go up first. He tried not to do too well although he knew he was the smartest kid in class and could show that he was any time he felt like it.

This did not help him to be liked by most of the other boys, however.

He managed to have the fourth or fifth highest marks in class; his average was about 90.

But the kids kept on calling him "Show-off." He was hurt when they called him this but he wouldn't let anybody know that it hurt him. If they knew that, they could really get his goat; they'd never let up and he'd be the goat all of the time.

"Don't you wish you had something to show off," Alec one day retorted to Beady.

A group of the kids were in an alley. Beady said he had something to show off. He opened his pants, took out his penis and urinated.

"Anybody can do that," Alec said.

"Your mother can't," Beady said.

"Don't talk about my mother," Alec said, angry. He knew that a kid should never let another kid insult his mother or talk about her.

"Your mother can't piss the way I piss," Beady said.

"His mother can't piss anyway," said Bobby Murphy, another of the first-grade boys.

They laughed at the joke but Alec knew they were laughing at him. Beady had been looking to pick a fight with him for a couple of weeks; and Beady was bigger and stronger than he was. Alec wasn't afraid but he didn't want to get beat up just to prove that he wasn't afraid to fight.

"What do you do, climb up on bathroom windows to find out how many mothers can take a piss?" Alec asked Bobby Murphy.

"Did you ever see your old lady piss?" Beady asked Bobby.

Alec was pleased with himself. He had turned the kids on Bobby Murphy instead of on him.

IX

As his early years passed, Alec became more and more sure that he was smart and clever. You could use your head and tongue to protect yourself much better than your fists, and it was easier, too.

In games, he was only average. He was neither the fastest nor the slowest runner. When sides were chosen for a game of ball, Alec was in the middle of the boys who were picked alternately for the two sides.

He didn't get much fun out of doing anything that he couldn't do well. He played with the kids a lot but he wasn't much interested in games and sports.

Ever since he was a tot, even before he started going to school, his mother had said that she wanted her son to be the first. Alec wanted to be first; it wasn't only to please his mother; he liked the feeling himself. It proved how smart and clever he was. He liked getting good grades. It made his mother happy too. He wanted her to be happy because of him. He didn't study very hard or long because he got things pretty fast; he had a good memory. But the kids didn't come around to liking him much. He was too smart for some of them. And others had heard their parents talking about his mother as a servant whose husband had deserted her. This made Alec not as good as they were.

X

Alec came to dislike school. He didn't like the neighborhood either. He was growing up, and growing ashamed of his mother and even more ashamed of his father. Not only was his mother a servant, but she didn't have nice clothes to wear either. She was neat and clean; but her clothes were old, and cheap—old dresses and coats, hand-me-downs. Her clothes were drab and she was drab, a drab woman.

But she was a good woman. She had her pride, too, and would take no help from anybody, except maybe her own kind, her relatives. Some admired her, others pitied her. The kids simplified what they overheard their parents say about Mrs. McGonigle. She was poor, a servant, not as good as their own mothers, and Alec wasn't as good as they were. He ought to remember that and keep his place, like his mother did.

Alec couldn't help being ashamed of his mother. He didn't want to be but he couldn't help it. The feeling

came, no matter how hard he tried to keep it out of his
thoughts, it wouldn't stay out. He didn't hate his mother.
He was just ashamed.

But he hated his father. He hated his father for going
away and leaving them alone. But no matter how much
he'd think about how he hated his father, Alec also wished
that his father would come back home to live with them
so that his mother wouldn't have to be a servant. Sometimes he imagined his father coming back rich, with a
fortune, and even buying an automobile. If that would only
happen. Wouldn't the whole neighborhood sit up and take
notice! He'd bet his boots, his bottom dollar, that just
about everybody in the parish would think a whole lot
differently about the McGonigles.

He didn't really believe that such good luck could happen.

When Alec thought about his father that way, he'd also
become afraid of the old man's coming back home. If the
old man did come back again and rule the roost, it might
not be so good for him. His father was a stranger to him
now. He didn't know what he would say or do. He had
left, just like somebody running away from home. He must
not have liked it at home; and not liked his mother, or
him either.

Maybe he didn't want his father back. His mother
wouldn't be able to treat him as well as she did now—not
with his father around. He didn't remember much about
the old man except he could remember him losing his
temper. Remembering these scenes, Alec decided no,
maybe it was best for him to stay away.

Alec remembered how the old man had belted him a
couple of times. It had hurt enough to make him bawl,
bawl like a baby. If his father came back, he might give
Alec a hard time. Maybe he would sock him around the
house and beat him up.

His father might or might not return; either way, Alec

worried about it. The only thing he could do was to grow up, and grow up fast; become a man and be able to protect himself. Then he could support himself, too, and do as he wanted to do. He could be somebody. He believed that's what he would be—Somebody, because he was smart.

Maybe he'd be a lawyer . . . or a doctor. He was smart enough. Doctor A. McGonigle, Dr. Alec McGonigle. It tickled him just to imagine the importance he would have carrying a doctor's black bag.

Then Alec would think some more and decide that he would become a lawyer and get admitted to the Bar. He'd rather be a lawyer than a doctor. Lawyers were smart. Doctors didn't have to be smart the same way, in outsmarting smart guys.

For criminy crickets' sake, he couldn't be what his mother hoped and wanted him to become—a priest.

XI

When Alec was only eight years old, he learned how smart he was. One day he got to thinking about God, and after thinking quite a while, he suddenly asked himself:

—Suppose God isn't?

Maybe God wasn't. Nobody ever saw God. Nobody in his neighborhood or in the city had ever seen God. God was supposed to have shown Himself to Moses; but that was a long time ago. Maybe Moses hadn't told the truth or had only thought that he'd seen God.

Alec couldn't figure out why God wanted people to do all the things that He was supposed to want them to do. Why did God want you to go to Mass every Sunday? What good did it do God? And why did God want to burn people in Hell forever because they committed a mortal sin? You could burn in Hell for Eternity if you missed Mass on Sunday because of your own fault.

This didn't seem logical somehow.

God was a mystery; and mystery was something that you couldn't understand by human reason. So you couldn't understand God.

—Suppose God wasn't?

Alec was fascinated by his own question and pleased with himself for having thought it up. He kept thinking about it and about God; and he wished that God "wasn't."

Before he was nine, Alec had decided that God wasn't. He didn't believe in God any more and even though he told no one, he preened himself on this new proof of how smart he was.

His mother. What if she knew? He couldn't tell her and he didn't. He couldn't let her know so he continued going to church. He pretended pretty well; well enough to believe that he was clever about it. He felt superior to the other kids in school and figured that he would always out-think them, the poor clucks.

But Alec McGonigle was still a boy. He wanted to be liked, to play with the other kids.

XII

Alec was still considered the "teacher's pet." He was in the seventh grade.

Gradually, growing up, there were disturbing changes in his body, particularly the growth of hair. Some kids talked of whipping the dummy. At first, Alec blushed when he heard this. But if he wanted to, why shouldn't he?

One day, after school, Beady McGuire and a couple of other kids talked about how a teacher's pet would not pull his pudding in private. Alec didn't answer. Beady suggested that they go down an alley and whip the dummy and see what teacher's pet was afraid of doing. Alec was afraid but he didn't want the other kids to know it; he went along.

They all went into the alleyway next to the gray brick apartment building where Alec lived.

"It's more fun doin' the pullin' in a bunch," Beady said. He turned around to the other kids, "All right, let's start the hand motions."

That was the first time Alec masturbated. He got excited but it didn't seem to be as much fun as it was cracked up to be. Afterward, he felt like one of the gang, now they'd take him as a regular kid. If they really accepted him as a regular kid, he'd organize the bunch, not like a gang, but just so that they could have more fun and play their games with a lot less crabbing.

When his mother came home from work that night, Alec was feeling independent. If he could do that, he could do the other, and even knock up a girl. He was as much a man as his father, goddamn him.

But he also felt ashamed. He'd feel like a louse if his mother ever found out. She'd be sad, then she'd get sore and would make him scrub his hands and go to confession next Saturday afternoon. She'd be very upset and he never wanted to upset her. He was getting old enough to understand more about his mother and to realize how hard it had been for her to raise him, and how hard it still was. His father was no good for clearing out. He felt sad because of the way his mother worked, and saved to send him to school. No, he couldn't do anything to make her cry and disappoint her in her hopes for him. And pulling it was something no kid would want to be caught at by a grown-up. If a cop caught a kid doing it, the cop would arrest the kid.

Girls were beginning to excite him, especially Teresa

Donlan, a plump girl with long black curls, playful brown eyes, and a smile that made almost everyone like her.

"Just let me keep lookin' at Teresa Donlan's legs and I'll even like school," Beady used to say.

She began to develop and the boys could see that her boobies bounced. They gawked at her and talked of her legs and tits, and they showed off in front of her to win her smile. She was a friendly girl who smiled quickly and would say hello to the boys, and since her father had a good job in an insurance company in the Loop, she was considered rich.

"Give me her legs and her old man's bank roll, yippie," Beady said.

"Which would you take, the legs or the bank roll?" Alec asked.

"The legs, Mac."

"I'd take both," Alec said.

Alec would joke around with the other boys about Teresa because he didn't want any of them to know how far gone on her he was. He started daydreaming about bumping into her, accidentally on purpose, when he could be walking her way. That would give him a chance to break the ice. He wasn't tongue-tied in front of a girl; all he needed was one chance to talk with her and he'd be off to a flying start.

If he could find out what she did on Saturdays, he could bump into her then. One day, Bobby Boland, a quiet, well-mannered boy, who was one of the smartest kids in class, was talking to Alec. Alec didn't shunt Bobby the way some of the other kids did. From Bobby, he found out that Teresa took piano lessons at ten o'clock every Saturday morning at the convent right next door to the school.

About eleven o'clock the next Saturday morning, Alec, accidentally on purpose, was hopping, skipping, and jumping near the convent house. When Teresa came out with her music in hand, Alec smiled and joked about how he didn't expect to see her going to school on Saturdays for extra lessons. Breaking out in one of her friendly smiles, Teresa explained that she had just had her piano lesson from Sister Catherine Marie.

Alec stepped to her right and took a few slow steps. He told her that he had nothing much to do and he liked walking. So did she. They strolled on. Alec offered to carry her music and she handed him the little briefcase.

His plan had worked; it hadn't even dawned on the other kids that he had a head start in the race to cop off the prettiest girl in class from under their snotty noses. He chuckled to himself.

They walked slowly toward her house, talking easily. She didn't mind taking piano lessons, and she liked Sister Catherine Marie, but sometimes she didn't like the lessons. But she guessed that a girl ought to learn to play the piano because that was one of the things a girl ought to know how to do. Her mother had been taught to play the piano when she was a girl.

Alec thought of his own mother with sudden shame. Mrs. Donlan went to church dressed like a lady and she wore big hats. She looked so different from his mother; she looked like the kind of a lady who could hire his mother to work for her as a servant. His mother couldn't play the piano.

He put these thoughts and his shame away quickly, dropping them in the wastebasket he imagined to be in his head. He dropped all the thoughts that bothered him there. This was a trick he'd learned when he was too bothered by his thoughts.

Teresa Donlan stood with him for a moment in front of the three-story tan brick building where she lived. She smiled and thanked Alec as she took her music back from him. He said he'd see her again, at school, and maybe next

Saturday. Her smiling response meant, yes, she'd see him.
Teresa hurried into the building and Alec walked off feeling
good, feeling cocky, feeling wonderful.

In the classroom the following week, Alec kept glancing over at Teresa on the girls' side of the room. Gee,
she was a swell girl and so pretty. She was like candy that
was sweet and soft and would melt in your mouth. And
she smiled at him. Of course, she smiled at almost everyone, but he thought that her smile for him wasn't quite the
same as the smile she gave the others. He'd outwitted them
pretty neatly.

On Saturday, he met her and again walked home with
her, carrying her music. He and Teresa became more
friendly. He was beginning to think of her as his girl, and
every time he looked at her, he wanted to kiss her.

Alec worked after school, delivering papers, but gave his
money, two and a half dollars a week, to his mother. Out
of this, she saved his tuition money of one dollar a month
and his dime for Sunday for the collection at Mass. Church
and Mass bored him more than it had when he was a young
kid. He was certain that God didn't exist; He was some
kind of joke that people put over on themselves and on
kids. But he was too smart for that one. And he was smart
enough, too, not to let on because he didn't know how
many damned roofs would fall in. His mother would never
get over it.

Teresa gave him a good reason for going to Mass. He
could think of her, of seeing her after Mass, and he could
think of the things he'd say to her. She could see him
dressed up and neat in his Sunday blue suit. No one could
tell that his mother had bought it secondhand. When his
mother had bought it, he'd been ashamed of himself and
full of mean feelings for her. He'd hated his father. Because
his goddamned father had gone away, he had to wear secondhand Sunday suits.

One Sunday at Mass he watched Teresa. He was bored. He went through all of the motions of the rituals. It seemed to take a long time. Finally, it was ended. Alec left the church, surrounded by others. As he blessed himself from the holy water font just by the back pews, he noticed three ladies dropping coins into the poor box.

—Boy, I wish my pants pockets were a poor box.

Alec thought of the poor box and his pants pockets for the next couple of days.

—Why not? he asked himself on Wednesday afternoon during his grammar lesson.

He woke up the next morning thinking of Teresa and of taking her to an ice cream parlor for a treat.

—Yes, and how? he asked himself.

He knew how. The answer came to him that morning during catechism lesson. There was no longer a question of why not in his mind. When the class let out for lunch, a few kids were bowled over when they saw Alec paying an extra visit to the church.

He took a good, careful look at the poor box.

It would be easy. And then he could treat Teresa.

Alec went into the church, nervous and shaking a little inside himself. He was ashamed of himself for shaking. He wasn't acting like the kind of a guy he wanted to be. What was there to be afraid of? Nobody knew that he was robbing the poor box. He wasn't afraid of God. He'd just have to be smart and not go to the poor box until the church was empty.

Damn it, there were some women in church. Two of them were old and had gray hair. Another woman who wasn't old, old enough to have gray hair, was kneeling in a pew near the back of the church. There was another old woman, taking all the time in the world before each station as she said the Stations of the Cross. That's all she had to do, say the Stations of the Cross and take more

time praying than Christ took carrying the cross up to
Calvary.

Alec went outside. He'd wait, but it looked like those
three women, particularly that old one saying the Stations
of the Cross, would take a long time. He took a couple of
jumps from a sidewalk square and landed just about on
the next crack. His legs were getting longer; he was growing up.

Alec didn't wait very long because he knew it would
be useless. He went off with the nickel and the bent hairpin in his pocket. Maybe he was in luck. Maybe there
would be more money in the poor box tomorrow. A lot
of other people would pay a visit before the church was
closed by cranky old "No-Good" Nolan, the janitor, at
six. And tomorrow, people would go to the six and the
eight o'clock Masses.

Alec went back the next afternoon with a hairpin in his
jeans. He'd spent his last nickel on chocolate drops. They
were all gone, and he couldn't have less money or be more
broke. He ought to get over three dollars, and pretty quick
and easy, if nobody was in church. Next Saturday, he could
buy Teresa and himself banana splits with chocolate and
strawberry ice cream.

The church was empty so far as he could see. He bent
down, certain that he was alone and safe. He used the
hairpin. It worked. He pulled out a handful of change;
there was a half-dollar, two quarters, and some nickels and
dimes as well as pennies. Alec shoved the fistful of money
in his pocket and reached inside the hollow for the rest.
He felt a crushed-up bit of paper; it took him a fraction
of a second to realize that it was a bill. He grabbed it and
a few more coins and jammed the additional money into
his pocket.

Just as he closed up the side of the poor box, there was
a soft swishing noise behind him. At first the sound didn't

register. Then, he knew that someone was behind him, inside the church. He became panicky and turned away from the poor box to take a couple of quick steps to the door. He saw the long, black habit, the dark beads, and the white collar before he saw the stern, angry face of Sister Benedict. He knew he had better get the hell out of church as fast as he could and run like hell as far from that church, as fast as he was able to.

"Aloysius McGonigle," Sister Benedict commanded.

Alec rushed through the inner door of the church, bolted down the few steps, almost losing his balance. Half-lurching because he was off balance, he brushed against the black outer door. He felt a slight sting of pain in his left elbow. He remembered that the door opened on the inside. As he grabbed the big iron handle, he heard the firm and angry voice of Sister Benedict.

"Aloysius McGonigle, stop! Aloysius McGonigle, come back here!"

But Alec couldn't have stopped. He was fleeing like an animal running for its life. He dragged the big door open, shot outside, blinked in the sunlit air and tore down the gray stone steps. He turned to his right and raced toward 47th Street, running for dear life. It didn't matter what he did. He had been seen; and he was running away only to postpone that awful minute when he would be collared.

Seeing Alec burst out of the church as if it were on fire, Beady and two other kids called to him. They tore across the street to the small white square of stone before the front façade.

Sister Benedict had hurried out of the church after Alec. She called out to him but he was already near the corner and running like mad. Beady and the two other kids stopped, with eyes enlarged with eager and cruel curiosity. They rushed up to Sister Benedict and tipped their hats.

Alec kept running. Pedestrians turned to watch him. He

didn't know where he was going. He was fleeing from the terrible exposure and humiliation which he would have to face. He ran on, feeling sick inside. The money was heavy in his pocket. It jingled and he felt the shaking coins and their weight. Maybe if he threw the money away, or hid it, they couldn't prove anything against him. No, it was too late. He had to run and never stop, run until he got so far away that nobody who knew him would ever see him again.

Alec turned around. Down near 47th Street but in the same block, he saw Beady leading a group of kids across the streetcar tracks. He knew they were chasing him to catch him and drag him back to Sister Benedict, or maybe to Father Flaherty. He turned east on 48th Street and shot on, not knowing where he was going. He heard more shouts and cries.

"Stop, thief!"

"Stop, McGonigle!"

"Stop, thief!"

He was breathing hard but he couldn't stop; he couldn't be caught. He ran on, panting for breath. He thought of his secret hiding place under the back porch stairs of the building two doors south of the building where he and his mother lived. No other kids knew of this hiding place. If he could reach it, he'd be safe. It was the safest place he could think of. He was gasping, his heart was pounding, his side was full of stitches, and the muscles in his thighs were hurting him. He wanted to give up to the shouting gang of kids.

"Stop, McGonigle!"

"Stop, thief!"

Alec dragged himself into the alley, staggered into the backyard, and heaving for breath, reached a gangway between the buildings. The darkness seemed safe but he knew that he wasn't safe; and he wouldn't be until he reached his secret hideaway.

Alec had to stop to catch his breath. He was so tired he ached. The cries of the kids seemed far away. He desperately hoped that they had lost his lead. He began to breathe more easily and to feel less weary. Maybe they had lost track of him.

Suddenly, he heard the cries again. They were louder. They were in the alley.

"Stop thief, McGonigle!"

"Give up, Alec!"

"We'll get you, McGonigle."

He ran for his life, cutting through the gangways of buildings, backyards and alleys. He raced on, his thoughts concentrated on getting under that back porch. Once he could crouch there in his secret hideaway, he'd be safe. Nothing could happen to him; they couldn't find him there.

He reached the back porch and crawled beneath it. He was stooped over, but snug in the dirt and dampness. For a few moments it was quiet. He was sitting with his knees together almost touching the black bottoms of the wooden stairs. A grocery wagon went by, cloppity-clop with noisy wheels, and the hoofs of the galloping horse rang on the alley bricks. It was dark under the stairs, near the damp cellar and damp stones, but he felt safe. They'd never find him here.

Alec didn't know what time it was. He didn't know how much time had passed since he'd gone into the church; it couldn't have been too long, not even an hour. But it seemed like it had been long ago since he copped the money out of the poor box. It was heavy in his pocket. He could bury it here and deny everything. He could say that he'd gone to pay a visit to the church and had seen the poor box open, and looked because he'd naturally been sur-

prised. Then, when Sister Benedict saw him, he had run
because he'd been afraid that he would be blamed. What
could they prove against him? He'd stick to this alibi no
matter what. But he knew that he couldn't get away with
it. Sister Benedict had seen him and he'd run away.

He wouldn't be in this fix if his mother had sent him
to a public school.

Alec became taut. His mouth popped open. He sat like
stone. He thought he heard the kids. Somewhere, there
seemed to be shouting. He waited, his ears cocked, expect-
ing that any second the gang of them would be in the
alley, looking around his backyard and maybe this one, too.

He couldn't think. He waited, numb with terror. Alec
was doomed and he knew it.

—I shouldn't have done it.

He thought of his mother and how hurt she'd be when
she heard the news. He didn't know how she would act. He
didn't think she'd cry but she'd take it hard; and she'd
suffer because of him. After all she'd done for him, it was
an awful repayment. He felt rotten.

He'd have to tell her.

—Ma, I robbed the poor box in church.

He couldn't do it like that. How would he do it? How
would he begin? How could he explain it?

—I feel like a bastard.

At that moment, the gang of boys came tearing into the
alley, shouting and shrieking. Alec trembled. He wished
that he could stop breathing. He pressed against the wood.

"He's around here somewhere."

"All right, McGonigle, we know you're here. Come on
out."

"Come on out, McGonigle, give up."

"Maybe he ran home."

"Sure, he's just the kind of guy who'd run home to hide
behind his old lady's apron," Beady said.

"Or under her dress."

Alec waited in torment, hearing them talk about him as they ran about his own backyard. A couple of the kids dashed up the back stairway, pounding their feet on the steps.

"Give up, McGonigle, if you know what's good for you," Beady called.

"Let's search his basement," Bobby Murphy suggested.

"Yeh, maybe he's hiding there with the other rats," Beady said.

"Let's go look for him," Tommy Riordan said.

"We'll find him," Bobby Murphy said.

"And when we do, we'll kick the shit out of him," Beady vowed.

Alec hoped that they'd give up and go away. He was hurt, hurt by what they were saying about him, hurt because he was alone and trapped. He didn't stand a chance if they found him. He felt that he didn't have a friend in the world.

He had to fight with himself not to cower and tremble. He didn't want to be a coward, or to be yellow. But he couldn't come out and dare them.

He waited, each second an instant of fright and menacing uncertainty. A minute was a torture that would never end. He would have to stay here forever, here in the damp and dirt. He felt stiff from having sat hunched up.

All was lost. Nothing would ever be the same for him again at school, or in this neighborhood. He was disgraced, marked. It was like having his forehead branded. He would be set apart, not trusted, not liked, not included in games. He wouldn't be invited to parties and he would have to be by himself, day after day.

And it would be the end with Teresa Donlan. Mrs. Donlan would forbid Teresa to even speak to him. He thought about running away; he could wait here until dark and then leave. What would happen to his mother? She'd be all alone. After all she'd done for him. If he ran away, she would suffer more than she had when his father left. He knew that he couldn't run away; he was all that his mother had.

The kids continued to look for him. They condemned and cursed him, repeated their boasts and threats about what they would do to him when they got their hands on him. They even talked about how he might be arrested and sent to reform school.

They came into the yard where Alec hid. They looked in the gangway and talked of searching the basement. Alec was curled up, stiff from having sat so long under the porch. Any minute now he would be discovered and dragged out into the open.

"Go on home where you belong," Mrs. Carter called to them; she lived on the first floor and had two kids who were too young for school.

"We're looking for Aloysius McGonigle. He's robbed the poor box and the Sisters want him," Bobby Murphy told her.

"Well, get out of this yard where you don't belong before I call the police."

They left the backyard.

—I knew they wouldn't get me.

—They're gone, they're out of the yard.

He was ashamed for having been afraid.

He remained under the stairs but sat in a more comfortable position. He wanted to stay here; as long as he did, he was safe. But he knew he could not stay here forever. He would have to go home. He would have to tell his mother. Having escaped the gang, facing his mother now seemed the worst of all. If Sister Benedict threw him out of school, he could always go to the public school and play with the public school kids. He liked some of them. But his mother! She would think that he had committed a sacrilege. And she loved him. He felt lousy.

He counted the money he had swiped—three dollars and twenty-three cents.

He looked to his left. It was dusk now; he'd wait just a little while longer and then he could go home. He knew he'd have to sooner or later. Maybe he ought to go now. Maybe his mother didn't know yet and he could kind of explain to her before they sent someone to tell her. He looked out again. It was almost dark. The kids had been gone for a while now. He only had to go two houses down to get home. He decided to take the chance. He crawled from under the stairs and stood up. For a second, he felt dizzy, his legs were stiff. But he knew it wasn't safe to stay here; he ran toward his own backyard.

He walked into the kitchen.

"Hello, Ma," he said, trying to sound natural, as though he'd done nothing.

She sat at the kitchen table. She hadn't touched the cup of tea before her. The kitchen was full of shadows. Outside, the sun had gone down. The melancholy of the day's ending seemed more pervasive, more like a permanent feature of the sky and the world than it had on many other days. He and his mother were alone as they had been for years; but now, they were like two people far away from everyone else in the world in their sadness.

"Son," she said.

Alec dropped his eyes and went closer to her.

"Son, why did you do it?" she asked, her sadness more unbearable to him than any anger could have been.

"I don't know, Ma."

"You know right from wrong. You know Our Lord has commanded us—Thou shalt not steal. And stealing from the house of God and from the poor who are blessed to Him is a terrible sin."

"I'm sorry, Ma. I'll never do it again. I promise, Ma.
I'll vow."

With all of the pain in her glance, she was still staring
at him with love. Somehow, he knew this. He felt safer
because of her love; but it made him feel more sorry, he
guessed, than he had ever been in his whole life. He had
done something to her which made her feel as sad as he
had ever seen her. He had disappointed her, failed her, and
brought shame upon her that would make it harder than
ever for her to hold her head high with pride, pride touched
with a quality of tragedy.

"Aloysius, why did you do it?"

"I wanted the money, Ma," he answered slowly because
these simple words were hard to utter.

"Ill-gotten money is the Devil's money, Aloysius. A sin,
a sacrilege committed in church, in God's own house, is
one of the worst things any person can do in the sight of
God."

Alec didn't speak. It was getting dark outside and the
McGonigle kitchen was in its dreary dimness.

"Why did you want money so badly that you would
steal it, Aloysius?"

"I wanted to buy sodas and I just wanted to have it in
my pocket."

"You know it was wrong, son."

"Yes, Ma. I'll never do it again. I'll never steal again,
Ma, I promise. I promise."

"You won't, Aloysius. If you ever do, I will put a strap to
you. You have been a good boy but today, you listened to
the voice of the Devil."

Alec knew he had done wrong, and he was sorry. But
he couldn't believe that the Devil had anything to do with
his stealing. He could have bawled because he had hurt
his mother. He wished that he could go to bed and wake
up tomorrow morning a man, free, and his own boss.

"You must never steal again. Anything stolen is ill-gotten and will never make a person happy."

"Yes, Ma."

"It's a sin. What don't belong to you isn't yours."

"Yes, Ma, I don't know why I did it."

"I'm not going to punish you, Aloysius. But you must go to confession this Saturday and do penance. You must pray for God's grace."

"Yes, Ma."

And then she told him that what he had done was one of the ways a boy grows bad, and does not grow up to be a good man; and that a boy who steals gets a bad name and is never trusted again and is unhappy all his life. She told him that they were poor, that he would have to be good and keep at his studies to make something out of himself.

He no longer felt that he was an outlaw. He knew that his mother would give him another chance. He knew that she would help him get straightened out at school.

And she did. The next morning, she took him to Sister Benedict's office. He told Sister Benedict that he was sorry, very sorry, and that he would confess his sin and do penance and pray for God's grace. He promised that he would never, not ever do anything bad again. Sister Benedict spoke sternly; she told him that he must write the sentence "It is a sin to steal." She said that because his mother was a good woman, she would not expel him from school this time but that he was on probation and if he caused any trouble in the future, any trouble at all, he would be expelled. Then she sent him to his class.

It was hard for Alec McGonigle to walk into the classroom. When he entered, there was a stir among the pupils. They looked at him with surprise, then hostility. Teresa Donlan didn't smile at him—she didn't even look at him. He felt uncomfortable. He knew that he would have to bear insults. He felt friendless but he tried to act as though nothing had happened or changed. In the lavatory and during lunch periods, he had to take it from some of the kids. This continued for a few weeks but then, the summer vacation came.

By the time summer had passed, Alec's crime seemed to the kids to be more human, and some of them even spoke of what he'd done with admiration. He tried harder than ever to make an impression on them, in everything. Most of all he tried to impress Teresa Donlan but she was chilly toward him. He guessed that her mother had heard of what he had done and had ordered Teresa not to walk with him.

Although Alec's crime seemed to have been forgotten by many of the other kids, he was never again really happy at St. Agatha's. The next fall, his mother, with the help of her relatives, was able to send him to St. Hilary's, a boarding school in Kickapoo, Illinois. He waited on tables to help pay his way. He felt some apprehension about leaving his mother and leaving Chicago, but he also felt that he had a new start, and escape from the unhappiness he'd known.

Sometimes he was lonely, but so were the others. Living in a dormitory with them, he was closer to his new schoolmates than he had been to the old ones. And they didn't know that his mother was a servant.

Chapter Four

I

In the week following his first brash intervention at the
Bohemian Forum, Eddie Ryan debated John Mason. He
had looked forward to this debate all week and had thought
about what he would say. He had checked snatches of poetry which he intended to quote and was confident that he
would speak well, that he might even be sensational. Eddie
believed that he was advancing himself in his intended
career as a writer by making his name known. Naïve about
Bohemianism, he believed that the people who attended
the Forum were interested in books, in writing and in
ideas; and that they would respect him and welcome him if
he could prove that he was well read and had ideas. He also
thought that he would be paid for speaking. If he could
earn money by debating, then he could quit his job as a
filling station attendant and devote all of his time to reading, studying, and writing.

About fifty people came to hear the debate. Among
them was Celia, the girl that Eddie had danced with the
Sunday night before. She was plump but he thought her
attractive and was ready to fall for her at the least oppor-

tunity. She had danced very close to him, pressing her body against his, and had excited him. From the way she danced, Eddie believed that she would not resist his advances. She had graduated from Jackson High School on Stony Island Avenue. Eddie had told her that he had gone to the University and he had spoken of poetry. She seemed interested and he had convinced himself that she was intelligent, serious, and loved poetry. He was glad she had come to hear his speech. He'd make a big impression on her, and dance with her later. Then, he would walk home with her, neck, and maybe she'd go over to Jackson Park with him.

Pat Cullen, Leo Donovan, and Michael Fontan, fraternity brothers of Eddie's from high school days, showed up. They thought he was a little goofy but they were amused. They sat, staring at him with friendly irony.

Eddie spoke well. He quoted passages from Matthew Arnold, Swinburne, and Tennyson with feeling. He argued that the life of man was futile; that it had begun and that it would end. There was no consciousness, no sentience in the universe, no God. Nature and the universe were indifferent to man. There was no life after death, no reward for goodness, no punishment for evil. History had no purpose, no end. The truth brought only disillusionment. Ideals were lies and illusions. The more we came to know and to experience, the more disillusioned we would become. The gods were dead, and all the idols were broken. Men lived in the ruins of the destroyed gods, broken ideas, smashed hopes. Men who hoped that progress was real, who believed that mankind could be saved, who felt that life was worth living—these men suffered pain and death as well as much disappointment and much disillusionment. He concluded by quoting from Swinburne's *The Garden of Proserpine:*

From too much love of living,
From hope and fear set free,
We thank with brief thanksgiving
Whatever gods may be
That no life lives forever;
That dead men rise up never;
That even the weariest river
Winds somewhere safe to sea.

Then Eddie Ryan sat down.

John Mason rose from his seat and faced the audience. He had had long experience as an agitator and a soapboxer. He tore into Eddie, he spoke of his inexperience, his immature cynicism, his lack of understanding of socialism. He orated. He dismissed Eddie's arguments as poppycock. He said that Eddie did not understand the great poets and yet he quoted them because he had no arguments of his own that would stand solid in the bright and shining light of reason and truth. He referred to Eddie as his "young opponent." He sympathized with his young opponent and felt very sorry that his life wasn't worth living.

John Mason was voted the winner of the debate. Eddie thought that the verdict was unfair; he felt that he'd won. John Mason hadn't answered one of his arguments. Eddie was saying this to George Raymond when old John Mason walked up and shook his hand, congratulating him. Eddie was surprised. Why should he congratulate him? Didn't he mean what he'd said?

"Say, that was some speech," Pat Cullen said.

"Yeah, you went after the old guy," Michael Fontan said.

"Maybe you're right, Eddie, life ain't worth living without a pint," Leo Donovan said. Pat Cullen and Michael Fontan were with him.

Eddie grinned as he stood talking to them. It had been

almost two years since their fraternity days. Pat was now
an oil salesman. Michael worked in an office on the Loop.
Leo worked, sometimes. Life was worth living to them,
and the best that life could offer was a good time. Most
of their talk was about what they had done, or what they
were going to do, or what they wanted to do. They didn't
question the way the world went. Leo regarded it all as so
much crap and horseshit and liked to talk of becoming a
beachcomber in Burma or somewhere else in the Far East.
Pat and Michael thought they had good jobs and they
wanted better ones. After they put in a full day's work,
they wanted to have fun. They thought Eddie was goofy
to do what he was doing—all that reading and studying.
And he wouldn't even get credit for it; he had quit the
University. Pat made some allowances for him for old
time's sake but he was sorry to see him like this. Eddie's
atheism troubled Pat, who disapproved, almost to the point
of resentment. He knew that Eddie thought of him as a
young Babbitt and this nettled him.

Poetry was all right, Pat thought, but there were interesting things to do in life besides reading it or talking
about it. If you could make some babe by reciting it to
her, that was something else. But the ties of the good old
days made them all nostalgic, none of them was free of
sentimentality.

They all stood and talked. It was as though there were
invisible veils between them. Even though some good-
looking girls were around the place, Pat and Michael didn't
feel at ease. They were in the wrong kind of dump. George
Raymond came up with a whoopee and took over the conversation.

The dancing began. Eddie Ryan noticed Celia and went
to her. They danced. They danced several dances together
and she pressed her body up to his just as she had the
last time.

Eddie walked her home later and he kissed her. That was all; he didn't get anywhere with her. She listened to him talk about poetry, about his ambition to become a writer. He wrote poems about her, bad poems, in free verse. After a few weeks, she stopped going to the Forum, and Eddie's fancy turned elsewhere.

After George and Eddie had visited the Forum a few times, Alec McGonigle's original apprehensions about them were quieted, and they became a trio of friends. George decided that he might be able to live off the Forum. He knew that John Mason and Wilbert Wilmer were living off the place. Old John slept in a little room in the back of the basement. Wilbert paid five dollars a week for a room upstairs, in the hotel. Alec lived at home but he expected to be cut in on the profits as soon as the Forum started making money. Alec, George, and Eddie started spending a lot of time together on weekends, and since Eddie was the only one who had a job, he usually paid for the meals.

On Saturday nights, there was dancing; on Sunday nights, there was a Forum with dancing afterward. It was an odd group who went. Most of them had only grammar school educations. They had no literary interests, or pretensions. Quite a few girls went regularly—girls who worked in offices, or as waitresses, or as salesgirls in stores; and girls who didn't work at all, such as Celia. It was a good time, or novelty, or sex that brought them in. Sometimes it was loneliness. They got in for fifty cents; some of them went in for nothing. They would sit through the Forums on Sunday nights, their minds empty, waiting for the dancing, the necking, the excitement. Some of them were virgins, half-desirous of defloration and half-fearing. They would allow themselves to be aroused. They would neck to the point of surrender, but then they would grow rigid, and even struggle if necessary.

Some of the girls came around for no other purpose but

to have fun. Bohemianism excited them and was romantic.
It provided an air that would have been absent at a public
dance hall. There was an informal atmosphere; everyone
talked contemptuously of conventions, and in favor of sin.
They talked about freedom. This made the girls who were
full of sex and hungry for thrills bold. Many of them lived
dull lives. Some had come to Chicago from small towns
or the country; and they found a chance to meet fellows
at the Bohemian Forum. They could go as far as they
wanted to go. No girl was ever raped; the most that would
happen would be a little wrestling when a girl would check
herself while in panting heat on the near side of her
sexual Rubicon.

The girls were a surprise to Eddie Ryan because he had
gone into Bohemianism with illusions gathered from hear-
say, legends, and reading. He had imagined a Bohemian
environment to be one of free spirits who were sincerely
in revolt against conventions, lies, and the false values of
the middle-class. Before he had met any of them, he had
had notions of Bohemian girls as the equals and companions of men with a love of art and ideas and a coura-
geous disregard of the standards which imposed sexual re-
straint on them. He didn't like the short hair of some
of the Bohemian girls, but he believed that they would
love a man, and that one of them would love him. Eddie
believed that if he would ever become attractive to a girl,
it would be because of his mind, and not a result of any
sex appeal. He regarded himself as graceless and awkward
on the dance floor and was unaware of any appeal that he
might have possessed in a purely physical sense.

Myrtle was one of the girls at the Forum. She was
scarcely a Bohemian girl; she was a waif, a stray; a girl
who drifted across states, working when necessary, and
sought only the ease which each day might provide. She
dreamed but little, a wanderer without vision, a creature

whose roots grew in marginal social soil, a girl who early
found that the intensity of sex wore thin. She could have
lived the life of a waitress or counter girl, but she found
in movement her easiest course in life. She was honest
and could be loyal. She was friendly and sympathetic to
people. The indulgence of her body, the protection of her
laziness, the temporary adjustments which gave her a place
and protected her from any eruption of feelings which
would have excited her imagination beyond the limits of
her capacities—these were some of the reasons why Myrtle
was a waif, a girl who drifted and floated from place to
place, from man to man or from men to men, job to job,
and from hotel to boardinghouse. She almost never com-
plained, was rarely bitter, and was ready to accept little by
way of keep and shelter as one more temporary stop in her
aimless journey. At fourteen, Myrtle had been seduced,
without struggle. She went to bed with a married truck
driver who lived in her neighborhood. She did this with the
same naturalness and acceptance with which she sat down
at a restaurant counter and ate a meal. At sixteen she was
married, but after six months her husband, a factory worker,
had left her. His mother financed the divorce. When she
was seventeen, a customer at the Greek-owned restaurant
where she worked, an accountant, thought that he was in
love with her and begged her to give him the love which
he did not get from his wife. She gave it, on a park bench.
She became pregnant. The accountant's love turned to
panic, and Myrtle paid for an abortion by a midwife, the
cost being thirty-five dollars. After this experience, she
could have no children. Myrtle felt no real bitterness,
neither could she feel deeply for a man. It was good when
a man roused her and she found pleasure in sex, but this
did not happen often. When she was nervous, she would
eat; and she was ten or fifteen pounds too heavy. She had

drifted into Bohemia and found it an easy world in which to live.

With her came Eileen, who at twenty-eight seemed to have been much battered and used by life. She had been married and divorced, had worked in restaurants. She had a fine, slender, and supple body but she often looked wan.

When Eddie Ryan and George Raymond started hanging around the Bohemian Forum, Eileen and Myrtle had already been there a few times. Eileen had gonorrhea but her desire seemed only to have been roused by it. She would dance, kiss, and fondle all night, refusing to do more. Eileen had been used, but she was not bitter and revengeful, and would not pass on her infection. She would not make love with Eddie Ryan although they danced and kissed and lay together one night, fully dressed, in a stuffy room of the hotel over the Forum. At dawn, they walked in the flower gardens on the Cottage Grove side of Washington Park, smelling the flowers and trees and grass, seeing the world awaken through thick gray mists, hearing the birds break into song and the unending chirping of the sparrows, watching the sun break through the walls of gray fog and sparkle on the drops of dew on the grass.

Relaxed and strangely sympathetic, they sat. Eileen's gray suit was rumpled. Her thin face looked tired, her eyes were haggard and circled. The beauty and the quietly dramatic growth of dawn, the freshness and appeal of the new day, the sky—vast and tranquil like a light blue sea, the sudden nearness of the world around them full of the perfume of dawn, seemed like an invitation to heartbreak.

Eddie knew that Eileen had been hurt by life. She had not told him; she had told her story to George Raymond who had repeated it to Eddie. She was disheveled and weary, with her hair half-mussed, her suit wrinkled, and in her brown eyes was a dull sadness. Life had betrayed her. Her head was on Eddie's shoulder and they sat until the sun was up and the park was glowing. Then they parted. Eddie walked home slowly. It had been a night of experience and that was what he needed. Even though Eileen had refused him, he was glad that the night had happened.

Eileen, like a number of the girls around the Bohemian Forum, was most interested in George Raymond. What love she was capable of giving, she had given him. For her, love had been a cause of betrayals and deceptions, and there was in her a sexuality turned frantic.

George had also been infected with gonorrhea, but was getting better. When Eileen refused him and told him why, he convinced her that she couldn't hurt him, and that even if she could, he wouldn't care because when he wanted what he wanted, he got it.

They spent a Saturday night together at the little decrepit hotel on Cottage Grove Avenue.

Eileen suddenly stopped coming around. Nobody ever learned why. She was forgotten.

Betty Everett was young, nineteen. She always wore a black dress. She had dark bobbed hair and sharp features, but her figure was good. The friendliness of her smile and her youth made her attractive. She was avid for dancing and would dance wantonly. She would also neck. But Betty was a self-admitted virgin and had no intention of sacrificing her virginity. Perhaps George Raymond could have changed her mind had he concentrated on it, because she seemed to go for him. But he didn't; and the others learned that she was impregnable. She would cling and kiss with passion, but then she would become stiff and rigid and refuse. No one became angry with her or called her a teaser. After a long night of dancing and necking, with her virginity intact, she would greet the fellow the next evening, smiling. She'd say "hello," ask how he was; and she was all ready to chitchat, to talk of people, dance records, the weather, or her day at work. She would act as though she had not been in his arms, like a girl abandoned to her instincts, one minute; and the next, a cold maiden who had thrown her body into stiff resistance. She gave everyone the impression that she liked them; and she did like people. She never gossiped about others and never had a quarrel or a tiff around the Forum.

Jane Foster was a filing clerk in an office in the Loop. She had gone to high school for a year. Occasionally, she read books but she didn't speak of them. One night, Eddie asked her:

"What do you want to do in life?"

She laughed, treating the question as a joke.

"I never think of that. Tomorrow will come, tomorrow. Today I'm having fun. Don't you have fun?"

"Yes," Eddie answered, not wanting to explain what he wanted to do with his life.

Jane Foster dropped around at the Forum almost every night even though there was nothing going on except on Saturday and Sunday nights. She'd sit and talk with Wilbert and Old John. Old John would reminisce about the days when he had been an active Socialist and had run for political office. He would talk about his plans to make a new start in the real estate business and earn a lot of money. He would bitterly denounce his wife from whom he was separated, and whom he blamed for his present state. Sometimes Jane would sit drinking coffee with little bald-headed Wilbert Wilmer while he would tell her that Herbert Spencer had been the greatest philosopher who ever lived, the man who had explained the full significance of Darwin's theory of evolution, and the man who had outlined how man could go on progressing endlessly and scientifically. Wilbert would talk about his great dream of founding a colony in the Ozark Mountains which would be run according to the principles and ideas of Herbert Spencer.

Jane Foster did not understand most of what she heard but she enjoyed listening. She said that the girls she knew, the girls in her office, went out with fellows who didn't talk about many things, that they went to a dance hall, or had a hamburger or chop suey, and maybe some drinks, and then they would talk about how important they were when they weren't. It was more fun to come to the Forum and meet all kinds of people that you couldn't meet going out on double dates with those girls. And if a fellow wasn't out after full payment for a date, and after he got it, forgetting you, he would be the kind who wanted to go steady and do the same thing with you all the time. But she, well she liked more excitement with lots of different things happening and with different kinds of people. That's why it was fun coming to the Forum and knowing everybody. The Forum was kind of wild. She liked it to be wild, in a way.

II

Eddie Ryan quickly discovered that the people that he met at the Forum were far from what he had expected. But he kept going, partly because of a kind of inertia and partly because of his friendship with George Raymond. But he knew that the Bohemian Forum was not the new environment he sought. Almost every time he'd spend an evening there, he would get moody afterward, and he would fret about wasting his time. He would dream of going to New York—of becoming a new Jack London or Maxim Gorky—and of bursting forth and taking his chances.

After George Raymond had decided that he could get a living out of the Forum, he convinced Alec, who had fallen under his spell. Alec had become closer to George and Eddie than to other fellows his own age.

John Mason and Wilbert Wilmer wanted no part of George's cutting in on the Forum; they were having a hard enough time scratching along. Wilbert had met Alec at the Wild Onion, a well-known and successful Bohemian Forum on the Near North Side. He had also run into him at the Bug Club. Alec had spoken at both the Wild Onion and the Bug Club. When Wilbert had decided to try to start a Bohemian hangout in the South Side, he thought that Alec was a young fellow who could be useful. John Mason had moved in because he was just about on his uppers—his needs were few and he could always be counted on to put on a show when he delivered one of his old-timey speeches.

Before George and Eddie had come to the Forum on that last Sunday night in March, it had been a new and struggling Bohemian establishment. The only thing that kept it going was Wilbert's money, which represented long years of saving while he had lived a bachelor life and worked in an office. Wilbert didn't have much money; no one knew just how much; but to run a place like the Forum had been his dream for over five years. He regarded this as a preliminary step and as a source of recruiting for the fulfillment of his big dream—the colony in the Ozark Mountains.

Eddie and George seemed like a strong gust of wind. They were lively, talkative, and young. Almost immediately Eddie demonstrated that he could speak well enough to be used as a speaker. George, on the other hand, seemed to be a threat; he was quick-tempered, attractive, and wherever he was, fights and trouble could happen at a moment's notice. However, he had charm and the girls really went for him.

At first, George suggested to Alec that he serve as the bouncer for the Saturday night dances. He guaranteed to increase business enough to allow himself to take a small cut and have enough left over so that Alec could start getting some money out of the Forum. Alec spoke to Wilbert. Wilbert did not want George moving in but he was a slow talker, and he couldn't think quickly when in conversation, especially with someone like Alec who talked at a rapid clip. Alec managed to convince Wilbert to take a chance on George. George borrowed five dollars from Eddie, five dollars from some fellow he had met in the Loop, and moved into the Kent Hotel.

His first idea to increase revenue was to sell bootleg gin. He borrowed some more money and bought raw alcohol at a drugstore, made some gin in an old washtub and bottled it. Before Wilbert knew what was going on, George had set up a bootlegging enterprise in connection with the Saturday night dances.

On the first Saturday night that George was bouncer and in charge, he dressed neatly in his one good brown suit. He danced with a couple of the girls and talked with some of the customers. The Saturday night crowd was different from the one which came to hear the lectures on Sunday nights. Unattached girls and young fellows came because they could dance cheaply—just a half a buck; and a fellow stood at least a fair chance of a pickup. Washington Park was just across the street and there was plenty of room for a young fellow and a willing girl.

After he had observed the crowd, had talked with some of them and sized them up, George began singling out likely customers. He'd take them aside and tell them he had some good stuff, gin, to sell at two bucks a fifth. He had a few sales that night, and he asked some of the fellows and girls to tell their friends to come the next week. He looked forward to the weeks ahead enthusiastically.

"It's better times, pal," he told Alec, grinning broadly.

"But you've got to be damned careful so we don't get pinched, George."

"Leave that to me, Alec, I can always spot a dick. There's nothing to be afraid of."

"I'm not afraid, but I don't believe in inviting danger or soliciting raids."

"I watched the crowd and I was very careful about picking my chumps," George laughed.

"Let's hope so. Wilbert is sitting on pins and needles. Old John and I had to convince him not to worry."

"He won't be sitting on pins and needles in a few weeks when the kale starts rolling in. There's real possibilities in this dump; and once I've got it in operation, I'm thinking of hiring a three-piece band."

"You'll be in big business soon. Listen, George, don't start pushing Al Capone around before you're set."

George chuckled.

"I can make a living, Alec, and increase the revenue for all of you. I don't want much. Twenty, twenty-five bucks a week will do me fine, and give me my time to read and start my book."

"I didn't know you were writing a book, George."

"Yes, I have decided. I'm going to do a very sardonic fantasy, in the Cabellian manner, more or less of a counterpart to *Jurgen* with a female hero."

"More power to you if you can do it," said Alec.

"Cabell is a stylist, a master stylist. Not even I would be so presumptuous as to think of being the equal of Cabell. But I'm going to read and study style—Cabell, Nietzsche—only writers who write beautifully."

"You can't write a counterpart of *Jurgen* with a female Jurgen as the main character," Alec said. "Women have no sense of humor."

"That's the point—that will be the source of my humor," George said.

"If you say so," Alec said doubtfully.

Later, Eddie Ryan and George Raymond sat having coffee in a small restaurant near 55th Street and Cottage Grove Avenue.

George chuckled, "Alec doesn't believe I can write a Cabellian satire on women."

Neither did Eddie.

"I'm going to begin with a dream. Before I do, besides studying stylists and carefully rereading Cabell, observing his style and making notes, I'll read Freud's book on dreams. I'll select a homely woman, a hatchet-faced old maid virgin, put her to sleep. She'll dream that she's an enchantress as beautiful as Cleopatra and Helen of Troy and all the famous beauties of history and legend. No, Eddie, she'll dream that she's Venus de Milo."

"Venus didn't have arms," Eddie said.

"That will give me wonderful opportunities for satire. She'll have two arms until she meets Zeus. He'll recognize her as Venus."

Eddie tried to think how George's idea could be developed; he wanted to believe that it could be, but he couldn't see much promise in it.

"I can tell you have no enthusiasm for my project, Eddie."

"My mind doesn't run that way. I don't think it's too promising an idea."

George frowned and Eddie wondered if a storm of anger was brewing within him. But then, George chuckled:

"Good old Eddie. You're my best friend, I can count on you for honesty. I made up the whole thing on the spur of the moment while I was talking to Alec back there at the Forum. Maybe, some day, if I do write books, and I learn the craft, then I might try it."

"I think you could write, George, if you tried and would stay at it."

"I think I could, too. Yes, I think I could do anything I wanted to do. That would sound conceited to anyone else, but you know me, Eddie, better than anyone else. You understand what I mean."

Eddie nodded. He was concerned about George's bootlegging of gin. He thought it was risky and dangerous. If George started selling very much of it, he could be caught by a dick or a revenue agent.

"Now that I have my little racket going, I have a means of getting the small revenue I need. I'll have time to read, to loaf, and invite my soul, as Walt Whitman would say. I'll think about writing before I make up my mind and decide if I have the urge, the *divine afflatus.*"

"Selling washtub gin is goddamned dangerous, George."

"Dangerous? I'm living dangerously, but there's no risk to selling gin. I'm careful about selecting my customers. It's easy money and it gives me what I need—time and leisure and the pittance I'm willing to live on."

Eddie didn't go for it. If George Raymond chose to sell gin at the Forum, it didn't involve him, Eddie. He wasn't in any danger; but he still didn't like it. He'd like to live dangerously, too; but he was afraid that he lacked the courage. He wished that he were as fearless as George.

Eddie remained dubious. The chances of arrest were high once George got his bootlegging on a profitable basis.

"Nietzsche didn't mean that by living dangerously, you walk into traps, or that you set traps for yourself," Eddie said.

"There'll be no traps if I'm careful; and if I really get this thing going, I can pay off the cops. Then it'll be like taking candy from babies or seducing virgins. It can't fail. What about you, Eddie, are you working tomorrow?"

"No, I get every other Sunday off at my station."

"That's right, I forgot. I'm going to sleep late. I wish I'd picked up some gash tonight. I had a chance to but I didn't want it. Now I wish I had. That's the contradictoriness of men. Who was the cute number I saw you dancing with tonight, Eddie?"

"She was some Lizzie Glutz. When I tried to talk with her, all she'd do was go 'Uh!'"

George burst into loud laughter. A surly unshaven fellow at the other end of the counter glowered at him.

"I don't like the look on that guy's puss," George said.

Eddie hoped that there wouldn't be a fight.

"If anybody doesn't like the way I laugh, he'd better stick cotton in his ears," George said loud enough for the fellow to hear.

But nothing happened.

Eddie walked with George back to the dumpy little hotel and then set out across Washington Park for home. It was late but he loved the night, with its blue haze reflecting the glow of a full moon. The grass was wet and all about him were shadows among deep black patches—spots which caught glitter from the moon, and ahead, a dark outline of shrubbery. The lagoon was glowing.

The silence of the night touched Eddie; it seemed profoundly serene. Eternity would be like this, he thought, quiet without end in a world of night. Then why is it feared and resisted, he wondered—this timelessness of peace without pain?

Eddie walked on, absorbed in his thoughts. He was dissatisfied with himself, with the way he was living. Why was he wasting time hanging around the Forum? And George Raymond—Eddie felt a vague disappointment in him. Why did George want to muscle in on the Forum; why was he selling washtub gin?

When Eddie had thrown away his past, when he had left the University, he had had a definite goal. He had made up his mind; he was going to become a writer. And what had he done? Nothing.

Suppose he should fail; he'd have nothing, he'd be nothing. He'd be like old John Mason, sleeping in a basement, in a stuffy little cubbyhole. There was something terrible in failure. It was a mortal wounding of a man's pride.

Out of his melancholy, came the resolution to study more, to write more and waste less time.

But he continued going to the Forum. George and Alec would talk about the future of the Forum. They believed that they could make something big out of it, as big if not bigger than the Wild Onion on the North Side.

"When we strike gold, Eddie, we'll finance you and let you write without having to work," George said during one of these talks.

Eddie didn't say anything; he was not able to share their enthusiasm. He couldn't understand how they mesmerized themselves.

George's small-scale bootlegging had increased the attendance at the Saturday night dances. These were getting crowded, as well as noisy and rowdy. More fellows than girls were showing up. The drinking was getting heavy and drunks staggered and floundered about. George had started getting his twenty-five dollars a week. He kept saying that now he had time to read and study, and maybe make a stab at writing. But if he did write, he said, it would be only for himself and a few friends.

When the Forum had been started, Wilbert and Alec both had hoped to be able to put on plays and do little skits. But they hadn't attracted talent or many aspirants.

However, Lenora Jackson was waiting for the time when the Forum would become a little theater. She would be the leading lady and would go straight from 57th Street and Cottage Grove Avenue to Broadway. Her father, Conrad Jackson, planned to manage her.

Conrad Jackson claimed to have been an actor in his youth. He was an aging ham with thick gray hair and a somewhat lined and solemn face. He always wore a flowing black tie. He would speak of his daughter's genius for the theater. Like an actor throwing away a line, he would slyly suggest that Lenora had not come by her gifts accidentally.

"We're a theatrical family," he'd say.

He constantly alluded to his own "thespian" past and said that he had been cast in plays of Shakespeare, Marlowe, and all of the "great playwrights of the classic tradition." He was never specific about these roles in his "thespian" past. Lenora, he'd say, even now could outstrip some of the well-known actresses of the American theater; but she could profit by a little experience and by his coaching.

Every time he'd make his assertion about his daughter's outstripping ability, the fellows would turn their heads and laugh. There were continual jokes and cracks about Lenora's talents in outstripping.

Alec was sensitive to these witticisms.

"That's a bum joke," he'd say, and he was often right. There were many jokes and remarks made about Lenora, thanks to her loving father's misuse of the word.

"He's practically a moron," Alec said, "but Lenora is good. Once we get started putting on plays, you wise guys will eat your bum jokes."

"You're in a position to know, Alec. You can talk with authority on Lenora's exceptional talents," Eddie said dryly.

"I'm no authority on the theater, but I've heard her read from plays; and I say she's good."

"Alec, I accept what you say as authoritative. I'd say it almost has the status of scientific truth," Eddie said.

"Listen, Eddie, what the hell are you doing, trying to be funny?"

"No. I am only saying that you ought to know if Lenora can outstrip many prominent American actresses."

"I like damned near everything about you, Eddie, but your sense of humor. It doesn't exist. You're one of the few Irishmen I know who's completely lacking in a sense of humor."

A moment later, Alec grinned broadly and said:

"I won't discuss outstripping, but after she is stripped, she has no lack of talent."

"She's well built and pretty," Wilbert said.

Alec was proud of himself for having won Lenora. A lot of the people around the Forum thought that she was beautiful. Eddie felt that this was stretching the truth a bit but he did think she was a fine-looking blonde, tall, well-built—almost statuesque—with a round and well-formed face. She had nicely proportioned, long legs; and her carriage attracted attention. She held herself erect, and had been coached in walking at a dramatic school on Michigan Avenue.

Lenora did stand out at the Forum. She was always dressed for show; and in that basement she appeared elegant and somewhat out of place. Most of the other girls were casually dressed, and a few were shabby. They were there to have a good time and did not stand about posing, did not turn their heads to give a profile view, nor did they indulge in other little gestures and mannerisms. They laughed, they talked, they teased, they danced with faces that changed from mood to mood. Lenora kept a masklike face that made her seem aloof. She spoke when spoken to; smiled often but not quickly, not with spontaneity. There was little to say to Lenora Jackson and she had little to say in return.

Her father usually stood watching her. She regularly turned toward him as though she were receiving signals.

III

When Riggs first appeared at the Forum, he struck almost everyone as being unwholesome. He seemed to be constantly peering at others and eavesdropping, instead of listening to their conversations. He'd hang around for a couple of hours and then casually invite one of the fellows to go home with him for a chat, a bite to eat—or to see a book or a painting that he had. He lived with his mother in an apartment on 55th Street.

Whenever he was refused, and he was, often, he acted as though he were impervious to insult; but he was hypersensitive to all that was said to him and about him. His memory was a warehouse of stored-away jibes and insults.

He fancied himself a poet and was convinced that his feelings were more rare and his sense of beauty more refined than those of others.

Riggs knew little about the theater and had no experience in directing or acting, but he believed that he could direct plays and run a little theater. For years he had harbored the ambition to write clever and sophisticated comedies—to become the Oscar Wilde of America. From time to time, he would dabble at playwriting; and in his room, there was a drawer full of scenes and fragments of scenes. Most of them were parts of a play on homosexuality which he had titled *The Love That Dares Not Speak Its Name*. Someday, in the future, he would complete this play and he'd write other plays, too; and the name Anthony Riggs would be famous. This he believed with desperate faith.

Riggs' eyes grew big and greedy when he first saw George Raymond. He introduced himself, and to Eddie's surprise, George engaged in a long talk with him. Eddie shouldn't have been surprised, however, because George constantly acted on sudden whims and would feign friendships for sundry and eccentric people.

Eddie stood nearby, half-listening to George and Riggs chat. He suspected that Riggs was homosexual and would probably try to make George. George often attracted homosexuals and seemed to be amused by this. He would egg them on, and then play them for fish, and inveigle money out of them.

George and Riggs continued to talk. Eddie Ryan stayed on the sidelines, impatient and bored. Riggs' desire was transparent. He seemed to have a driving need, which he could not check or control, a lust which could shatter his pride and his dignity and make him a beggar for love and sexual gratification.

Eddie recalled a sketch of Ben Hecht's which dealt with such an uncontrollable lust. Suddenly, Eddie felt pity for Riggs.

At one point, George Raymond turned around to Eddie and introduced Riggs to him; but Riggs, after barely acknowledging the introduction, turned back to George:

"You have made a singularly strong impression on me— I should have known that you are intelligent. By happy accident, and I tell you this with assurance because to eavesdrop would be a breach of taste, I overheard you talking. Are you a poet by any chance?"

"I dabble in poetry, and aphorisms, epigrams, and I make notes for stories I might one day write. It suits my whim to live poetry instead of write it. You asked me if I am a poet. You mean not merely am I a poet, but who am I and what am I? Is that not so?"

"Precisely, if the intrusion of one whom you do not know does not rouse ire in you or cause offense."

"In this dump, anybody can talk to anyone else," George said.

"It isn't an elegant place and I cannot give utterance to

any enthusiasm about it as it now is. But that is why I have been bold enough to approach you."

"I can make it exciting but I can't envision myself adding any elegance to the joint."

Riggs became a bit fluttery.

"Elegance is of the manor borne," he said but there was an unsureness in his voice. "May I call you George?"

"Everybody else does. Even my mother."

"I ask you first because I do not become familiar enough to use a first name before I know a person. It is not my custom to accost."

"Think nothing of it. What are you called? Tony?"

"I'm known as Riggs. I admit that I prefer it to Tony. I've become so accustomed to hearing myself called Riggs that that's what I think of myself as."

"My buddy here is Eddie," George said.

"Eddie," Riggs said, turning toward him for a moment.

"What's in a name, as Shakespeare asked," said George.

"Yes, names never make the man," Riggs said.

The conversation went on like this for a few more minutes.

George stood with his hands in the pockets of his unpressed blue pants, his feet spread wide, the collar of his white shirt open, sometimes watching Riggs and then glancing off to his left or right, his manner easy and nonchalant.

The scene was strange to Eddie Ryan. His interest quickened; he wanted to know and to write about all kinds of people. He began to feel some excitement and he hoped that George would keep the conversation going. He had never heard a man try to pick up and make another man. He couldn't fully believe in the reality of this kind of attraction although he knew that there were many men who were drawn to men just as he was drawn to girls. On principle, he couldn't consider this wrong or evil—it would be inconsistent with what he thought. By judging Riggs' desires, Eddie would have been violating his Nietzscheism. He could not have remained "beyond good and evil." Too, it would have contradicted his motto taken from Max Stirner's *The Ego and His Own*— "All Things Are Nothing to Me."

"Have you ever felt the urge to be an actor?" Riggs asked, pronouncing the word "urge" with intensity.

"Life, the world, is the only stage on which I want to act and strut. Life is my stage."

"Yes, but I think you could be an actor, a gifted one if you were trained and directed."

George gave a deprecating short laugh.

"I wouldn't have the patience to rehearse the same lines, night after night."

"Patience is an acquired virtue."

"I've never learned it."

"You could be taught," Riggs said. He paused. "I could teach you patience . . . and how to project yourself on the stage."

"Hey, Eddie, can you imagine me, George Raymond, an actor?" George asked, turning to Eddie.

"I've never thought about it, but . . ."

Riggs interrupted: "The reason I'm here and the reason I approached you is that I am going to direct plays and manage the productions here. I think I could make you my leading man if you are willing to give it a try."

"I'll give anything a try," George said, lighting a cigarette. "But acting up there on that stage, I'll have to think about it."

"But you will think about it?" Riggs asked, gushing.

"Oh, yes, I'll give it some thought."

"I hope you do, George. I can just see you on that stage, holding the audience enthralled, your magnetism radiating across the footlights."

"Oh come on, Riggs, I couldn't be that good."

"Give it a try, George, you'll have no regrets."

With this, Riggs left.

At first George chuckled and then he burst into loud laughter.

"That sawed-off pansy thinks he can make me."

"You certainly made a conquest, George."

George bent over, still laughing, "I strung him along. I gave you some good material, Eddie. My acting wasn't bad, was it?"

"He's good material all right. He'd be good to do in a story written like the pieces in Ben Hecht's 1001 *Afternoons in Chicago*. He's sort of grotesque, and a little pathetic."

"I'll string him along and let him think he's going to make the grade. Why not? It's a new role and it might be amusing for a while. Maybe we can use him before I dash ice water in his fairy face. Fairy face—that's a good description of his mug. I'll give you a full account, Eddie. Maybe you'll be able to write a story about it and sell it to someone—like Mencken at *The American Mercury*."

Eddie wasn't enthusiastic about this idea. He felt that he had known George long enough not to be surprised at anything that he did; and yet this plan to string Riggs along and toy with him did surprise Eddie.

George went on talking about the farce he planned—he'd gain some understanding of the fairy mind which would be of help should he decide to write. He'd get Eddie material, too. And it would be fun to watch. He could get Riggs to proposition him in embarrassing circumstances, and then expose the pansy.

Eddie didn't say anything—he hoped that George would abandon the idea. He couldn't understand what pleasure there would be in this game. But he knew George Raymond well enough to know that the best way to have him turn a game into a project would be to try to talk him out of it, so he said nothing.

After his first meeting with George, Riggs had hopes. He would seek George out at the Forum and was even becoming casually friendly with Eddie. When George and Eddie sat alone at the Forum and discussed writing, Riggs would join them. Eddie suspected that he was trying to give the impression that the three of them were friends with common interests. Riggs had not read much. He spoke of how one should be as selective of one's reading matter as of one's friends. Fewer books could be appreciated more because the mind would be free of too many impressions. In the same fashion, a man with a few friends rather than many could know them better. The good things in life were rare. Figuratively speaking, the truly good things were like rare wines. That reminded him—he had some exceptionally fine wine at home. Why didn't they come on over later and share it with him?

George said that they'd like to. The three of them left the Forum and went over to the five-room apartment that Riggs shared with his mother. There was nothing exceptional about the place. The furniture was big and ugly. There were a few dime-store prints on the parlor wall. There was a random collection of books behind glass in a clumsy but ornate bookcase. There were some small figurines of nude men on the mantelpiece.

Riggs introduced them to his mother, a small pale woman with tight lips; she was dressed in black. She merely acknowledged the introduction and then left the parlor to go sit in the dining room. She had managed to convey her resentment of their presence. She sat there for at least an hour before she could be heard moving about.

"Mother doesn't take to people on the first meeting," Riggs explained. "She has to see a person two or three times before she becomes friendly, but she's a doll of a mother."

He lowered his voice, "She always thinks that I might associate with bad companions."

"My mother is afraid that others will associate with me," George said, trying to be witty. He knew that this was not at all true.

Eddie said nothing.

Riggs served some red wine and then sat down in a big upholstered chair.

"It's a treat to talk somewhere where it's quiet. There is so much noise at the Forum, so many interruptions. There are too many people around to permit satisfactory conversations that enable civilized human beings to know one another, to discover the width and length and depth of their friendship. Friendship blooms in quiet hours and quiet conversations," Riggs said with an air of thoughtfulness.

Eddie tasted the wine. It tasted no different than any dago red. He wished he hadn't come, he couldn't think of anything to say.

George and Riggs spoke more of friendship.

"It's the finest thing in life," Riggs said and then he quoted Walt Whitman.

George said that one needed a few friends but one really needed many enemies.

Riggs declared that he had his share of enemies, all right, even at the Forum.

"Who?" asked George.

Riggs answered that he would not pay them the honor of naming them; but if he did, he would venture to say that the two of them would be surprised.

Eddie's curiosity was aroused, he wondered who these enemies were. He thought of Alec McGonigle. A few evenings earlier, Alec had said that Riggs was the kind of a person who not only got in other people's way, he got in his own way. Alec had asked Eddie what the hell he saw in such a pompous fool. Eddie had pointed out that it was Riggs who sought them, especially George. Alec had shaken his head and said that he couldn't understand how anyone could be friendly with the little weasel.

"Friendship can be called another kind of love, a pure love, don't you think?" Riggs asked George.

"Friendship comes from the brain. Love is a product of glands," George answered.

"Physical love, yes. But the love of friends, George, which—as you clearly expressed it—is an outgrowth of the brain, that's a purer form of love."

"I place a high value on friendship," George said, "but solitude gives fibre to the soul. Of course, I don't mean the soul literally. I mean to your character, to whatever you are."

"Oh, yes. A man who is not lost in the crowd, a man who aspires to fly above the dirt—a man of this kind must commune with himself. I need my own solitude. But after those hours of rare refreshment, a man needs a friend to see," Riggs said, his voice and eyes full of the appeal he was making to George.

Eddie continued to sit there, silently. Riggs didn't impress him as having much intelligence, but he found himself wishing that he could say something to impress on him the fact that he, Eddie Ryan, was intelligent.

Too, he was embarrassed. Although Riggs and George were only exchanging generalities, Riggs was revealing his feelings. In that dreary parlor, he was uttering a plaintive cry.

George Raymond was amused. He was stringing Riggs along. He was helping Riggs make a fool of himself.

But the scene, the artificial situation, seemed pointless to Eddie. He felt that his presence was even more pointless. Why had he come? Why was he wasting his time as a spectator of this kind of farce? And why was George playing such an elaborate joke on Riggs?

"Eddie, what do you think about friendship?" George asked, turning to him.

The question surprised Eddie, he hesitated to speak. "I don't know. Friendship is important. It's a disinterested relationship. You can be yourself with friends; you don't have to be on guard. It's one of the highest, no, it's one of the most satisfying kinds of shared experience."

"I like that," George said, and turning to Riggs, "Eddie Ryan is the most loyal of friends."

Riggs nodded and he and George resumed their conversation.

Eddie just sat. He was wondering what a friend really was. What did he mean when he said that George Raymond or that Alec McGonigle or anyone for that matter, was his friend? He considered George his best friend, but he did not tell him everything that was on his mind, all his thoughts and dreams. He guessed that was one of the reasons he wanted to write, so that he could express more.

Chapter Five

I

"It's early," George said as he and Eddie Ryan walked along 55th Street, past the dark store fronts.

"What time is it?"

"It's only ten-fifteen."

"I thought it was about midnight," Eddie said in surprise.

"You were bored, weren't you?" George asked, a vague note of reproof in his voice.

"I felt that I was wasting my time," Eddie answered.

"You don't approve of what I'm doing, do you?"

"I wouldn't say that, George, I just don't see the point."

"If I could call myself a student of anything, I'd say that I was a student of human nature, Eddie."

"Maybe so, but I can't study everybody."

"Riggs should be fascinating to observe."

Eddie thought that George probably was right but he felt resentful because of the wasted evening, and resentful of George because he'd allowed him to induce him into wasting it.

"Didn't you think it was funny, Eddie, when he gave me his gabble about friendship when all he was doing was trying to proposition me?"

"A little," Eddie answered.

"Are you going Puritan on me and morally disapproving of my conduct, Eddie?"

"Why the hell should I want to be a Puritan?"

"Sometimes I suspect you do. I wouldn't say this to you, Eddie, if we weren't such friends."

"That's not it at all. I'm not reading enough or writing enough. I feel I've got to do more."

"You have to experience life before you can write, Eddie."

Eddie became depressed. George was probably right. Not only had he read far too little and not written anything worthy of being published, but he had had so little experience. How much did he know about people and about life? Suddenly, his aspiration to become a writer seemed arrogant. He was ridiculous in imagining that he could succeed. He was as ridiculous in his way as Riggs was in his.

"I'm not going to let that ugly little pansy make me," George said.

"I know that."

"But I want to know what makes the wheels go around in his twisted head."

George went on talking about how he was learning by stringing Riggs along. Eddie wondered, what should one do to gain experience to write: How far should one go?

George started singing *The Prisoner's Song*. They walked on along 55th Street. Eddie's mood became more melancholy and he thought of how hopeless life was.

II

Riggs kept making a play for George. He would flatter him by telling him that he was one of the exceptions, one of the rare few who had wings and could fly into the

purified air which was above the many who made up the
vulgar herd. He told George that he had the physique of
a young Greek god, and that the beauty of his appearance
was matched by that of his intelligence. Riggs confessed
that he was a pagan spirit and wished that he had lived
in pagan times. Occasionally, he would allude to the plays
that he would stage and direct. It would take time to acquire the means to put them on; but by then, Riggs hoped
that he would have his own play completed, one with a
part in it that would be perfect for George. The play would
be set among Roman temples.

George recounted to Eddie everything that Riggs said.
He was keeping Riggs at arm's length, finding excuses to
postpone invitations to visit him alone, but leaving the
door slightly ajar so that Riggs would keep hoping.

Alec was let in on the game. Eddie began to lose all
interest. George's descriptions were becoming monotonous;
and even though Eddie couldn't morally disapprove of using people because of his proclaimed views, he found that
he didn't like to see it done.

III

After George had started running the Saturday night
dances and selling his bathtub gin, he and Alec decided
that something more was needed. They decided that a skit
or two should be put on every Saturday night. George said
that he'd write one. He did fill about two pages of a note-
book but then he gave up. He showed his notes to Eddie
and asked him if he could write the skit. His idea was to
build it around a beachcomber in a dive in Singapore.
George Raymond would appear as the beachcomber.

"It's for the morons who come to the Forum on Saturday nights and it has to be on their level. Of course, I

wanted to give it an original sardonic twist, something that would be over their heads," George said.

The beachcomber would be sitting with his head on the table, drunk, while two men at a side table bargained over a woman. One of the men was in white slave traffic and the other was buying a captive woman for his whorehouse.

"That will tickle the morons," George said.

The white slaver would talk of the charms of the woman he was selling—her figure, her beauty, and her technique. He would declare that whoever had broken this woman in and trained her had known his movements and positions. The whorehouse owner would try to get the price down. He'd swear that no woman could be as good as the new one was supposed to be. The white slaver would then propose that the customer have a free trial. The whorehouse owner would suggest that the trial take place as soon as the woman was brought in—the whorehouse owner could jump her right there on one of the tables.

"That's an enticing bit for the morons. They'll think that we're going to put it on right there before them. And the white slaver can say, 'She's better on a hard table than most molls are on a bed.' I like that line."

The whorehouse owner would nod his head in the direction of the beachcomber and ask about him. But he'd be told that the guy was a derelict who was always so drunk that he didn't know what was going on. The free trial would be agreed on and the price would be determined by the results of the test.

"By that time, the morons will all have hot pants," George said.

The captive woman would be brought in with a sheet over her head. Then, George corrected this detail.

"No, she'll have a towel around her face. That'll win some laughs."

The woman would be told she had to strut her stuff

good or else she'd be killed, taken to the jungle and fed as breakfast food to some baby tigers. She would plead and wring her hands.

"Take 'em off, lady, and take 'em off fast. I ain't got all night."

The woman's sobs and pleas would fail. Her captors would surround her and start to tear her clothes off. She would struggle and scream:

"Is there no gentleman in this joint? Will no hero save my honor?"

The beachcomber would spring up from the table and shout:

"I'll save your honor. Unhand that lady, you dastards, don't undress her."

"I get a chuckle out of that—'Unhand that lady, don't undress her.'"

Then there would be a scrap but the beachcomber would succeed in getting a gun from one of the villains. He would shoot them all, and he would take the towel off the woman's face, saying:

"I've saved your honor, fairest one."

Then he would see who she was, and he would be struck with consternation.

The woman would say:

"You always were my hero, darling."

And the hero would put his hands to his ears, face the audience, and cry out in despair:

"My God, I've saved my wife again."

While the wife would tug at him, he would bend down over the dead men sprawled all over the stage.

"Rise from the dead like Jesus Christ," he would tell them frantically and desperately.

"That's the end. It ain't art, Eddie, but what wise men cast pearls among swine? The morons will like it and that's the purpose of my skit. Maybe I'd better not use the name of Christ. I'd better not offend their religious sensibilities."

George decided that he could "use" Riggs by asking him to write the skit for him.

"If I ask, Riggs will obey," George chuckled.

Riggs did agree to write it. He remarked that there were touches of true sardonic humor in the idea as George had explained it to him. After some discussion, they decided on a name, *Femme Fatale in Singapore*. Riggs went home immediately to start on the skit.

Watching him waddle along Cottage Grove Avenue, George said:

"Look how big his ass is. The poor chump, he's got more ass than he has sense."

Riggs wrote the skit. George lined up three other fellows to take parts in it. Alec had told him that there wasn't a dog's chance of getting Lenora to play the wife. Her old man would balk, and Alec didn't want to rub the wrong side of the old faker.

"She's too good in bed," Alec said, "I don't want to risk my pleasure. There are plenty of girls who come around here. You can get one of them easily. Hell, Raymond, with your sex appeal, you can get most of them to do anything you want."

Riggs finished the skit and brought it over. Alec looked at the manuscript and said:

"It's too long. The audience doesn't want to watch anything that long, especially when it's acted by amateurs."

Riggs looked at Alec with resentment.

Alec went on, "It's clever, Riggs. It's funny, it makes me chuckle, but the three guys we've picked can't learn this many lines. And you have to remember, the gang we're getting here now, you can't hold them for more than five or ten minutes. They want to drink and shake with girls on the dance floor."

Riggs' eyes filled with hatred as he stared at Alec.

The skit was put on before a big Saturday night crowd, almost a hundred. The only props were tables, chairs, and glasses. George stood at the front of the low stage and gave a brief explanation.

No disasters happened, the skit ran smoothly. Some of the spectators laughed. George Raymond was stripped to the waist for his part.

Later, when the dancing was resumed, he wandered about with his chest still bare. He had good shoulders and was well-built. Quite a few of the girls noticed him.

George sold about fifteen bottles of washtub gin that night. Many of the fellows, and even some of the girls, got drunk. They staggered around, bumping into each other, shouting. Some were necking openly. As the evening wore on, a few grew surly. The atmosphere in the hot and overcrowded basement was tense.

"Stick around, Eddie, we may have to pound lumps on some of these monkeys," George said. Eddie was sober and didn't like the prospect. Some of the fellows looked plenty husky and he didn't want to fight them but he knew that if anything started, he'd have to pitch in.

Even though that was the best evening, financially, that George had had so far at the Forum, his own mood was mean. Eddie was afraid that he might touch off trouble. If a fight was started, it might turn into a free-for-all or a small-scale riot. Either way, it could be nasty and dangerous. Anybody could be slugged and trampled upon and the girls might be injured. The place would be wrecked and the cops would come.

The blare of the jazz records being played on the victrola filled the basement. The talks and shouts rose to a roar. The small floor space was jammed with couples dancing. They looked like an eerie swaying mass in the darkness. Fellows and girls kept leaving and returning through the door at the right, mainly to drink the raw and vile-tasting stuff that George had sold them. The basement became stuffier and stuffier and the cigarette smoke began to look like a gray cloud.

Eddie started to have a headache. He moved toward the side door; he thought that some fresh air would help his head. A fellow was dragging a girl through the door, shouting at her:

"If you two-time me, bitch, I'll kick your tits into pulp."

"Let me go," she screamed.

Outside on the sidewalk of Cottage Grove Avenue, they shouted and cursed at each other. A small group rushed out to watch them.

"Any two-timing broad ought to have her teeth smashed down her throat," a fellow who stood near Eddie said.

George walked by, still naked from the waist up.

"Who do you think you are, Tarzan?" a husky fellow sneered.

George turned around quickly and faced the fellow.

—Now it will begin, thought Eddie.

"Yes, you sonofabitch, I think I am Tarzan. What do you want to do about it?"

Eddie drew near. So did others.

"Hell, I don't care if you are Tarzan."

"I don't happen to like loudmouths. I do the bouncing around here. You put a silencer on your tongue when I'm around or else you'll find out damn quick just who I am."

"I was only kiddin'."

"And I'm not kidding."

George faced the fellow for a few seconds. Then he turned to glare at the group that had crowded around. No one spoke. He sauntered off.

There were no fights on that Saturday night. As midnight approached, the fellows and girls started to leave.

George stood, watching them. When they had all left, he turned, lit a cigarette:

"Who can waste his pity on humanity?"

Riggs was standing a few feet away. He was watching George.

IV

On the next day, Sunday, Alec and George sat on a bench in Washington Park near the 57th Street entrance. They were having what they jokingly called "a conference."

"I was thinking in church this morning," Alec said, "you know, I'm as much an atheist as you and Eddie Ryan, but I go to Mass on Sunday mornings because of my mother. If I told her I didn't believe in God, she'd be terribly hurt. And damn it, I get some of my best ideas at Mass on Sundays. This morning I got one that I'm proud of, even if I do say so myself."

"Spill it, Alec," George said.

"Here, do you want one?" Alec asked, holding a package of cigarettes out to George.

"Thanks. I can buy my own now, but I'll smoke one of yours," George said, taking one.

They lit up.

"Listen, George, because I know this is a damned good idea and it'll work, too."

"If that's the case, it means that the church and the ritual of the Mass have some use," George said.

"Well," Alec began, "I was thinking that it's about time for a reaction away from the ideas of flaming youth."

"What do you mean, Alec? Do you mean we've had too much sin and that the pendulum will swing over until we have too much virtue? I can't see that."

"Listen, goddamn it. I listen to you a hell of a lot."

"That's more than I do to myself, Alec. I don't usually listen to myself talk."

"There's been a hell of a lot said and written about the Jazz Age, flaming youth, and the revolt of youth. The newspapers have been pretty full of it and there must have been dozens of articles in magazines about it. It's been in books. What was the name of that book written by a professor named Percy Marks? I didn't read it but I remember there was a lot written about it."

"*The Plastic Age,* I think that was the book."

"Of course, the older generation always thinks that youth is going to Hell and the world is going to the dogs; and the wowsers, people like that, decry how fast youth has become. I was thinking about all this at Mass. I asked myself, why don't we start a movement to slow down youth?"

"Jesus Christ, Alec, have you been reading Eddie Guest and Dr. Frank Crane?"

"I'm serious, George. I was watching the crowd last night. In a couple of weeks if we keep getting a gang like that, we're going to have a goddamned rowdy joint. They'll be fighting and yelling and guzzling gin all over the place and damned near screwing in the middle of the dance floor."

"Good, we'll make more money," George said.

"We both agreed that there's something lacking, something we need. There aren't enough Bohemians on the South Side to make the Forum pay and Bohemians aren't good spectators. The Bohemians don't pay the freight for the Wild Onion on the Near North Side. They merely provide the atmosphere. They serve as the substitutes for the real writers and poets and artists. It's the tourists and the college boys who are the paying customers for the Wild Onion. We can't pull in tourists. We haven't any attractions for them."

"Except Raymond," George joked.

"Yes, except for Raymond, we have no other attractions that will draw tourists, gapers, hicks and, what the hell, you know what I mean, George."

"Yes, I get the drift, Alec, but we're doing pretty good. We pulled in about ninety or a hundred bucks last night. That's not bad. In fact, it's damned good. For us, business is booming. And we'll have just as big a crowd or bigger next Saturday night and I'll sell more of Raymond's own specially made washtub gin."

"I know but we're starting to attract a lot of goddamn riffraff, and if we ain't goddamn careful, we'll end up running a joint for street corner and poolroom hooligans."

"I wouldn't call the gang we had last night a gang of Nietzschean supermen, Alec."

"Many of them were nothing but riffraff. And if they keep coming and drinking that potent rotgut you sell them, we're going to have nothing but fights every Saturday night until there is a big free-for-all and the place is completely wrecked. When that happens, the cops will come and we could all get pinched." Alec paused and broke into a smile. "You know, Mr. Raymond, or did you, that there is a law prohibiting the sale of spirituous liquors?"

"You know, I had forgotten. My memory never was very good, especially in matters pertaining to law. My mother must have dropped me on my head when I was a baby. Or else my memory was jarred when I was dropped off the freight car in that fight I had about four years ago. I told you about that fight, didn't I, Alec?"

"Yes you did."

"If you ever write my biography, remember that, my poor memory for the laws of the land. But come on, let's have it, what's your bright new idea, Alec?"

"If we want to keep going and make some dough, and

be sure that it comes in pretty steady, we've got to organize something—a club."

"That's damned near a stroke of genius," George said.

"Of course it is. Who the hell do you think thought up the idea?"

"I almost thought that I did," said George. "If we organize a club, we can collect dues. I might even get myself elected treasurer."

"We could organize a club to slow down fast youth, the Slow-Down Club, that's my idea for the name. How does it strike you, George?"

"That's not a stroke of genius, Alec, that is genius. You ought to attend two Masses on Sunday. It tickles my fancy—George Raymond and Alec McGonigle organizing a club to slow down the fast, Jazz Age, flaming youth. That's a card, Alec. We'll sell them Raymond's gin, made with George Raymond's own hands, and maybe we'll cop a cherry or two ourselves on the side, just to keep our consciences clear of virtue."

"I thought you'd like my idea."

"The Slow-Down Club," George said, "I like that."

Alec beamed.

They talked about how they would organize a Slow-Down Club and how they would keep the control of it in their own hands. They offered the presidency to each other. Both of them wanted it, and Alec believed that he deserved it—it had been his idea. But George convinced him that they ought to control the club from behind the scenes and place others as officers. Alec then suggested Old John Mason as president. With his age and his dignified manner, he was an ideal choice. They both laughed as they talked about the hell-raising speech that Old John would probably deliver, denouncing the evils of youth. It'd be better than most of the sermons on the Jazz Age that you could hear in churches around town on Sunday. Alec

then asked George what he thought of naming Wilbert
Wilmer the treasurer. George didn't like this idea, he was
afraid that Wilbert would pocket all of the cash. Alec
was sure that Wilbert was a square shooter. George agreed
that he might be but explained that Wilbert might have
too much power if he were treasurer. He might even want
rent from the Slow-Down Club for the use of the hall.

They sat in the sun, smoking cigarettes, absorbed in
their discussion. Each believed that he was proving how
clever he was to the other. Alec was especially proud of
himself—for once, he Alec McGonigle, had proposed a
plan. George was the one who usually appeared stronger,
cleverer, more daring, more charming, and frequently,
more intelligent. But it wasn't George who had produced
the idea of the Slow-Down Club. Alec rose in his own
self-esteem and found new proof to justify his belief that
he was very intelligent.

They both felt a thrill of power as they continued their
discussion. They would control the Slow-Down Club, and
they would do it in a conspiratorial manner from behind
the scenes, using others to do their bidding. The two of
them, especially George, kept bragging about how they
could "use" people. They thought of an undifferentiated
group, a small mass of members without any distinguishing
or individual characteristics.

They sat on the park bench and talked and laughed and
sometimes kidded each other. They envisioned scenes of
meetings and imagined every chair in the hall filled. In
their minds' eyes, they pictured the human outlines and
forms but not the faces of the members. They were the
ones who would pay dues, buy George's washtub gin, and
provide them with enough pocket money. They felt the
fascination of conspiracy. They considered the members
suckers and it didn't occur to them that they would act as
anything but suckers.

V

The Slow-Down Club was formed, and Alec, because he had been a law student at night school, worked out the constitution with advice from George and John Mason. The old man had instantly warmed up to the idea when they had explained it to him. He saw himself playing a bigger role than he had been playing around the Forum. To many of the young people who came to the Forum, John Mason was merely an old man. They would listen in a vague way when he spoke and sometimes they didn't listen at all. They were bored by what he said. Through the Slow-Down Club, he would be able to make himself more important and respected. The young people would look up to him and he could associate more with them. He was stimulated by them and able to enjoy the illusion that he was a little younger. And yet sometimes he was saddened because he felt the loss of so many years and he would think how he would die soon. These young people had so many years before them; they had not yet learned of the swiftness of time.

John Mason needed no persuading when Alec suggested that he serve as president of the Slow-Down Club. He considered it a big honor. The possibilities of the club excited him and he dreamed about the future. The idea of the club might spread through the city or even the whole country; and he, as president of the first Slow-Down Club, could acquire fame. He saw himself as the president of the Slow-Down Clubs of America. He thought of the comforts he would have, a decent room, even a home. He would travel in Pullman cars with meals in the diner, and stay at first-class hotels. He'd have women, too.

Wilbert Wilmer also liked the idea. It would give him

some increased revenue and help him pay the rent and electricity bill. He hoped that this idea of slowing down would catch on—at least a little. He had begun to get jittery because of George Raymond's bootlegging operation. There was too much drinking at the Saturday night dances. There were dangers of fighting and rioting and this could bring the police down on their heads. Some of the girls who came to the dances looked young, like minors, who must be jail bait. Suppose a fellow picked one of them up in the Forum and laid her—if she got caught, she'd probably tell her mother and father. Then he'd really be in trouble, they might even close down the Forum. Wilbert was all in favor of organizing the Slow-Down Club. And who knows—perhaps the club might start bringing in a different class of young people. He might find a possible recruit or two for the colony in the Ozark Mountains that he hoped to found one day.

Eddie Ryan was the only one who didn't respond to the idea of a Slow-Down Club with enthusiasm. He refused to be an officer. At first, George Raymond tried to convince him to serve as treasurer, then as secretary. Eddie backed away from both suggestions. He explained to George that he could not serve as an officer because it would interfere with his writing. Actually, Eddie was getting very little writing done, although he was trying, mostly when he was on duty at the filling station. George took Eddie's aspirations to write seriously and whenever Eddie used his writing as an excuse to get out of some proposal or scheme, George never urged him.

Eddie didn't think that George and Alec would succeed. He didn't think that they would follow through even if they made a good start. And he didn't share their confidence about being able to attract large numbers of fellows and girls by proposing a slowing-down of Jazz Age youth.

The fast ones would remain fast; and the Boy Scouts and virgins wouldn't join.

"Where's your sense of humor, Eddie?" Alec asked. He and George laughed, they had no serious intentions of slowing down anyone; they were merely using this idea in order to organize a club in connection with the Forum that would increase the Forum revenue.

—Besides, we can have some fun playing around with the Slow-Down Club, George thought.

Eddie didn't approve; he couldn't understand the feeling of power they were experiencing. He didn't have any desire for such power and couldn't really believe that there was any satisfaction in it. Eddie thought that the club could lead to trouble; and although he tried to appear as reckless as his friends, he didn't like trouble and was anxious to avoid it. He couldn't understand why they would waste time organizing a club and then run it from behind the scenes. For that matter, he couldn't understand why they'd spend so much time organizing a club for people they considered suckers. He was disappointed; he thought that George would have preferred to spend his time reading and writing, and that Alec would rather read good books. There were so many to be read. Almost every time Eddie stepped into the library, he would have a gloomy fear of dying with a staggering number of them unread. Even though he was still young, Eddie felt the oppression of time. His life could not be long enough for him to read all the books that he wanted to read. And how would he ever have the time to write all that he wanted to write?

George and Alec weren't as serious as he had thought they were, or as he had wanted them to be. If the Slow-Down Club did turn out to be a success, it would be a waste of their time and a waste of his time too. Because in his own mind, Eddie Ryan did not fully face up to the simple realization that he did not have to allow them or anyone else to waste his time if he didn't want them to. He wished that the Slow-Down Club would fail.

But the Slow-Down Club started off with surprising success. There were at least fifty young people present at the first meeting. Alec was chairman. He and George had prepared an agenda but most of the items on it were Alec's contribution. He had never before participated in the organization of a club and he prided himself on his intelligence. He also drew satisfaction from the fact that it was he and not George who had had the most ideas for the preparation of the meeting. While they had been making all of the plans, Alec suddenly regretted having quit law school at nights. Maybe he had made a mistake and ought to go back in the fall. Alec had personally thought that Eddie had been a damned fool for quitting the University since he had had a scholarship, and had been pretty sure of winning a second one. What would George and Eddie think if he went back—they'd probably think that he was afraid to burn his bridges behind him as they were always claiming that they had done. But still, the way he was able to think about organizing an agenda and a club helped to convince him about something he had believed—that he ought to enter politics. And if he were a lawyer he just might do that.

Alec had not been nervous before the meeting. He was confident that he could handle the crowd even though most of them were strangers. He knew that he was smarter than nearly all who would be there. Most of them would be like sheep—they wouldn't really know what was going on. He knew that he could think fast on his feet, much faster than these loogins. He knew that he'd demonstrate his intelligence and would impress those who count— George, Eddie, Old John, and Wilbert—and possibly a choice few who might have strayed into the meeting. He liked to speak in public and believed that he did it well.

He could get up on his feet and talk extemporaneously with cleverness and fluency. He had a need to speak. George and Eddie were convinced that this was a sign of an inferiority complex; but Alec knew that damned few fellows his age could come anywhere near him as a speaker.

Conducting the first meeting was a high water mark for Alec. He circulated only in Bohemian circles but he didn't intend to spend his whole life doing this. The examples of John Mason and Wilbert Wilmer struck him and provoked frequent reflection. It was fun doing what he was doing in his early twenties and it provided him with more intelligent and civilized amusement than he could find, say, running around with some gang that hung around poolrooms or went to public dance halls and whorehouses. But he knew that the kind of life he was leading couldn't be permanent.

Alec enjoyed standing before the crowd, running the meeting and making himself the most important person in the basement of the rundown Kent Hotel. He was controlling the crowd before him as though there were reins in his hands. He was pulling their minds to him, managing them, and he held authority over them. He experienced the thrill of power—he had not realized how keenly a person could enjoy doing this.

George Raymond and Eddie Ryan sat in the last row of camp chairs. They slouched in their seats and put on an air of indifference, but they were paying attention. George enjoyed the meeting, laughing to himself at Alec's success. Alec was fooling all of these suckers. He and Alec were pulling strings and George had his own assurance that he would be able to control the club, and Alec. But he had to give him credit—Alec was doing a damned good job.

Although Eddie was following the meeting, his mind wandered from time to time. He'd stare at the backs of people and wonder what this person was like or that person.

He realized that he not only didn't know their names but
he didn't know what they were like, what their thoughts
and dreams were, what their homes were like, their parents, their work—their whole lives.

Eddie noticed some of the pretty girls. He hoped that
he would get a chance to speak. George had asked him to
be ready to if something should go wrong, and Eddie had
agreed. Maybe he would make an impression on some of
them and they'd be curious about him and wonder who
he was.

Alec was still talking. He promised a constitution and
a set of by-laws for the second meeting. Officers were
elected: John Mason as president, Alec as secretary, and
Wilbert Wilmer as treasurer. He and George had discussed
this for some time before they decided on Wilbert as treasurer. Bill Pfeister, a thick-chested young laborer of twenty-
two, was named sergeant-at-arms. He had dark brown hair,
closely cropped, and a large head with a round face. He
looked stupid, and honest. George Raymond had remarked
on this to Alec.

"He looks muscle-bound, even in his head," Alec had replied.

"That's why we can use him. I picked him out of the
crowd. He's only sergeant-at-arms and that will save me the
effort of throwing out some sonofabitch who becomes dis-
ruptive. The poor slob really believes we mean it when we
talk about slowing down."

Alec had laughed.

George continued: "The poor chump's brains are slow,
like a watch that nobody thinks of winding. It ticks slower
all the time. Anything that's slow appeals to him."

They both laughed, not only at Bill Pfeister but at the
Slow-Down Club—the whole idea of it. They had found
the trick which would give them a kind of a career, at least
for a while.

The success of the club surprised everyone. The membership jumped to seventy-five the first week. There were enough cute girls, cute girls who were willing, to attract the fellows. Before the second week had passed, George and Alec took their success for granted.

"It's better times, friend," George would say to Alec with a broad grin.

He kept on selling his washtub gin. He counted on a steady intake of money from this. He and Alec teamed up with a twenty-eight-year-old salesman, Phil Dumont, who had come to Chicago from Quebec. The three of them rented a two-room apartment at 47th and Drexel Boulevard. Alec didn't actually move out from home; he intended to but had to prepare his mother for the blow.

Alec still had Lenora. She very rarely talked about her future career on the stage any more, even though her father kept it up. But Alec had also ended up with Myrtle one night and was laying her in the apartment. George had quickly cut in but nobody seemed to mind and it was satisfactory to all three. Whenever Phil would have his girl at the apartment all night, George, Alec, and Myrtle would sleep in the other room.

George was making money and suggested that Alec quit his job. Alec did.

Alec McGonigle felt the need of taking a chance, of "living dangerously." He was influenced by George and Eddie, by their Nietzscheanism, their appearance of having severed family ties and obligations. Neither George nor Eddie seemed to be under psychological pressure to succeed in order to please their families, especially their mothers. George had already held and quit so many jobs that a recital of them sounded like a reading from a phone directory. He had left home the first time when he was sixteen. He had been a traveling salesman in Texas, had hitchhiked to New Orleans and shipped out on a freighter

bound for London and Liverpool, had made fifty dollars a
week as a salesman for an advertising agency, a job far more
promising than those which most of the fellows around
58th Street had ever gotten. And he had thrown up all
these jobs and taken his chances. When Eddie Ryan had
abandoned his faith, George Raymond had followed suit,
after having put up many arguments. Eddie Ryan had introduced George to *Babbitt* and to the writings of H. L.
Mencken and Nietzsche. George Raymond had already
launched forth on his own, scorning the security of a job.
He began to talk about becoming a writer.

And although Eddie Ryan still lived at home and still
had a job, he had rejected religion, "the gospel of success,"
as George now called it, and had quit the University to become a writer.

Alec had abandoned the Church by the time he was ten
years old, but he had guarded this as a secret for years—
from his mother and others. He made no pretensions to
becoming a writer. There was no bitterness in him. He felt
that he had been lied to, that false values and ideals of
success had been held up to him, but he bore no resentment about this.

Eddie Ryan and George Raymond did bear resentment
about all this, and George would sound off bitterly about
it. But in this, as in so many other angers, he would
overdo himself. His emotions did not seem to be rooted in
any urgent needs of his own personality. His outbursts
would sometimes puzzle Eddie and touch off doubts in
him. Vague questions would occur to him and he would
wonder for a brief moment if George meant what he was
denouncing in such energetic and concentrated anger.

Eddie would dismiss these thoughts; he didn't want to
believe them—he would not recognize the hollowness that
George sometimes exhibited when he sounded off.

VI

Like Alec, George and Eddie had discovered the Bug Club in their teens. They had been drawn to some of the Bug Clubbers' personalities, and especially to Wallie Brockton, a towering man in his early thirties with blond hair and a likable smile which put you at ease and thawed away any fears that his size and powerful physique might have inspired.

Eddie had first heard Wallie Brockton when he was still a high school kid in short pants dreaming baseball dreams. He didn't understand what Brockton meant when he would address the Saturday or Sunday crowds. Eddie put him down as another radical, an I.W.W. "I Want Whiskey" and "I Won't Work" fellow. Eddie didn't distinguish between wobblies, Communists, and other radicals—he considered them all crackpots.

Wallie Brockton appeared regularly at the Bug Club. He was usually coatless with a clean white shirt, open at the collar, and brown slacks. He didn't look like a bum or a hobo; and he never shouted or ranted when he spoke in the big circle, or even when he disagreed with others in one of the direct arguments in which the Bug Clubbers engaged.

Wallie Brockton's attacks on the system and on America's participation in the War made Eddie apprehensive. He didn't like this kind of talk; he didn't want the government overthrown.

One warm summer evening when the sky was a thick and heavy blue, Eddie Ryan had stood at the edge of a small group listening to a discussion. Wallie Brockton's head and shoulders loomed above the people clustered around him. He was smoking a cigarette and listening to the discussion. Now and then, he would lean his head toward someone who was talking. There were six or seven men arguing and explaining what they thought; but each of them was riding his own horse, heedless of the others. Wallie Brockton started talking. He explained that there was always action and reaction, that the pendulum must always swing back to the opposite end of the arc. In history, there was action and reaction. In business, action and reaction. In politics, too. Eddie listened, he was impressed, Brockton was right.

It wasn't until later that Eddie realized that this notion about action and reaction was empty.

Wallie Brockton had committed suicide by turning on the gas in the small apartment where he and his wife were living on the Near North Side.

Alec talked about Wallie Brockton often. He told George and Eddie what a wonderful guy Wallie had been. Alec couldn't understand why he had killed himself. There had been no forewarning, none; and Wallie Brockton had been a fellow who loved life. He hadn't seemed morbid or cynical; nor was he the kind of a fellow to rack his brains out with problems and worries. He'd had guts, Wallie had. Riding freights, working in the fields at harvest time, participating in the struggles and battles of the wobblies. Wallie had lived in freedom and loved it; no man had ever been his master. If he hadn't liked things in one place, he'd hop a freight train and move on. He'd been flung in country jails and had battled with cops, sheriffs, and deputy sheriffs. He had spoken to agitate workers from soapboxes, from freight cars, and on street corners—urging them to unite and let no man be their master. He had sat by jungle fires, listening to and telling stories, a happy outcast, a man free to roam, unafraid of danger, unworried about tomorrow or the next town—unencumbered—a romantic and adventurous figure.

Alec spoke of the stories Wallie had told him, descriptions of the road, characters he had met, escapes from death, and of Big Bill Haywood who had died in Russia.

Eddie would be filled with nostalgia for the days when the I.W.W. was waging its heroic struggles. To be a tramp, to ride the rails, wander over the face of America; to ship out and see the world. If he could do that, he would gain experience for writing; he could write like Jack London or Maxim Gorky. His life was so small. He had not faced danger or taken the risks that came with the freedom of a hobo. He had often been afraid of small dangers, like the danger of getting a bust in the nose in a fist fight.

Chapter Six

Alec McGonigle felt bound at home because of his mother. His memory ached with recollections of all his boyhood years. He had looked ahead with the age of twenty-one fixed in his mind. Then he'd be free, independent, on his own. The unexpected return of his father after fifteen years had freed him of the duty to support his mother. She no longer had to work.

Alec had reached the age which had been the time of promise for him back in the unhappy years of his boyhood. He was twenty-one years old. But Alec remained at home.

He had started going to the Bug Club, the Wild Onion on the Near North Side, and the Forum. Some of those he met were the most intelligent men in his experience— they had roamed and traveled. Many had been homeless and some still were. They made up a world of their own.

And then he had met Wallie Brockton who had lived the free life. Alec had been close to him, seeing him often, drinking with him, listening to him talk, admiring him as a hero, the greatest man he'd met.

It was not long after he had known Wallie Brockton

that he had become friendly with George Raymond and Eddie Ryan.

After the immediate success of the Slow-Down Club, Alec and George were convinced that they had it made. There was no problem that could develop that they couldn't master by getting together for a brief huddle and deciding how to handle. Alec's confidence grew—even his walk became jaunty. He was completely unaware of the fact that a growing number of people around the Forum were beginning to consider him conceited, and were beginning to resent him. Wilbert Wilmer was frightened by this change in Alec—maybe Alec, with George as his ally, would take the Forum out of his hands.

And even though Conrad Jackson continued to speak of his daughter, Lenora's future as an actress, he realized that Alec and the Forum could give him no help in advancing her. The Slow-Down Club threatened to absorb the Forum, and there was rarely talk any more of establishing a little theater. Alec tried to assure Conrad Jackson that the club would give them the means to launch a theater in the fall and that they should begin to seriously plan to stage plays with Lenora as the star.

Lenora herself began to fret. Her father was nagging her about Alec and criticizing her because she wasn't controlling him. Alec was seeing less of her and her vanity began to suffer. She wasn't in love with Alec but he was attractive to her and she had been quite willing to go to bed with him. Beneath her masklike appearance and aloof manner, there was a quiet but urgent need for attention and praise. It was this need as well as her fear of her father that made Lenora want to become a great actress. And it was this need that made her bold enough to sneak away from her father and go out with an older man who was married but who swore undying love to her. Alec knew nothing of this affair.

Conrad Jackson was nursing another grievance against Alec; he had been left on the sidelines. He had no role to play in the Slow-Down Club. He smelled money in the club and saw possibilities in it both for Lenora and himself. She could be presented as a model girl who believed that young people should act morally and live clean lives. And he would come forth as her proud father, the man who had brought her up and guided her in purity and modesty. He envisioned her picture in the newspapers, and his own. Once the two of them broke into the newspapers with good publicity, new possibilities would be opened for them. They would be interviewed and he would explain how he was training her for a career on the stage. When her photograph appeared, she might be described as a "beautiful young actress" or the "beautiful daughter of a retired actor." He wondered why he had not seen such possibilities sooner, at the time this crazy club was started. Once he and Lenora made the news, he wouldn't need that squirt McGonigle, he'd be a hindrance. McGonigle had left his daughter in the background. All he'd wanted was to use Lenora for his own pleasure. Conrad Jackson had first thought that the two young people were in love, and he had sanctioned their union. Maybe he had been a fool. McGonigle had changed in the last couple of months. In the beginning, McGonigle had struck him as a fine, clean-cut and intelligent young man. He had even thought of him as an acceptable son-in-law, one who would cooperate with him in helping Lenora have a career, because of her beauty and the ability she had inherited from him. Had he deceived himself? Or had McGonigle changed? Had McGonigle come under the spell of that conceited pair of upstarts—that George Raymond and that Eddie Ryan fellow with the glasses and long hair? Ryan didn't count so much; he only tagged along with Raymond and McGonigle. That

Raymond, he was the one, he was charming, like a snake. He had to watch his Lenora and protect her so that she didn't fall into Raymond's coils.

II

Conrad Jackson started spending more time around the Forum. He would drop in unexpectedly in the afternoon. He would come without Lenora, leaving her free to see her married lover whom she even risked bringing home one afternoon for a rendezvous. Jackson tried to become friendly with old John Mason but they had too much in common to trust each other.

"These young people could profit by more guidance from those of us who have had the experience of life, don't you think, John?" the old man asked John Mason one afternoon.

John Mason was sitting on the bed in his little partitioned room, with his stiff, starched white shirt open at the neck. He had not put on a collar. The gray-black stone basement floor was damp. A slit of window near the ceiling let a feeble light trickle in through crusted dirt and dust. Two suits hung on hooks on the wall and a suitcase was open in a corner. On the small dresser top was a row of books. Old John had not turned on the single light bulb hanging from the ceiling. The room was almost dark and the two old men could not see each other clearly. In the dim light, John Mason looked old and strange, not fully real.

"Young people come out better when they're left alone. They'll come out all right if they grow in freedom. All my life I've been a champion of freedom and the friend of youth."

"Yes, yes, that's what I mean, John. I, like you, am a

friend of the young folks. That's why you see me around
here. And I admire you for what you're doing to help
these young people. I was wondering if I couldn't give you
a helping hand. After all, John, I'm a father myself."

"There's not much to do. The young people are managing themselves quite successfully."

"Yes, yes. It was a fine idea, the Slow-Down Club."

"Yes, a worthy idea. McGonigle is a smart boy. He often
comes to me and I talk to him by the hour."

"I'd take a young man like him to my heart, just like a
son-in-law."

John Mason didn't answer. He sat, looking down as
though lost in thought. Conrad Jackson waited for him to
speak. John remained silent.

"Yes, it's a fine thing being done here, John. Well, I'll
be off; but if I'm ever needed to help promote this idea,
you can count on me. I'm always available, John."

"Yes, I'll remember," Old John said, like a man who
had not heard.

Conrad Jackson left the dingy little room. John Mason
was racked by a fit of dry coughing. His rasping coughs
continued and could be heard in front of the basement.

Eddie Ryan could hear him. A new paroxysm seized
Old John and he gagged, making sounds as though he were
trying to talk but couldn't. His suffering struck Eddie like
some shame, a secret revealed that no one should know.
Eddie felt pity for him. Old John was an old, old man
coughing in a damp dingy basement room with cardboard
walls. This seemed to strip John of all dignity.

Gradually, the coughing stopped. Eddie felt saddened. In
the end, bodies were but poor, weak things, the source of
pain and suffering; and all were equal in the helplessness
before the final destiny of death. Death was ugly, an insult. He remembered the lines from Swinburne that he had
quoted in his debate with Old John:

> *That no life lives forever;*
> *That dead men rise up never;*
> *That even the weariest river*
> *Winds somewhere safe to sea.*

Eddie wondered, would he suffer the pains of dying? Would he be humiliated by that last and biggest insult to man, would he die with his life unjustified? Would he die without having written anything to live after him, some work free of all the ravages that time imposes?

"Oh, how are you, Ryan?" Conrad Jackson asked.

"Oh!" Eddie exclaimed, lost in his mood.

Conrad Jackson stared at him as though he were someone strange.

"I'm all right," said Eddie finally.

"Are your friends around?"

"What?"

"Are Alec and Raymond around this afternoon?"

"I suppose so."

"The Slow-Down Club keeps them busy. They're busy young fellows. How about you, Ryan? Are you slowing down too, like a good member of the Slow-Down Club?"

"Should I?"

"Yes, I guess so. I'm no old fogey. I guess you know that, since you see me all of the time with you young folks. But a little slowing down is wise."

"Yes, it's the golden mean; and we have to practice the golden mean."

"That's a fine way of putting it. The golden mean."

"I really think youth should mend its ways. I'm thinking of joining the YMCA."

"They do good."

"That's why I might join."

Eddie was bored; the conversation was stupid and he wasn't really being clever.

"Don't you think this golden mean idea of the Slow-Down Club would catch on if we got the newspapers interested, and got it written up? We could have a photograph of some girl. I could ask my daughter, Lenora, to help out by having her picture taken. She comes out striking in a good picture."

"I suppose so," Eddie answered disinterestedly.

Riggs walked in. He called to the old man. Eddie walked outside. He blinked—it was a bright day and the basement had been dim. He stared, vacantly, at the streetcar tracks. They gleamed in the sunlight. He wondered what to do, maybe he'd try to write a story about Old John Mason. How would he start? Several men passed. A Negro maid pushed a baby carriage. The baby was asleep. He thought of how much living was going on in Chicago, away from the Forum and the Slow-Down Club, and he was missing it. Time and life were slipping through his fingers. He sunk into a despondent mood. There just wasn't enough time to learn everything there was to know; and then to write, to freeze forever all of the moments of time that slipped through man's fingers. What was he doing here?

Across the street, Washington Park ended in a line of trees. The east side of the street, on which he stood, was ugly. The Kent Hotel had once been an apartment building. The stones looked old and dirty. There were weedy lots on both sides of the hotel. The sidewalk was dirty. It was a forlorn block. And in it, in the basement of that dirty-looking building, Eddie Ryan was crowding his life.

He was a spectator, watching George and Alec play around with the Slow-Down Club. He hadn't even been able to find a girl. He felt frustrated. Somehow all this mattered and it didn't matter. He was not only a spectator at the Slow-Down Club, he was a spectator watching himself. He was watching time slowly move toward death.

George and Alec came along. George broke into a snatch of song. Alec's thin and slightly pale face was full of smiles.

"We thought you'd be here, Eddie," George said.

"We took a long walk; I wanted to get away from this goddamned place for a while," Alec said.

"Our conversation was fascinating. We were both brilliant because the subject of our conversation is one which makes us brilliant—we talked about ourselves," George said.

Eddie was glum and could not respond to their mood.

"What the hell's the matter with you, Eddie? Are you sore because we talked about ourselves instead of you?"

"You're wasting my time. I don't read enough or get enough writing done because both of you waste my time," he lashed out.

They were both startled for a moment. Then Alec spoke:

"Look, fellow, nobody makes you come around. If we're wasting your time, what the hell are you doing here now? We're not stopping you from reading and writing as much as you damned well please."

"You don't understand Eddie, Alec," George explained, "he always feels that he's wasting time unless he's writing or studying."

Eddie laughed. "Let's eat," he said.

"Were you at the Forum, Eddie?"

"Yeh."

"Who was there?"

"John Mason, Riggs, Conrad Jackson . . ."

"Yeh, let's eat," Alec said scornfully.

III

"I want to lay her because she's a virgin," George said. He sat on one of the unmade In-A-Door beds in the

apartment at 47th and Drexel. Alec was sitting on a chair
with his elbow on a folding table. Eddie Ryan was slouched
in another chair. Eddie had closed up the station where he
worked at 8 P.M. and had gone to the apartment instead
of going home.

"Isn't she Bill Pfeister's girl?" Alec asked.

"He thinks so. He met her at White City at the dance
hall. He's been dating her and brought her to the Slow-
Down Club. But for Christ's sake, if I can't take a girl
away from a dumb ox like Pfeister, then I'm sure as hell
going to the dogs."

"He's our sergeant-at-arms and you ought to treat our
officers with respect," Alec joked.

"That's something to ponder and mull over," George
said.

"How do you know she's a virgin?" Alec asked.

"She told me."

"Does that make it true? Maybe she isn't."

"I ought to be able to make Nora Lewis in three weeks.
Three weeks from tonight, I'll tell you if she lied. If I
discover that she's committed the sin against the Holy
Ghost and lied to me about her virginity—Hell hath no
fury like the wrath of a Raymond deceived by a female
of the species."

"Jesus, you're a fair bastard with girls," Alec laughed.

"I'm fair because all's fair in love and war."

"Cut it out, Raymond."

George laughed.

"That is an old saw. But Nietzsche wrote—'Thou goest
to a woman? Take thy whip.'"

"How old is she?" Eddie asked.

"Unfortunately, she's not jail bait. Nora is eighteen."

"She's old enough to give you her all," Alec said.

"That's all I want—her all."

"Now that you've told me about Nora, have we any important matters to discuss?" Alec asked.

"Yes, Riggs asked me to come to his house. He has a dirty movie which he will allow mortals like me to view."

"That little bastard hates my guts, but what the hell, the feeling is mutual. No it isn't; who can hate a worm?"

George lit a cigarette and threw the pack to Alec who caught it and lit up also.

"You're unusually quiet tonight, Eddie," George said.

"Are you taking notes on us?" Alec asked.

"I was just thinking."

"Even though you slouch around and flop into a chair with that far-away look in your eyes, I can tell you take in everything," Alec said.

Eddie was flattered. He didn't deny what Alec had said but he didn't really believe it. He thought that he probably missed a lot—so many times while he was listening to them talk, he'd find himself thinking about something else.

"Eddie doesn't miss much. He's deceptive. He'll always surprise you. I once was boxing tip-tap with him and before I knew it, he had caught me with his right. I almost got sore. Do you remember that, Eddie? It was on 58th Street in front of the Greek's poolroom."

"I remember, George, it was in 1923."

"Just think, it's 1927 already," Alec remarked.

"Time flies," George said with mock solemnity.

"*Memento mori,*" Eddie added.

"It's fascinating to think about time," Alec mused. "What did it mean to man before watches, or hourglasses? What did they do before they had invented calendars? Before the Greeks, or the Jews or the Phoenicians? Before the Egyptians, before man could write?"

"There always was night and day," George said.

"Yes, there was night and day. And in some climates, the change of seasons."

"And women had the monthlies," George laughed.

"Before clocks were invented, man could tell time by the position of the sun," Eddie said.

"Yeh, that's right," said Alec, "but it's still fascinating to think about. We're all three sitting here, and we're pretty much the same as we were two minutes ago. But two minutes ago is gone. Time is last minute becoming this minute becoming the next minute. Time is every minute, every one of them."

Eddie and George kept quiet. Alec went on.

"Time goes on. It will always go on, even after the second law of thermodynamics leaves nobody. There'll be a universe of equalized energy with no life, the globe will be uninhabitable by any form of life; and time will go on. The earth will be run down, the sun cooled down, and for years upon years forever, everything will be the same. I suppose that's the way the world will end. It's what science tells us and science knows best. It won't matter once it's happened. But it makes life meaningless. I know I'll have to die some day, but I don't believe it. I don't think about it. I act as if I expected to live forever. And you think the world will go on forever, but it won't. Why should anyone give a damn about anything?"

He turned to Eddie.

"Why should you want to write so that you'll be remembered? I, of course," continued Alec, "have been influenced by George Bernard Shaw and am inclined to think of evolution as leading to higher stages. I never gave much thought to what then."

" 'What then' reminds me of 'as if'," George Raymond said. "You should read Vaihinger's *The Philosophy of As If*. The world is really as if it were the world we think it is—it's inside our heads. What isn't inside our heads is only as if it were outside our heads and as if it happened to be the way we think it is. Time is one of man's *as ifs*.

There's nothing right nor wrong nor anything else but thinking makes it so, just as our fellow superman, Billy Shakespeare, might have indicated to mankind."

"Everything in the world isn't as if it were what it is," Eddie said. "Rocks aren't as if they were rocks. They are rocks. They are something which feel hard if we touch them; they'll go through a window if we throw them." Eddie paused, groping for the right words. "What I mean is that, to us, the world is as we see it and think it to be; but the world is still a real thing. We can have illusions or false notions about it, but we still are in a world which is what it is."

"Of course. I meant that what we consider to be the truth is only *as if* it were the truth," George explained. "But I know that I have to read more philosophy. To penetrate the fundamental questions of life gives more enjoyment than to penetrate the vagina. Woman, of course, is man's greatest illusion, his greatest *as if*."

"And they're cute, too," Alec said.

"They're cute all right, but they have feet of clay. And they aren't so beautiful either. Their hips are too wide, they aren't harmoniously proportioned. The male figure is more beautiful, actually."

"But we still want to see a naked woman, not a naked man," Alec said.

"That's because it excites us. It's our glands that are affected, not our sense of beauty. A naked woman makes the old sailor stand up. And if you don't let sex out of the door, it'll break out the window."

"Listen, Raymond, you and I are supposed to be organizing a movement to slow-down sex," Alec said.

"That's as if," George laughed.

"I think the Slow-Down Club will end as the Knock-Up Club," Eddie Ryan said.

They all laughed.

Eddie was supposed to open up the filling station at 6 A.M. the next morning. It was almost midnight when he left the apartment. As he walked along 47th Street, past the unlighted stores, he thought about the conversation that they had had. He, George, and Alec had all accepted as fact the purposelessness of life. He brooded about this.

He arrived at the El station. As he climbed the steps, he told himself that life seemed to be senseless.

He didn't have to wait long for a train. Eddie sat down in an almost empty car and started reading a story by Anton Chekhov. He almost missed the 58th Street stop. Walking down the station steps, he thought:

All men are caught in a trap of time.

IV

The Slow-Down Club flourished. It didn't slow anyone down, decrease drinking, or de-sexualize dancing. It didn't keep the fellows from trying to make the girls and it didn't impel the girls who wanted to say "Yes" to say "No." The membership jumped to over a hundred. The basement of the Kent Hotel became a lively place on Saturday nights. The crowd was noisy and there were always some drunks. Most of them came because they wanted fun; the club provided them with a feeling of identity, they weren't strangers, they all belonged to the same club. Bill Pfeister took his position as sergeant-at-arms very seriously, and he, along with some of his friends, helped to preserve order. There were no fist fights.

People started coming around to the Forum almost every night. The Slow-Down Club was a success. The fact that the aims of the club were ignored seemed to trouble no one.

Very few of those who joined the club had any interest

in Bohemianism. Most of the fellows were clerks, factory workers, or truck drivers. The girls were stenographers or salesgirls; there were some telephone operators.

The girls came because they found an illusion of romanticism, a feeling that they were bold and an excuse for more boldness—it was different. The fellows were there because the girls were there.

They formed small groups that stuck together at the dances. Eddie didn't get to know many of them and was met with suspicion whenever he approached some of them. He didn't understand this reaction but made no effort to find out the reason. The reason was that Eddie was identified with George and Alec; and the three of them were missing what was happening.

Wilbert Wilmer considered the Forum his. He was becoming increasingly alarmed because he feared that George and Alec would ease him aside and run it as though they owned it. He was particularly afraid of George—he was convinced that George had turned Alec against him. He didn't know what to do. If he tried to get rid of them, he might lose the new crowd; and he was making money.

He listened to Lenora's father, Conrad Jackson, who wanted to take old John Mason's place, as well as get rid of George and Alec. Alec and Lenora had lost interest in each other and the old man felt sure that he could have his daughter end the affair without arousing suspicion.

And Riggs began talking to Wilbert about Alec. He regarded him as an evil influence on George Raymond and felt it was because of Alec that he was being thwarted in his pursuit of George. Riggs had developed a fierce hatred of Alec and told Wilbert that he had overheard Alec talking about a scheme to throw Wilbert out and run the Forum by himself. Riggs was very careful when he told this lie to Wilbert not to mention or accuse George.

Conrad Jackson and Riggs were no match for George

and Alec. Wilbert would listen to them but he didn't dare take action. Bill Pfeister was friendly though and Wilbert began to hope that Pfeister would bring him support from the members and help him get rid of Alec and George.

He asked Pfeister if it didn't seem that George Raymond, who wasn't even an officer of the club, had too much influence in the running of the club. And he wondered aloud if George might not be endangering all of them by selling washtub gin. Bill Pfeister agreed that George shouldn't have so much say in the running of the club, and he shouldn't risk all their necks by selling gin. Pfeister had already been worried about George Raymond, and Wilbert's questions alarmed him. He was proud of his office as sergeant-at-arms. He felt important and he hoped that this office would impress Nora Lewis. He had fallen in love with her; but he didn't try to go too far with her. She was a good girl. He believed that it would be wrong to try to destroy her purity. In loving her, he loved her innocence.

Bill Pfeister worried. If George Raymond wrecked the club, he would lose his own importance as sergeant-at-arms. He wanted George out of the picture but he didn't dare make an open effort to have him kicked out because he was afraid that George and Alec together were much too smart for him. Bill wanted to have it out with George, man to man, because he didn't like a guy like Raymond. Raymond was supposed to be a whale of a scrapper but Bill Pfeister didn't believe it. He was convinced that underneath, he was yellow, pure yellow. But Wilbert Wilmer and Riggs had told Pfeister not to pick a fight with Raymond because it might disrupt the club and break it up. Even if he did pound lumps all over Raymond, it wouldn't solve anything if the Slow-Down Club was broken up. If that happened, he wouldn't be sergeant-at-arms any more. Bill started talking about George and Alec to his friends in the club and he brought in several additional

friends to help him. A whispering campaign had been
started and had gained momentum before George and Alec
were aware of anything. They were far too confident to
suspect that they were being undermined.

V

It was at this point that George Raymond began his
campaign to seduce Nora Lewis. Nora was the daughter
of a factory worker who worked at a carburetor plant. The
family lived in a wooden frame house on 35th and Peoria.
She was a small girl and neatly put together. Her bobbed
hair was brown, on the darkish side, and her small face
was pretty in a very ordinary way; yet with her brown eyes,
she would sometimes have a look of childlike wonder.
There was a special appeal in Nora Lewis.

She had taken a commercial course in high school and
worked as a typist downtown in a Loop office.

Nora's childhood had not been unhappy—merely drab.
Everything in her life had been drab and ordinary and she
had lived with dreams of romance and a hunger for excitement for over four years. She had dreamed of a lover—
strong, tall, dark, handsome. He'd be tender, with curly
hair, and would take her in his arms, kiss her, hold her
tight with his strong arms, and then he would take her
and she would know the raptures of love. Nora believed
that if you wished for something long enough, hard
enough, and with enough faith, you were bound to get
that something. She wished and believed that she would
meet the tall handsome lover of her dreams.

On her eighteenth birthday, Bill Pfeister had taken her
out to dinner and dancing. Nora told herself that her eighteenth birthday was an omen, and that she would soon
meet him, the wonderful man of her dreams.

The orchestra played "Wonderful One," and Nora fell
into her dream. Her expression grew tender and full of
yearning; she was entranced. Bill glanced down at her as
they danced and believed that the love which caused her
eyes to glow was for him. A happiness came over him that
he could not understand. It was something that he had
never known. He had never known how you could worship
the ground a girl walked on, kiss her feet.

Bill felt Nora's body close against him. In her dream,
Nora felt such an unbearable hunger that she pressed her
body tight against Bill. She moved her abdomen against
him from side to side, slowly and sensuously. She felt him
pressing her but she couldn't stop, not until it happened,
making her feel wonderful and more wonderful. She had
known in a way that she was dancing with Bill, but the
tall handsome man in her mind had seemed more real to
her. And even though she was dancing with Bill, she had
been appeasing the hunger for "him" that she could not
control or deny. It was an omen that the day was near,
the time had come for her to be loved by him. She would
meet him soon and every day of her life from then on,
and for always, would be wonderful with love.

When they walked off the dance floor, Nora's eyes were
shining. Her face seemed to glow. Bill gazed at her with
worship. He had never known what love was. Now he did.
How could a beefy, clumsy lug like him make a girl as
fine and pure as Nora so happy that her face could shine
like that? And the way she had danced did not spoil her
innocence. She had done this in love. He would not rob
her of her innocence, not until he had put a solid twenty-
four karat gold ring on her finger, a ring just like the ring
his own father gave to his mother.

Nora's feeling of a sweet flowing inside her, her feeling
of being so content, of being in softness, quickly gave way
to shame. It had happened so fast—she hadn't had any

control of herself—it was like "he" was more a real person
inside her heart than Bill was a real person dancing with
her. It was like when she dreamed. The people she saw
in her dreams were real in the same way, as long as she
was dreaming. She didn't know how to describe it. She was
sorry. Oh, she'd make it up to him when she met him and
she would meet him soon.

Bill Pfeister watched her, wanting to tell her how he
felt, that he loved her and would protect her, but he didn't
seem to be able to talk. He knew what he wanted to say,
but, heck, he couldn't manage to say it. He looked at her.
He'd always known that he would find the girl of his
dreams, and he had. Nora Lewis. She was so quiet. Her face
was full of her thoughts, a girl's thoughts. How could a
lug like him know what a girl's thoughts were? If he hadn't
seen the wonderful way she had looked at him on the
dance floor just a minute ago, he might think she was
sad. She looked kind of sad. Maybe a girl felt sad when
she fell in love because she was a girl. That was about it,
he guessed. But he was surprised because he had kind of
thought when a fellow and a girl fell in love, they talked.
That's what he thought you could expect. But how was
he to know? He'd never been in love before.

Nora Lewis wished that Bill Pfeister wasn't so much in
love with her. She was flattered, but only in the way that
any girl was flattered when a fellow fell for her. But a girl
didn't want the fellow loving her to get to be a nuisance.
And Nora was awfully worried that Bill would get to be
one. Bill acted like she was in love with him and wanted
her to say "I love you, Bill." But she couldn't. She couldn't
say those words to anyone but "him." She couldn't explain
this to anyone, not even to Evelyn who was her best girl
friend at the office.

It would be nice to go out with Bill if only he wasn't so
head over heels in love with her. She didn't want to stay

at home, on the shelf. No girl wanted to. Bill was reliable. She would even let him kiss her, hard on the mouth, and touch her breast. Of course, outside her dress, not any more than that. A modern girl had to have some necking, if it didn't really count and mean going the limit. If a fellow worked and earned money and spent it taking a girl out on a date, the girl ought to give him a little something. Bill Pfeister worried her. She and Evelyn both agreed that Bill Pfeister was not the kind of a fellow that a girl couldn't handle, but still, she worried. But not so much that she couldn't give him any more dates.

Bill would not have taken Nora Lewis to the Forum had it not been because of the Slow-Down Club. He was puzzled by her. He would bet his last dime and his friend's last dime that she had fallen in love with him on that night of her eighteenth birthday when he had taken her out dancing.

He couldn't make it out, not for nohow, why she held him at arm's length and would stiffen and draw a little back when he put his arm around her. He wanted just a little loving up, no more than that. He couldn't dope it out. He'd still damned well bet his last dime that Nora Lewis loved him. If she didn't, why did she let him date her, on Saturday nights and on Sunday nights? Of course, she was only eighteen and it might be that she was making up her mind. Maybe her mother had told her she was too young, or given her some kind of advice. You never could tell with girls.

George Raymond spotted Nora Lewis the first night that Bill Pfeister brought her to the Slow-Down Club. She looked pretty cute and there was something fresh and innocent about her. She wasn't bad, not bad at all; and if his hunch were right, he'd say that she was a virgin. The cute little trick, she had come with Pfeister, and if Raymond couldn't Pfeister Bill Pfeister, then Raymond may as well surrender to that wormlike fairy, Riggs, or better yet, enter a monastery. George and Alec had selected Bill Pfeister to be sergeant-at-arms. Already the moron was showing signs that he thought he was too big for the boots Raymond and McGonigle had made for him. George knew that sooner or later, he was going to have to knock Pfeister down a dozen or so pegs. Pfeister was said to be a good scrapper, and if the two of them were going to stick around the Slow-Down Club, they'd have to tangle, and it would be knock down and drag out when they did. But he could take Pfeister on. He'd dance all around Pfeister and the slow-slower-slowest sergeant-at-arms of the Slow-Down Club would wonder where in all unholy Hell so many jabs had come from.

Pfeister was getting popular with the suckers who came to the club. There was only one way to handle Pfeister so he didn't crab the act that he and Alec had carefully planned for themselves. He'd have to handle him with his fists. The moron was too dumb to be handled any other way. And the best way to hasten to this conclusion was to take Pfeister's girl away from him. George liked the idea. First, he'd Pfeister Pfeister, then he'd fister Pfeister.

When George Raymond walked over to Nora, she blinked and looked at him with such an expression of puzzlement that it was almost a look of pain. She stared at him, trying to remember where she had met him before. She thought she was going to faint, or that she ought to faint; but she wasn't at all weak or dizzy. He was smiling down at her. It must be him. Him. And here she was, wearing her blue suit that she'd even worn to work. Bill Pfeister had told her that she didn't need to dress up to come to this place tonight. Now he wouldn't want her. She wasn't looking her best and he'd be sure to notice her old suit.

"You impress me as being a person that we need around

this dump," George said. Nora immediately realized that
he was sure of himself, poised. He didn't look any older
than the rest of the fellows but he seemed older. And he
had called her a person, not a girl. She liked that. She
didn't know exactly why.

"Me?" she exclaimed questioningly. Nora didn't know
what to say, she didn't exactly know what he meant. She
was afraid she'd say something silly. And she was afraid
she looked too young. Oh, she wished she was twenty-one
instead of eighteen. And she wished she had known she
was going to meet him tonight. She could have dressed
up and made herself look older.

"This is the Slow-Down Club and we need sweetness
and light here to shed a beneficial influence and still the
savage blood of youth. May I dance with you?"

"I like to dance."

She liked the way he talked, even though she didn't
know what he meant, exactly. None of the other fellows
she knew or had gone out with on dates, talked like he
did.

She was a good dancer. She was glad that she could
show him some of her advantages. She knew it must be
Him.

They danced. George didn't dance as well as Alec or
Eddie Ryan. He was rather stiff and took short choppy
steps. A partner had little opportunity to show how well
she could follow or how she could help make dancing an
exhibition of gracefulness. Nora was disappointed because
of George's dancing, but not disappointed in him, not at
all disappointed in him.

"You dance well," George told her.

"Thank you."

He pressed against her slowly, closely. She didn't pull
back as she usually did, especially when she was dancing

with a fellow for the first time and didn't even know his name.

She knew it was Him.

George decided that Pfeister's girl was a nice morsel. He asked her name. She told him and asked him his.

"You haven't heard of me before? You don't know my name?" he asked, tightening the pressure of his arm around her back.

Nora shook her head bewilderedly and thought with a pang of worry that she ought to know about him and his name.

"Well, now you shall," he said softly and leaned his head down, close to her ear, "I'm George Raymond, often known as Brimstone."

"I'm pleased to meet you, George . . . Raymond," Nora said, smiling weakly. She didn't know how to talk to him.

"How did you happen to come here tonight, Nora?"

"Oh I sometimes go out with a fellow, Bill Pfeister . . ."

"Good old Bill. He's the sergeant-at-arms of our Slow-Down Club," George interrupted. He shimmied against her as he spoke.

"You know Bill?"

"Yes, he keeps order. He's our sergeant-at-arms, the man elected to slow down the Slow-Down Club. Do you go with good old Bill, Nora?"

"Oh, you know, a girl doesn't like to stay at home on the shelf, and if a fellow asks her out and there's nothing to do, that's the way it is. Bill's a good friend but I don't go with him. I mean I don't exactly, serious and steady."

"He's your escort," George said.

"My what?"

"Escort. He takes you places."

"Kind of, yes, I guess so."

"Good old Bill, I like him. If he was not your escort,

I wouldn't have met you and that would have been calamitous."

Of course, this was a line; but he was different. He had personality.

"But you would have met some other girl, a prettier one," Nora said, a little in self-dismissal.

"There's always another girl," George told her and he laughed from his throat. It sounded like a half cough.

She wanted him to compliment her, even if it was only a line. She was tingling, she didn't want the dance to end. The way he pressed her made her tingle all the more, all over. She was afraid that he knew how she felt.

She wanted to press herself closer to him and to be held tighter, because he was so strong and she wanted him to keep dancing like this, this way, against her, only it made her lose her breath and would show him what he was doing to her and then, he'd think that she was easy.

He was talking to her and it was like he was kissing her with his voice almost.

"I can always meet another girl. But even though I can, another girl isn't . . . Nora Lewis."

"But you don't know me. I'm only, oh, just a girl."

She had been able to say that all right, not excited. But then she sighed.

"You don't know me either."

"I'd like to," Nora said before she realized what she was saying. She shouldn't have said that to him.

"I'll attend to that, Nora. I'll allow you to know me," he told her, almost in a whisper.

Just then the record ended.

They walked off the dance floor. Nora was hoping that he would ask her for her telephone number. She was hoping that he would ask her for a date.

"Thank you, Nora. And shall I be rendered the happiness of seeing you here again . . . at the Slow-Down Club?"

"Yes, I suppose so," Nora answered. To Nora this was like she was saying yes to anything he would ask her to do.

Nora didn't turn to glance after George as he walked away, lighting a cigarette. Bill Pfeister was watching her. She knew that he'd be jealous. She didn't want Bill to think the dance had been anything at all but a dance.

"I was looking for you," Bill said, his voice strained.

"Oh, a fellow came over and asked me to dance while you were talking to that little bald-headed man; and you know me, Bill, I like to dance."

"The fellow you was dancing with, he takes advantage of girls. I wouldn't let my sister dance with him, that is if I had a sister."

"He just danced and he told me his name. That was all. A girl dances with a fellow; you say one thing or another thing and he says something or other; and that's all. I just like to dance."

"Raymond better not try monkeying around with my girl," Bill said with a threat in his voice.

Nora was alarmed but she didn't say anything. She was afraid for George Raymond because Bill Pfeister was so strong. But if Bill Pfeister hit George Raymond, or even laid a finger on him, she would never speak to him again, ever, as long as she lived.

When Bill and Nora were leaving the basement that night, Eddie Ryan was standing with George. Eddie saw Nora give George a quick, furtive glance.

"Eddie, do you see that petite morsel going out with Pfeister?" George asked.

"Yes, she looks cute."

"That, my friend, is the first cherry that's going to be copped at the Slow-Down Club."

Any girl who wasn't fat or deformed was attractive and desirable to Eddie Ryan. He could recognize a truly beautiful girl as such; but any girl, any female body that other

fellows would regard as almost ugly, was sufficient for
Eddie. To him, most girls were pretty. Nora Lewis looked
very good to him. He wished that he had met her first;
but he knew that if George had set his mind on making
her, he didn't have a chance.

Eddie was far too inexperienced to hold fixed views on
women; his yearnings and hunger for love were too great
for him to be detached and critical. He could not sacrifice
his feelings of romance and beauty, of the wonder and
mystery of girls. Girls were to be loved; there was something shy, sensitive, and glowing in them. Their physical
appeal and his own romantic idealization were mixed together in his mind. He had not gone through the experience of knowing, assimilating, and accepting love and sex
in their many physical and psychological significances.

Eddie Ryan was a young man, chronologically, physically, and intellectually. Emotionally, much of his adolescence lingered with him.

VI

Bill Pfeister phoned Nora Lewis for a date. He caught
her at supper time. She guessed that that was just what
he wanted because he thought if her whole family could
hear her talking to him, it would have some kind of influence on her and she would give in and go out with
him, maybe to a movie, to see something that she didn't
care two pish-pish for.

"Some fellow giving you the rush and paging you, Sis?"
Joey asked. He wore a white shirt with the collar open.
His face was shining and reddish.

"It's only Bill," she replied but she didn't like his smart
buttinsky teasing.

"What did you tell him, Nora, huh?"

Joey didn't talk as refined as George Raymond did, Nora thought. And his jokes weren't funny, neither.

"Give the fellow a break, Sis, throw him a kiss over the phone."

"Will you please cut it out, Joey." There was a sharpness to her voice as she spoke to her brother.

"Sorry, Sis, sorry, I was only foolin', didn't mean anything by it," Joey answered.

"There's a time and a place, Joey."

Nora's sentence broke off, and she spoke into the phone: "Oh, Bill, supper's just been put on the table."

Joey's face gestured Ha-ha-haw but he didn't laugh aloud. Nora frowned.

"Oh, I'm sorry, Nora. I just wanted to ask you what you're doing tomorrow night," Bill asked.

She caught herself just in time—before she said "Nothing." She answered after a short pause that threw Bill Pfeister off balance.

"I'm sorry, Bill."

"Just so you're sorry, kid," Bill said but his voice didn't sound right. He knew what it was, that shitheel Raymond.

"I can't, but thank you for asking, Bill."

"But, Nora, I was figuring . . ."

Bill Pfeister's voice was interrupted by the sound of coins dropping into the phone.

"I just can't, Bill, but thank you anyway."

"No chance of changin' your mind tomorrow?"

"I'm sorry, Bill, but I can't."

"Well you see, Nora, Augie Ziedler at work is having a birthday party, and . . ."

—Why hadn't he said this first?

"No I couldn't, Bill, much as I'd like to but thank you for calling me up."

"But, Nora." Bill sounded bewildered.

"Goodbye, Bill, supper's on the table."

"Goodbye, Nora."

"Call me again, Bill, another time."

Bill was hurt.

Nora knew he was hurt but she couldn't help it. She was relieved that he was off the wire.

"Now, I'll finish setting the table," Nora said.

"Sis, you're the cat's canary," Joey kidded.

Nora frowned again. She didn't like to deceive anybody.

She wished that it wasn't necessary to hurt anyone; and it wasn't as if she had something else to do; suddenly, it dawned on her. George Raymond would be at the Forum tomorrow night. She could maybe be with him, be with him alone.

That's what she'd do, she'd go to the Forum.

What was Joey saying, she hadn't been listening . . . "I give you credit, Sis, you've got all the makings of a vamp."

VII

The next night Nora Lewis didn't go home for supper. She ate in Wintner's Restaurant with Evelyn. Nora chatted and told Evelyn about George Raymond, but she was careful about what she said.

Evelyn wanted to see a movie but Nora said she couldn't, she had to go out on the South Side.

When they left Wintner's, they walked together to the corner. They had just reached the corner when Nora's streetcar arrived, she ran and jumped on the platform. Evelyn waved goodbye to her.

Nora could hardly wait for the streetcar to get to 57th and Cottage Grove. She wished she could fly there.

It seemed like *such* a long ride.

VIII

George Raymond looked like he had been waiting for her. She guessed he must have been . . . waiting for her, Nora Lewis. And in his own perverse way, George had been waiting for her.

George danced with her and charmed her. He told her exciting things about himself, his shipping out to England and traveling as a salesman in Texas. He invented some travels, including a trip to California. He asked Nora about herself and she told him what little there was to tell. He had guessed her age so she couldn't say she was twenty the way she'd planned.

Dancing with him was wonderful to her. He held her as she wanted to be held. He talked so interestingly and made her smile and laugh. No fellow had ever talked to her as George Raymond did; but then she had never met a fellow like him.

He must be Him, he must be.

IX

They left the Forum together. They crossed the street and walked into Washington Park and sat on a bench. George put his arm around her and his hand touched her left breast.

She was helpless, she didn't know what she'd do when he kissed her, how could she refuse him anything? She was all his, her all was his if he wanted it.

But George said that they'd better be on their way. He'd take her home and see her to her door.

On the Cottage Grove Avenue streetcar, George put

his arm around her. She felt wonderful all over again. They rode to 35th Street and then changed for a westbound 35th Street trolley car. George was more proper on this car. Nora couldn't wait for the ride to end so that she could be alone with him, and be kissed and held and touched by him.

"I'm next," she said.

"What street?" George asked.

"Mine's next," she repeated, not hearing his question over the noise of the trolley car.

The streetcar stopped. They got off and George guided her by the arm across the street.

When she stopped in front of her house, he turned her to him, and kissed her, holding her tightly, acting like a lover.

"Nora," he said, very softly and gently.

She was limp in his arms. She had the sensation of something flowing through her, flowing like waves. There was some thought or word in the back of her mind; and it was going to come to her the next second—the thought or word that would bring her a bliss that would give her the greatest happiness possible.

"Nora," he said again.

She looked up at him, full of hunger.

"You're lovable."

She spoke his name in a gasping breath and clung to him. He kissed her again, breathing hard.

"My sweet, I told you I'd let you know me."

He kissed her again, and then, almost abruptly, held her away from him, and then released her.

She walked up the wooden stairs slowly, too dazed to think. She turned on the landing and saw him watching her. The dim beam of light from the lamp post fell by his feet. He waved. She waved a limp hand. She was weak and dizzy.

"Come back to the Slow-Down on Tuesday night, sweet."

She nodded. Her head seemed to be going up and down against her will.

George blew her a kiss, turned and lit a cigarette as he walked to 35th Street.

Nora could hear him whistling. It sounded lovely in the night. Then she heard the lonely whistle of a train from the Rock Island tracks. The engine whistle sounded sad, like someone calling and calling, trying to speak. As a little girl, she had sometimes cried when she heard the whistles of the engines at night. There were tears in Nora's eyes when she pushed open the door and entered the dark hallway. The house was silent. She closed the door softly. Very quietly, she went up the darkened stairway to her room, where she would sleep in her virgin's bed.

X

George had not left the Forum with Nora unnoticed. Riggs had watched them go, and had pressed his teeth against his lower lip. His hand had trembled as he reached for a cigarette. Wilbert Wilmer had also seen them go. So had one of Bill Pfeister's buddies. The fact that George Raymond would take Nora Lewis home had struck them all as some kind of sin. Wilbert thought it was rotten that George would leave with a girl so young and innocent. It proved that he would do anything, anything at all for his own pleasure, even ruin a nice, sweet young girl.

Wilbert knew that Bill Pfeister would be sore as hell and would line up his pals and everyone he could in the Slow-Down Club to kick George Raymond out. If George could be kicked out, so could Alec. It didn't matter much about Eddie Ryan; he'd probably go out with them.

Riggs' hatred was directed at Nora Lewis. She was a deceitful little female animal who was as innocent as the Devil's daughter. She would betray her sweetheart, Bill Pfeister, for the Grecian god body of George Raymond. She was too stupid to understand him or want anything else from him. George must be saved from that little female animal and from being expelled from this foolish club. If he were to leave and go elsewhere, Riggs might lose contact with him altogether. He didn't know how he could bear this. He had waited years for George Raymond, lonely years, when he had known only defilements and the depths and the nadirs of life's pains and anguish. And then George Raymond had come into his life. He had been so near, he knew it. Pfeister must save George by taking back his she-bitch. But he, Riggs, would have to be cautious and clever. He could not expose his true feelings. In this insensitive and unpoetic world, his own lofty affection was the love that dare not speak its name. He must not endanger George Raymond and lose the soul that he wanted and had to save. But that McGonigle, with a soul of Irish mud and a spirit as poetic as corned beef and cabbage, was the real evil influence to be combated. McGonigle and that corrupt little daughter of Eve, Nora Lewis.

Pfeister's buddy thought that any fast-talking cocksman who would try to take his girl away from Good Old Bill, a true blue pal if ever there was one, why that fast-talking bedroom polo player was a sonofabitch. Bill would be told about it, and Bill Pfeister would know what to do. Bill Pfeister didn't talk fast, but he had guts and as mean a set of dukes as any fellow needed.

XI

"How did you make out last night with that cute little gal? Her name's Nora Lewis, isn't it?" Alec asked George the next day. They were having toast and coffee at the apartment at 47th and Drexel that they shared with Phil Dumont.

"I have her drawers on fire," George said. "If I'm not careful, I'll melt her cherry before I can cop it."

"Congratulations. When are you going to perform the sacrificial rite of the virgin?"

"My move now is to play her along for a short while."

"What in hell for, George? If she's ready to give you her all, well, that's her all, and you might as well take it before Pfeister does."

"Pfeister beating my time? Alec, don't you have any respect for my technique even if you don't appreciate my charm and manly beauty?"

"Take all the credit you want for your manly charms. I don't want them but Nora Lewis apparently does and damned bad."

"That's precisely and specifically the point. If I can give free rein to my peculiar genius—by withholding my manly charms for a time—she'll not lose her eagerness to have them. She'll appreciate them more and her virgin's passion will reach the proper degree of high intensity that is one of the Raymond requirements from the female of the species."

"Jesus, you use a lot of words, George, to describe screwing a girl."

"I might use a lot of words when I talk about it, but I use other tools for the operation itself."

"That's your business."

"You mean my penis, Alec."

"Maybe the two are synonymous. Anything else new?"

"No, I haven't robbed any banks, or been baptized a Baptist by total immersion. And the Slow-Down Club isn't slowing down."

"I was wondering while I was walking over here. What

the hell's the matter with Wilmer? He hardly spoke to me last night. He seems to be avoiding me lately."

"He's got Herbert Spencer on the brain," George said.

"He's had that disease for a long time."

"We'll sound out John Mason. Old John's around him more than we are."

"I think I'll do that." Alec said. "How about coming along down to the dive? The two of us can talk with Old John."

"I'm going to shave and go out North to see my mother and the gaffer."

"My old man was trying to tell me I'm not home enough. He has his goddamn nerve. He goes out and stays away for over fourteen years," Alec said. "Such goddamn nerve. I won't see you tonight then?"

"No, not unless you stay around here late."

"I think I'll go home and catch up on my sleep for a change. I'll see you tomorrow, George."

XII

Alec walked down to the Kent but John Mason wasn't there. He found Wilbert Wilmer having ham and eggs in the kitchen in the back of the basement. The table, covered with oilcloth, was cluttered with dirty dishes.

Wilbert looked up from his plate but didn't speak. He took a big bite out of a piece of burned toast. Alec suspected that Wilbert had done this so that he wouldn't have to speak first. Alec looked around. The frying pan on the stove was crusted with dried egg. There were cockroaches scurrying across the board by the deep tublike sink.

—What a hell of a way to live, Alec thought.

He wanted to get the hell out of his home and live alone, but not like this.

"Hello, Wilbert, how are you?" Alec said, trying to sound cordial and casual.

"Hello."

Alec sat down on an old chair at one end of the narrow kitchen table. Wilbert continued eating.

"Is something wrong, Wilbert?" Alec asked bluntly.

"No, no, why do you ask?"

"Are you sore at me?"

"No, no, I'm not sore at anyone," Wilbert said, but he was plainly embarrassed.

"You seem to be avoiding me lately. When I walked over to talk to you last night, I got the impression that you turned and cornered that little Riggs in a hurry just so that you wouldn't have to talk to me."

"I don't remember," Wilbert said uncertainly, and with growing embarrassment. "Oh, yes, I did have a little matter that I had to take up with him."

"Wilbert, don't kid me. I've known you for a couple of years now. What's on your mind?"

"What's on my mind? I don't know what you're getting at, Alec. Is something bothering you?"

"The only thing that's bothering me is that I'd like to know what in hell's bothering you."

"If something wasn't on your mind, Alec, you wouldn't talk that way."

"I'm not talking any differently than I ever do, Wilbert."

"Well, then you're imagining things."

Alec felt frustrated. He knew that something was eating at the guy and he didn't like the idea that he couldn't figure out a way to get him to open up about his gripes.

"I've always considered us friends, Wilbert. But for the past few days, you've been avoiding me. That's why I came around now. I thought I'd see you and find out if there's anything you're sore at me about, or if there's something you don't like. I thought that if you'd tell me, we could talk it over and straighten out any misunderstanding. It would be a damned pity to let gripes or grievances stew now when the place is going so well, much better than we hoped for when we opened up last winter."

"It's going well but we can't have any horsing around with the young girls and that sort of thing."

Alec was surprised for a few moments.

"What the hell, Wilbert, are you becoming a Puritan?" he asked.

He had guessed that Wilbert meant Nora Lewis and George Raymond. And he realized that he had suspected all along that Wilbert was sore about George Raymond, about something that George was doing.

"Guys come here because they'll find girls. What the hell do you think they want to do with girls?" Alec had almost added "Talk about Herbert Spencer?" but he checked himself in time.

"That's not what I mean, Alec."

"Well what is it then? What do you mean—horsing around with young girls?"

Wilbert had finished eating. He sat silent for a moment, looking away from Alec. His lips twitched.

"Nothing's the matter, Alec," he said, turning to glance past Alec rather than look at him. "I've been urging you to read Herbert Spencer for two years now. He was a greater thinker than Darwin. The principles of evolution are not only true about the origin of the species, but all through society. The principles of evolution are the key, the clue, the laws that give us the truth. That's why I keep telling you that you ought to read Herbert Spencer."

Wilbert Wilmer's thin, pale face had come alive. His voice had changed, losing its flatness and it now throbbed with feeling.

"All right, Wilbert. I think I will. I'll go to the library

right now and start reading something of Herbert Spencer," Alec said as he rose from the chair.

"You'll never be the same, Alec, once you start reading Herbert Spencer," Wilbert said as Alec left.

XIII

At about ten o'clock the next morning Alec went to the apartment at 47th and Drexel. Phil Dumont let him in. George was still in bed. He woke up, rubbed his beard and yawned loudly.

"Gimme a cigarette, Alec."

Alec handed George his pack. George lit a cigarette and said:

"Coffin nail. What's new, Alec?"

Alec told him about his visit with Wilbert and their talk, and said that he was certain that something was up.

"We got to have a conference, George."

"Yeh," George exclaimed, yawning widely again. "He advised you to read Herbert Spencer, did he?"

"Listen, you lazy bastard, we've got to have a conference."

"What do you think is cooking?" George asked.

"They're going to screw us some way, that is they think they are."

"That's better, Alec. They only think they are going to phrigg Raymond and McGonigle! Who do you think is in this shitass cabal?"

"Wilbert for one, and I think Riggs. Haven't you noticed how he's been playing up to Wilbert?"

"You mean asshole-ing up to the greatest living disciple of Herbert Spencer."

"That numbskull, Pfeister, is dumb enough to be used

by Riggs. Wilbert and Riggs may not be brainstorms but they're intellectual wizards alongside of Pfeister."

"That's true, Alec, and it isn't a *De Profundus*, either. It's as plain as the hole in any ass what Riggs sees when he looks at the stars."

"We've got to figure out what to do and then, break it up, George. If we aren't intelligent enough to do that, we'd better . . ."

"Go to work and make an honest living," George interrupted.

"Yes, that's the punishment we'll deserve if we let those half-ass brains outwit us."

Phil Dumont came out of the bathroom.

"What bank are you two Al Capones going to hold up today?"

"You know, Alec, that's what we ought to do, rob a bank." George said this with a serious and thoughtful air; at the same time, winking at Alec.

"Yeah, say, George, that's something I've never done, held up a bank."

"Neither have I but I've always wanted to," George said.

Phil Dumont's rugged face seemed to be painfully caught between incredulity and belief.

"Come on, George, let's do it. There's a hell of a lot of money in the bank.

"We can get that dough. Sticking up a bank is no harder than doing anything else; that is if you know how to do it, and use your brains," George said. "We might get as much as fifty grand. We can take it on the lam, and shake our tails out of God's country. Then as for the Slow-Down hards, Phooey and Pfeister!"

"Where would you like to go with the dough? Rio de Janeiro ought to be an interesting and exciting city. We could have one hell of a good time on twenty-five thousand bucks apiece in Rio de Janeiro."

"My whimsy and sentimental fancy make me lean toward Paris. I'd like to lay some French broads. The Raymonds never came over on the *Mayflower*, because they came from France. That's a black mark on my escutcheon, Alec. I've never laid a French broad."

Phil Dumont frowned and said:

"You two bullshit artists—you'll rob a bank just as quick as I'll . . . oh as quick as I'll become President of the United States, or of the bank you're gonna rob."

"Phil always has to be one of those doubting bastards who wouldn't believe there was a hole even if he fell into it," Alec said dryly.

"I'd get out of the hole and shovel your horseshit in it," Phil said.

The doorbell rang loudly.

"Phil, answer the door, please, and even if it's Jesus Christ, don't let Him in. I owe everybody else money, and I might even have borrowed a fiver from Him," George said.

The bell kept ringing. Phil hopped to the door. Ed and Alec watched him open it. It was a special delivery letter for G. Raymond.

"Alec, sign for me, will you? I've made it a strict rule to sign nothing but the checks I forge," George said.

Alec signed and took the letter, which was in a light blue envelope. As he handed it to George, he said:

"It's perfumed."

"Of course it is. You don't think Raymond would have an untrained harem, do you?"

Phil Dumont put on his hat and coat and said:

"The bullshit's floating again. I'm up to my ears in it already. I got to go out and make my livin'."

As Phil picked up his worn briefcase, George held the letter up, smelled it, toyed with it. All the while, he speculated aloud as to who might have been the sender.

"There is something about this letter that strikes a note of alertness in the most perceptive Raymond of the extraordinarily perceptive Raymonds. The handwriting is funny, not ha-ha funny, but funny as is not usual, peculiar. In other words, Alec, my friend, it doesn't look like a girl's."

"What man would send you such a goddamned letter?" Alec asked. "Unless it was Eddie Ryan. Yes, Eddie, with his sense of humor might think it'd be some joke."

"It's not his handwriting."

"Well, you know, George, there is a way to find out. You could start by opening the goddamned letter."

"A perfumed *billet-doux*," George said, smelling the envelope. "It's cheap perfume."

George tore open the envelope. Alec leaned forward, curious in spite of himself. George read for a moment or so and then an angry frown appeared on his face.

"What the hell is it?" Alec asked impatiently.

George flung his head back and let out a roaring laugh. "It's from Riggs," he said.

"I'll be goddamned! What does the little rat say?"

"Listen," George said.

Chapter Seven

I

Riggs had gone to the Forum on the previous night, after Alec had left. Conrad Jackson and Wilbert Wilmer were the only other ones who happened to be around. Old John Mason had gone over to the Bug Club in Washington Park.

Bill Pfeister had walked in, looking for Nora. He was distraught. His buddy had told him about George leaving the Forum with Nora the night before. He had telephoned her home, but Mrs. Lewis had told him that Nora was out someplace, she didn't know where. Nora had just said she wouldn't be home to dinner. After she had put the receiver back on the hook, Mrs. Lewis remembered that Nora had said she was having supper at Wintner's with her girl friend, Evelyn.

Bill Pfeister had gone on a streetcar and headed for the Kent Hotel, cursing George Raymond. He imagined himself pounding George into lumps, mashing his face into an unrecognizable pulp, even kicking him in the balls. Then he reminded himself that you never kicked a guy in the balls, not even a shitheel like Raymond. But if any guy ought to be kicked in the balls, it was that shitheel. If he

found Nora at the Forum with George, he'd slap her face
and drag her out of the place and take her home. She was
too pure and innocent to understand a shitheel like Raymond. Raymond had a fascination for girls just like niggers
were supposed to have. Raymond was as bad as a nigger.
All the way over, Bill fumed and raged. He flipped the
Cottage Grove streetcar before it stopped and almost fell
as he jumped off. He regained his balance, and then ran
the half block to the Kent Hotel. His big chest was thrust
out, his elbows bent back toward his shoulders, and his
fists clenched. He thought of how strong he was; he was
stronger than Raymond. He was more decent, too. He
didn't go around trying to ruin decent girls from good
homes like that shitheel did.

Bill Pfeister had plunged down the basement steps, hoping to find Nora there, without Raymond.

She wasn't there. The place was practically empty. Nobody was there but that old Conrad Jackson and Wilbert
Wilmer and that pansy Riggs. He wanted to ask them if
Nora had been around but he didn't. He might give away
the way he felt and he didn't want any of them to know.
A man didn't wear his heart on his sleeve; he didn't let
nobody know how he felt, except maybe his closest buddies.

Bill sat down with the other three. There was a lost
look in his eyes. All of sudden he felt low. He wanted his
girl. Maybe she wasn't his girl any more. If Raymond fascinated her and had charmed her, she might never care
for him again. Suppose Raymond ruined her, laid her—he
hated the idea of a decent girl like Nora Lewis being laid.

He wanted his girl.

Raymond, that shitheel!

Bill Pfeister looked around at the group. He wondered
if they suspected what he did about Nora and Raymond.
He noticed Riggs; he had no use for that fruit.

Catching Pfeister's glance, Riggs turned aside quickly; he almost shuddered. Pfeister, what a vulgar name. And he was vulgar, almost like an animal. He was the right sort of animal for that little she-bitch Nora.

"I don't see the bedroom artist around tonight," Bill Pfeister said. He had to say something about Raymond because he felt like knocking that shitheel's teeth down his throat. Maybe if he said something about him, he could find out if Nora had been around and gone off someplace with him.

"He hasn't been around tonight. I haven't seen him," said Conrad Jackson.

"His side kick, McGonigle, was here this afternoon," Wilbert Wilmer said.

"That's the root of much evil," Riggs said snidely.

"I don't think McGonigle is the bad one. I think it's that Raymond. I didn't like him the first night he came around here. I wish he had never set foot in the Forum," Wilbert said.

"If he just came around, that would be perfectly fine," remarked Conrad Jackson. "If he behaved, that would be one thing. But if I know anything from what I've seen, and I've seen every part of this country while I was traveling during my Thespian past, then I say this: that young man, Raymond, is headed for jail."

"I don't know where he's headed for, and I don't give a damn. I'll be satisfied just to see him headed away from here," Wilbert said.

"If I was, if I were the president of the Slow-Down Club, I'd do something about it. I'd take action. You'd never find me sitting around twiddling my thumbs, wondering what to do," Conrad Jackson said. "No sir, not on your tintype, that's not the kind of man I am." He looked pleased with himself after this statement; but suddenly, he cast a fur-

tive glance in the direction of the small bedroom where
Old John Mason slept.

Riggs kept jamming his upper teeth against the skin
under his lower lip. He didn't like the way the conversation was going. McGonigle was the one, he was the root
of all evil here. He would have to convince George Raymond that McGonigle was an evil companion, a pernicious
influence.

George Raymond was a beautiful person and he could
become more beautiful. His spirit could become a golden
eagle, soaring high in the clearest blue air.

Riggs was lifted into a state of exaltation. He knew that
the poet in him was directing his thoughts.

"Riggs, do you have any idea about what would be the
best way to get rid of them?" Wilbert asked.

"No," Riggs answered slowly in what he considered his
Mephistophelian tone of voice, "no, but I soon expect to."

Bill Pfeister slammed his big right fist into his left palm.

"I just want to plant one of these right square between
Raymond's eyes," he said, stretching out his large-knuck-
led fist. "That'll take care of him once and for all, I'll
guarantee that or my name ain't Bill Pfeister."

"I know how you feel, young man," Conrad Jackson
told him, "I know, because that other scamp, McGonigle,
chased after my daughter."

Bill Pfeister listened. The old man's voice, his benign
face, and his gray hair, seemed to Bill just like a father
on a calendar picture, bestowing wise advice upon a son.

Bill didn't need the old man to tell him how to get rid
of George Raymond. He knew how to take care of that
drugstore cowboy; but maybe the old fellow could help
talk to Nora and bring her back to her senses.

But Bill Pfeister didn't really believe this. He was only
trying to convince himself. If he asked the old fellow to

talk to Nora, he'd be asking the old man in a backhanded way, kind of, to convince Nora that she should love him, Bill Pfeister, instead of George Raymond. What was that saying? Faint heart never won a fair maid. Look at Raymond. That four-flusher just walked up to Nora and asked her to dance and he'd shot her his line. But how did he know that Nora was out with Raymond? All her mother had said was that she was out and wasn't coming home for dinner.

"That's the only way to do it," Wilbert said.

Bill Pfeister suddenly looked straight at Wilbert.

"Isn't it, Bill?" Wilbert asked.

"Do what?" Bill Pfeister asked, blinking. He didn't want Wilbert to know that he hadn't been paying attention to what they had been saying.

"The only way to get rid of them is to have them thrown out by a vote."

This was a new idea to Bill. He'd always gone along on the principle that the way to throw a man out was to do just that—throw him out, kick him out, give him the boots. He stared at Wilbert, blank-faced.

"I can throw 'em out, Wilbert. Me and my pals, we can take care of the two of them, or the three of them if that four-eyed one, what's his name, Ryan, if he sticks his nose into the picture."

"I haven't got any doubts but that you could, Bill, you alone or you and your friends."

"You don't want 'em hangin' around, do you, Wilbert?"

"No, Bill, they don't give this place a good name."

"If you ask me, I'll tell you what I think of 'em," Bill Pfeister said. "They're full of horse manure. They act like they was too good for the rest of us, because what are we? We're just ordinary people."

Riggs knew that the time had come, the time had come.

II

George read aloud:

"*Dear George:*

In the darkest hours of the night, I am writing you to tell you of the message of the dawn and the sun. For you are one of the dawn and the sun, not of the night and inky blackness which can only weave the shroud of death around your soul.

You live today in a nest of iniquity, an eagle that will not spread its wings. Through the mud and slime of the desiccated valley, crawls a snake that will spit its poison into you and wind its vile body around you, tighter and tighter, until you are constricted to death.

That snake is Aloysius McGonigle. Like all who are low in soul, he cannot rest until he drags down to his own level one who is lofty in spirit. He is not your friend. He works like a thief in the night to rob you of your Grecian grandeur. His mind is cunning, his tongue is glib and his smile is false.

Beware, George, of McGonigle, the snake in the grass who will kill all that is fine and noble in you. With him, you can only live with broken wings, lost among the multitudes, where the air is foul. It is he who will betray you and bring degradation upon you. It is he, who with base and foul treachery seeks to blacken your heart and mind.

Hearken unto me, George, for it is I who am your friend. It is I who sees your finer nature and who will never betray you. Do not waste yourself in the valley of mud where the base and vulgar earthbound wallow. That is not for you whose soul is as fine as your face is fair. You were fashioned by the gods for rarer, purer and headier air. And it is I who can give you wings to reach that air

*and accompany you above the mountains to the sun which
is your true and destined home. Come with me, like
eagles we will spread our wings and fly to all the beauty
that is aloft. Come and be the eagle that you are.*

With heartfelt hope,

Riggs"

When George had finished reading the letter aloud, he and
Alec had both laughed. They passed it all off as a big joke,
but each was affected by what Riggs had written. George's
vanity was flattered by Riggs' description; and Alec was
stung, more than he would have admitted, by Riggs' ref-
erence to him as a snake. They continued to laugh, however. George read the letter aloud for a second time, with
exaggerated emphasis on his superior qualities. Alec found
himself liking the Machiavellian cleverness that Riggs attributed to him.

"He sure gives me a pair of horns," Alec laughed.

"And he endows me with godlike attributes," George
said.

"One thing is certain, George, he's a lousy writer."

"Yes, his style is more repulsive than his intentions."

"When I think about it, Riggs' letter is a little sickening."

"It's too droll to nauseate, Alec."

"The ugly little sonofabitch is crazy," Alec said.

"The arrogance, the conceit of him to think that he
could guide me to be a sportive fellow eagle. If there is
one thing I can spot and recognize, it's conceit. After all,
Alec, I am not without conceit myself. I have so much of
it that I can always recognize it in my fellow man," George
laughed, "or even in a fairy fellow who is not a man."

"The simple fact is, of course, that Riggs is crazy."

"That's no excuse for his bad style."

"I have no interest in his lousy style. I'll leave that to Eddie. He's the one who's interested in writing."

"I'm half-tempted to go out and find him and kick his teeth in. It's an insult to send me, George Raymond, such a lousy love letter. If I ever receive a love letter as badly written from a girl, I'll jilt her. To send me, George Raymond, such a letter, such inferior writing—I call it an insult."

"For Christ's sake, Raymond, be careful or you'll believe you are a Grecian god. Why the hell don't you get out of bed, put on your clothes so we can go walk a little."

"Yes, I think I will. I'll walk along 47th Street, and along Cottage Grove Avenue with godlike grace, under the rays of the sun which is my 'true and destined home,' in a pair of shoes that cost five bucks."

He got out of bed.

After he had dressed, they went out and walked. Neither of them had much to say—they were talked out. After a little while they separated.

III

Alec walked over to the Forum. Old John Mason was there. He told Alec that something was going on, he didn't know what it was, but something was up. He didn't like the way that Conrad Jackson was beginning to nose around the place like a gumshoe. Old John didn't like the way that faker was behaving—he was beginning to act as if he owned the place.

"If he ever was an actor, Alec, then John Mason, like Tom Johnson, was Mayor of Cleveland, Ohio; and yes, the Governor of Ohio, too, for good measure."

"You should have been," Alec told him.

Old John was touched by Alec's words. Alec appreciated

his qualities and what he could have been. He knew something of the real John Mason, not the unlucky old man that he was in the eyes of almost everyone who met him. For a few seconds, Old John imagined his life as having taken a different course, the course it should have taken. He envisioned himself in a silk hat, and a black coat and striped trousers, shaking hands with important and powerful men, even with the President of the United States.

Suddenly, his daydream vanished. He looked around at the drab basement where he lived. He felt shame and hurt, a silent sense of misery which made him aware that he was now in the black night of a life that had gone nowhere.

Old John felt like weeping. He wished that he had had a son like Alec.

"What specifically do you know, John?"

"Wilbert is up to something. I've known him a long time and rarely, rarely have I seen him smile. Now he goes around smiling with an air of mystery. He acts like he has a rich uncle about to die and leave him a million dollars."

"Has he said anything to you? He's been giving me the cold shoulder lately and I know he's got something besides Herbert Spencer on his mind."

"He did say this morning over coffee that if any young smart alecks thought they were more clever than he, they were fooling themselves."

"That means me, and George Raymond. That dumb moron! Without me, this dump would be an empty cellar with rats running around in it."

"The rats are running around in it, Alec. Two kinds."

"What do you think he's up to?" Alec asked.

"That pious old man who pimps for his own daughter is putting him up to getting me out of here. It won't do them one iota of good, not with my interview tomorrow with Mr. Cordwood of the big Lakeside Dunes Realty Company."

"Do you have any more facts?"

Old John didn't. Alec asked him to keep his ears open. John promised to. Alec loaned him a dollar and the old man said that soon, he'd be in a position to light his cigars with brand-new dollar bills fresh from Uncle Sam's mint, if he so wished.

IV

Nora Lewis told George Raymond that people around the Slow-Down Club basement had warned her against him. One had been a funny old man who talked to her as if he might be her grandfather. At first, George thought she meant Old John Mason; but her description made it clear that she was speaking of Conrad Jackson. The old man had told her that a young girl like her should be careful of gay blades who were flashy and acted like matinee idols.

George frowned so angrily that Nora was frightened. For a moment, George thought that for revenge, and for his own amusement, he might seduce Lenora Jackson and jilt her. That would teach the meddling old fool to stay out of his affairs.

George soon learned that Wilbert Wilmer and others whose names Nora didn't know, as well as Bill Pfeister, were warning her to watch her step with him.

"If Bill Pfeister doesn't shut his stupid trap, I'll make his puss look like a pot of cranberry jelly."

Nora was locked in fear again. She was afraid that George would be hurt if he and Bill Pfeister fought. She begged George not to say a word to Bill and please not to start a fight with him.

"Anything they tell me goes in one ear and out the other," she said.

But George was in a fury.

Nora trembled. She could see him, his handsome face all bleeding. She couldn't bear it, she just couldn't bear it if he was beaten up just on account of her. No she couldn't, even if it did mean that he must like her to fight over her. Gosh, as much as six months ago, she never imagined that she would become so important and, well, in a way, such a romantic person that two fellows would fight over.

Nora promised to tell George everything she heard. George decided to delay what he had labeled in his mind as the "Rites of the Defloration of Nora Lewis, Virgin Un-Extraordinary."

V

Eddie continued to go around to the Forum but largely because of George and Alec. He was beginning to feel a growing dissatisfaction with himself. He knew that he must see more of the world. He'd have to get away, have experiences, live where the excitement about writing and literature was keen. Word had gone around in his neighborhood that he wanted to be a writer, and he was regarded as crazy. At home, his Uncle Larry laughed at him, called the books he brought home to read "dirty," and laughed at the manuscripts of stories that Eddie had tried to write and left lying around the apartment.

—Where will it ever get you? his Uncle Larry kept asking him.

At least the atmosphere at the Forum was different, unconventional, and perhaps shocking in the eyes of the people that Eddie had known. He was pleased to know that the word was going around that he was crazy, an atheist who wanted to be a writer. This gave him a sense of importance that he hadn't felt before his break with all of the values of his past.

Even though Eddie Ryan was still a spectator, he did have some importance at the Forum.

But the Forum was being divided into two factions. Wilbert Wilmer, Conrad Jackson, Bill Pfeister, Riggs, and a number of nondescript members who took the Slow-Down Club seriously, at least as a club if not an uplifting organization, formed one group.

George and Alec were collecting an entourage around themselves too. George's younger brother, Charles, who worked in a gas station, often came over to the apartment. Sometimes he'd spend the night there. He seemed to take Myrtle's presence for granted whenever she was there for the night.

And there was Ken Gilmore, a tall lean fellow that George and Eddie had known in the "old" days. The three of them had gone to Marguerita Mooney's Dancing School together. Ken was a fun-loving fellow who loved to go gash-hunting in his old secondhand jalopy. Eddie had always liked Ken and had wished sometimes that he could be the same devil-may-care kind of fellow that Ken was. Once in a while, Ken liked to read. He was one of the few from the old gang who didn't laugh at Eddie's ambition to write. Eddie had run into him one day when he was on his way to the Forum and invited him along.

Another fellow who took to going to the Forum was Philly Benton. George and Eddie had known him from their early days around 58th Street. He had gone to Carter School. One day, he had fought Davy Armand, a good little scrapper, for over forty-five minutes under the 58th Street El station. Philly was an easygoing, slap-happy kid. He wasn't too bright and never thought seriously about the future. He had married a girl who had a pretty face and a plain soul. They had a one-year-old child and lived in a

five-room cottage made of wooden clapboard not too far
from the filling station where Eddie worked. George and
Eddie told Philly about the Forum and he promised to
drop in to see them one night. He did, and much to their
surprise, he took to it. He seemed to like everything about
it—even the discussions of books and ideas that George,
Alec, and Eddie would sometimes have. Philly began dropping by almost every night after work. He could have more
fun with George and Eddie than he could in a speakeasy,
and it didn't cost as much. He hated staying home. Grace
was no longer a broad. She was his cook, his housekeeper,
and the mother of his kid. The meek and usually silent
wife who bore his name and took his pay envelope, giving
him a daily allowance, made him feel he had been hooked.
He couldn't go riding the rods, seeing new places, finding
broads where he went, layin' 'em and leavin' 'em. A couple
of years ago, Grace had been different, not a broad, not
gash, but someone who had put the moon and the stars
inside of him and had given him a terrific feeling that a
man could never admit to another man. She had made
him think all kinds of goofy things. The moon was even
something that you felt different about when you kissed a
girl and stuck your tongue in her mouth until you both
got super hot pants. And kissing on a park bench or under
a tree in a park at night with the stars coming inside your
head—that was love. Love was all of this with a girl who
had a twat like all girls but her twat wasn't a twat. He
didn't know what it was, but it made her the girl who
put the stars in your head. It happened to you and made
you go to work and mope, thinking and dreaming of it, like
you weren't all there. It made you think that a girl could
keep you living with the moon in your head until the old
pecker drooped and drooped away until it couldn't start up
again, not even for all the dough of John D. Rockefeller.
And it made you put the ring on the finger of a girl, a girl

like Grace. Then after you banged away at her like she was
Lulu, you had the feeling that the stars and the moon
had gotten drunk in your head. But love was like breaking
a crap game by rolling sevens and elevens, until you broke
the game, once in your life, and then you couldn't count on
it again. And you found out that the girl who had put the
stars in your noggin was the girl who had put the ball and
chain on you. That's when you went around getting whatever you could out of a bender or a poker game. The only
love that was left was the stuff you saw in the movies.
Grace was all right as a hump of tail, better than putting
calluses on his hands swinging them in the pudding and
better than making himself so nuts the squirrels would
only want him in the winter.

Now Philly was having fun again with his old pals
George and Eddie. It was almost like it was in the good
old days in the good old neighborhood, the days that were
good like brown crap when the chain was pulled, but that
you never could forget because they were the best damned
days in the best of all the shooting matches of neighborhoods that there had ever been.

Another two who showed up at the Slow-Down Club
were Henry Jones and his younger brother, Mark, a dull,
skinny boy of nineteen. Eddie had thought of Henry as a
goof when he had known him in high school. He had been
a shy and awkward boy who had weighed less than a hundred and twenty pounds. He was a freshman and nobody
had paid any attention to him except the football coach.
Eddie had been a senior and had gone on to graduate that
year. Henry had stayed on, almost becoming a football star,
despite his weight handicap. He smiled almost constantly
and clearly liked almost everyone. He gave the impression
that the whole world was jolly.

These were the fellows—Charles Raymond, Ken Gilmore, Philly Benton, and Henry Jones and his brother

Mark—who most often visited the apartment on 47th Street and Drexel Boulevard that George and Alec shared with Phil Dumont.

As the struggle at the Slow-Down Club developed, the apartment became the headquarters.

One afternoon, they were all together in the apartment drinking some of George Raymond's homemade gin.

"They're calling a special meeting of the Slow-Down Club and their aim is to vote us out as immoral," Alec said with a laugh.

"How gallantly these champions of virtue and maidenheads have accepted a pansy as an ally, a pansy who would pretend to be a Superman. Thus spoke not Zarathustra, but Raymond, the menace to fair females of virtue, who lurks in the basement of the Kent Hotel," George Raymond said, holding a glass in his hand.

"Hell, George, if you want to go down now and have it out with them, I'm game. We've got three of the boys from 58th and Calumet—and there's you and Eddie." Philly Benton was counting.

"What about me?" asked Charles.

"Four," Philly corrected himself.

Eddie didn't say anything. He felt that any brawling, any slugging, would be a compounding of moronishness. Unless he were pushed into it, he wanted to avoid a fight, but he suspected that before the Slow-Down struggle ended, there would be a big fight. He knew that he should be writing now, writing every minute—and yet there he sat, in the noisy apartment, listening to plans and gossip about a struggle over the control of the Slow-Down Club, a plain fraud.

They were all talking, laughing, and drinking.

Eddie sat quietly, in a somber and gray mood. Would he ever know kisses? Would love never be his lot? He had daydreamed of walking through life, as though it were a

garden with a girl, her hand in his. In grammar school,
the girl had been Gertrude Dawson. There had been others.
But Gertrude Dawson was the abiding image, the girl. Eddie thought of her often. He felt lonely. They were all
young in that room. Eddie looked around.

He wondered which of them would die first, especially
which of the three of them, George, Alec, or him. He
could not think of any of them as dead—they were still
young and strong, their lives had yet to be lived. And then
the road would end. And:

Even the weariest river winds somewhere safe to sea.

Did George and Alec think of their futures? Eddie Ryan
knew his goal. But he was walking toward it very badly.
He took a drink of the liquor. He didn't like it. He felt
very much alone in the crowd.

"Riggs," George said, his voice full of contempt, "Riggs,
that dirty-minded little fairy."

"He's an asshole bandit," Eddie said. His phrase went
over big. He had heard it four or five years earlier when
he had worked for the Express Company; but he accepted
the laughter as though he had thought of the phrase at that
very moment.

"That asshole bandit. He, too, has decked himself in the
white robes of virtue," George said spitting out scorn.

"The question is this," Alec said. "We've got to decide
what we're going to do. Give up the Slow-Down Club or
fight for it."

"I say let's go down and take it over," Charles said with
an anger he didn't seem to really feel.

"Sure we're going to fight for it," George said. "Can you
imagine George Raymond walking out on such a pack?"

"It's not only George Raymond, it's me, too."

"Yes, pardon me, Alec; I was so goddamned exercised
that I thought only of myself. George Raymond and Alec
McGonigle."

"They've got the property. It's going to be hard as cracking walnuts with a baby's teeth," Alec said. "Possession is nine-tenths of the law."

"That's why I say—take it over. Kick 'em to hell and gone out of the joint," Charles said.

"I'm game," Philly said.

"We can't get away with it," Alec said. "Wilbert can get warrants out for us and we'll all be in the clink—on serious charges, too. We've got to beat them on a vote."

"Counting noses when Riggs' flat little nose will count as much as my beak," George said bitterly.

"We can get votes," Charles said. "If each of us gives a broad a couple of good screws. She's yours for life after that. Aren't we men? If not, what the hell are we?"

"I'm game," Philly Benton said.

"We can win with the use of Riggs' letter," George said.

"How are you going to use it to beat them?" Alec asked.

"I'll read it aloud at a meeting."

"I wouldn't do that, George. You'll lay yourself open to accusations and suspicions. Gossip and scandal-mongering have already been started about both of us; and if you read the letter, you'll probably stimulate more talk. Some of the goddamned fools will start saying something as profound as 'where there's smoke, there's fire,' " Alec explained.

"I suppose you're right, but such filthy hypocrisy nauseates me. It makes me want to puke up the whole goddamned mess."

"Wilbert has the lease in his name. If we take the club away from him or not, he's still got that lease and we can't get away from the fact," Alec said.

"You don't want to give up the fight, do you, Alec?"

"I've been thinking, George, what the hell are we fighting for?"

"They're trying to gang up on us and kick us out of our

goddamn Slow-Down Club. The club is only a fake and a farce."

"That's just it, George, is it worth fighting over?"

"It's demeaning and degrading—scheming and fighting over who's going to bamboozle some young morons," George said.

"Hell, George, I'll go along with any fight you want, but we ought to ask ourselves here—what do we want, what are we fighting for?"

For a moment, George didn't answer, then he laughed and asked:

"What the hell are we fighting for?"

Both he and Alec suddenly changed their attitudes concerning the Slow-Down Club and the Forum. They decided that they were not getting into any fight where the stakes were not high, that it was in their power to damage the Forum and seriously impair, or even wreck the Slow-Down Club, without fighting.

"This is like shooting craps for pennies," George said.

"And according to the latest reports from our spies who have infiltrated the headquarters of the enemy," Alec said, giving a heavy play to his words in order to strengthen his irony, "the newest addition to the enemy general staff is— Riggs."

Everyone in the room hooted. The atmosphere lightened and all of them had a drink.

"We don't have to beat them, we can wreck them," George said.

"The goddamned fools don't know it yet, but they're already wrecked," Alec said. "Among them all, there isn't one person with a useful idea that will help enlarge the Slow-Down Club or even keep it functioning at its present level."

"And don't forget, George Raymond's good stuff right out of the old washtub kept the Slow-Down Club a going

business. Without it, and us, the organization is going to
fall apart. Riggs can't contribute anything." George paused.
"Imagine him telling Bill Pfeister that the two of them are
a pair of eagles flying away from the mud of the valley to
soar above the mountains. That's a card."

Everyone laughed. Eddie Ryan's interest quickened. If
the struggle should take on the aspect of humor, then he
could participate. He could exhibit his own cleverness and
bring his wit into play.

Just as they were approaching hilarity there was a knock
on the door. Alec got up, walked over and opened it. Nora
Lewis stood there.

VI

Nora brought the latest information from the enemy
camp. She had gone to the basement of the Kent looking
for George. She had been surrounded immediately and was
given so much advice that she simply couldn't remember
it all. Even Wilbert Wilmer had chipped in with his two
cents' worth. He told her that she was too nice and sweet a
girl to allow herself to fall into the clutches of George Raymond. While she was telling George about this, she gazed
at him with loving eyes.

George met her gaze coolly. Up to that moment, he had
not specifically told Nora that he wanted her to give her
all to him. He had been leading up to this proposal and
had planned to make it when he had her in his arms, alone
in the apartment. George wanted to develop the relationship between them, to keep rousing her and intensifying
her girlish love for him, and to fix in her mind the fear
that she could not, she dare not risk losing him. He had
started explaining to her the beauty of true love, and the
wholesomeness of a perfect union. He had decided that

when the time came, if she made an issue about her virginity, he could threaten her with the loss of him forever. He had no doubts of the outcome.

The little group at the Forum had jumped the gun on George. They had openly made her purity and her virginity a stake in their fight against George and Alec. Wilbert had warned her that if she allowed herself to fall into the clutches of George Raymond, she would never be the same again, not as long as she lived. Conrad Jackson's advice had followed Wilbert's. He had told her that he was speaking with all of his long experience in mind. Not only was he the father of a girl whom he had raised to become a shining example of virtue, but he had seen much of the ways of the world during his thespian past. It had been his fate to witness the fall of more than one pure girl, girls such as Nora herself who had been caught in the cleverly contrived snares of a seducer, one who took his cruel pleasure from women and then abandoned them in ruin, seeking out more young and innocent girls upon whom to play the same cruel fate. He always told his own daughter, Lenora, that the virtue was to young girls as perfume was to the flowers in the garden.

When Nora repeated all of this, a howl went up. She looked bewildered, almost frightened. Her eyes sought George. He asked her to tell them more. She did and she kept turning her head toward George. With her eyes, Nora was begging him for approval.

Bill Pfeister had warned her. He told her that he would protect her. He said that George Raymond did not love her, but that he did, with all of his heart. George would only use her like a toy and then throw her away, a broken toy. If she ever gave in to him, he would lose all respect for her and treat her like "the girl that men forget." But Bill Pfeister was jealous. He had told her that he would save her, save her from becoming a toy to enjoy for a while by George Raymond who shot girls like her a line, turned their heads, and then when he had his way with them, left them, even if it meant that they would end up in the gutter.

Nora was overexcited. She didn't know what to think. She had come over to tell George. What had been said to her had only increased her desire for him. And while she was afraid of what would happen that first time, and had heard that it would hurt her and be terrible, everything in her cried out "yes, yes" and "yes, yes" again for her to give herself, body and soul, to George Raymond.

But somehow, she seemed to be changing, and thinking that maybe it would be George who would be giving more of himself to her than she would be giving to him. Nora still thought of it as "if," but she was beginning to feel that there was no longer any question of "if," and that she would do it if George Raymond wanted her to. It was kind of exciting to know that Bill Pfeister and the men down at that basement were trying to protect her, but all of that was kind of like a play or something and they didn't reach her, not inside. It was like something that wasn't real, not exactly a dream but still, something that wasn't really and truly, and honest-to-goodness happening.

When she was with George that was honest-to-goodness happening. And it was real and honest-to-goodness when he held her in his arms and kissed her.

Nora felt more important than she had ever felt before in her whole life. It made a girl feel important to know that she was loved. Maybe George Raymond did love her. She wasn't sure that he did, not all the time, but maybe he did. He acted like he loved her, the way he'd kiss her and hold her. He was so experienced. Who was she, little Nora Lewis. She was afraid she might lose him, and she couldn't bear the thought of that because it seemed to her that if she lost him now, it would be like her life was over, at eighteen.

She was afraid to let him do it, afraid of what would happen to her. It was supposed to hurt you and once it happened, you could never, ever be the same again. If she did it, would she ever be able to look her mother and father in the eye? Nora was afraid; but she still wanted to. She wanted to know what it felt like. When George held her and kissed her in front of her house, she would have let him. She had wanted more, and not just more of being held and kissed, but something more to happen to her.

She was puzzled and afraid. Sometimes she had the most wonderful dreams she had ever had and sometimes she felt sad, like she was waiting for a terrible thing to happen to her.

This must be the way it was to be in love. She kept thinking that if she didn't let George, she would lose him. She couldn't bear to lose him, and all that she had to give him was that. She would just have to give it to him no matter what happened to her or how it would hurt, and no matter if it ruined her and made her a bad girl.

Nora had hurried to the apartment from the hotel, nervous to see him. She had hoped that he would be alone and would kiss her. She had even thought that maybe it would happen then. And once it did happen, she wouldn't worry any more and be afraid. And then, wouldn't he love her more, wasn't that what made lovers more in love than ever and the reason why love was so wonderful?

By the time she had arrived at the door, Nora Lewis was prepared to surrender her all. The presence of so many in the apartment had been a disappointing letdown for her; but at the same time, she felt a kind of relief. It meant that nothing could happen to her then, and George couldn't blame her; and no matter how much she thought and dreamed, and how much she loved George, she had never done it before and she couldn't help being afraid.

Nora kept looking at George. She'd rushed to tell him what she had heard. She had done something for him, and all she wanted was to keep doing things for him; and the more things she could do for him, the happier she would feel. And maybe, she hoped, that would mean that he would love her. After Nora had told them what she knew, the conversation became excited. There was impending danger. At moments the most important thing in the world was the struggle and rivalry between the group at the Forum on one hand, and George and Alec on the other. Nora was in the center of all this fuss. She liked her role, but she didn't really understand what it all meant. Some of the talk confused her. The conversation turned on Riggs. She didn't like him. There was something nasty and ugly about him and she wished he wasn't at the Slow-Down so much. Sometimes when he spoke to her, she was almost frightened. She knew that there was something the matter with him, he was different. But when she heard that he was in love with George Raymond, she couldn't believe it. Yet it was true, she knew it.

VII

Every day, the bitterness around the Forum became more intense. Those involved in the fight stopped speaking to one another. Wilbert Wilmer cut Alec at the Washington Park Bug Club on a Sunday afternoon. George was told that he could no longer run the Saturday night dances and sell his washtub gin; and that if he tried to, the cops would be called. Alec and George decided that they might smash Wilbert and his small group of allies at a meeting. They demanded a meeting, which had already been planned by the other side.

Since Wilbert had the lease in his name, they didn't have any hopes of getting control of the Slow-Down Club but they were certain that they probably could wreck the club, and maybe even the Forum. Wrecking the club became their objective. George said that he had gotten all of the amusement and entertainment he wanted out of the club; now it was beginning to bore him. He couldn't fancy himself going on working with a thick-skulled moron like Bill Pfeister or a treacherous weakling like Wilbert Wilmer. They weren't satisfied with their own faults, they had to associate with Riggs, a pansy. He denounced their hypocrisy in calling him and Alec immoral while they plotted with Riggs and said nothing of the letter that Riggs had written him. George had had Nora make copies of the letter, which he had distributed around the Kent Hotel basement. He fumed when he was told that Riggs denied having written the letter; and then, had claimed that it had none of the significance attached to it by George and Alec. He had described himself as a poet and had said that he had merely written to George in a poetic vein, warning him about McGonigle. It was even reported to George that Riggs had insinuated that Alec's interest in George was a homosexual one.

Alec treated all of this as though it were humorous, too ridiculous to merit notice and too far beneath his dignity to warrant a reply. But he was hurt, not only by the rumor attributing homosexuality to him, but also by all the other things that were reported to him in the cluttered Drexel Boulevard apartment.

Although Riggs spoke of Alec as the evil genius deceiving George, the others, including Bill Pfeister, talked of Alec more or less in contempt, as the cat's paw of George Raymond. He was described as one who jumped at

George's bidding and was lacking in any will of his own. Alec smarted under these reports but he laughed and said that nothing else could be expected from such sources.

Alec was losing all pleasure in the whole thing. There was very little at stake and regardless of what happened, he was finished with the Slow-Down Club, which had been his idea. He knew he couldn't go back to the Forum and feel as important as he had when it had just been opened. He had liked Wilbert, and those first weeks of the Forum began to seem happy, almost idyllic. He had been unchallenged as the outstanding young person there. He had looked forward to Sunday evenings as occasions when he could make an impression with his intelligence. Strangers coming for the first time would eye him. Wilbert Wilmer and John Mason and many others had been impressed by his wit and intelligence. Lenora had seen him treated with respect and importance, even by men as old as her father. And when they danced, the two of them would stand out and be noticed.

All that was over now. He and Lenora were broken up and although this did not cause him any sorrow, his vanity was wounded. And he missed her sexually. She had been the first girl he had had regularly, and he had felt a great assurance in the knowledge that he had her. The uncertainties of the chase, the fear of being rejected, had been spared him. If he did try to make some other girl and failed, he still had Lenora and this would take away the sting of failure. He remembered how it was sometimes before Lenora. To have desire without gaining satisfaction made you feel degraded, weak, a ridiculous kind of a failure. And it made you think about sex too much. Against this memory, his affair with Lenora had loomed as a big success. Sometimes he would tell himself that some of the fellows from St. Hilary's ought to see him and know what he'd copped off.

And Lenora had become familiar to him. He had acquired a satisfying knowledge of women from her, which had erased all of the strangeness he had once felt with them. He was at ease in her bedroom. He had watched her dress and undress, seen her move about in her chemise and her underwear. He knew how she went about dressing and where she kept all the various articles of her clothing. He knew the bureau drawers where her underthings were neatly piled, her closet full of dresses, her nightgowns and robes, the cosmetics and perfumes on the top of her dresser. The little secrets of a woman were his knowledge. Sex was more satisfying when it could be carried on in her own bedroom instead of in a car or in the park. He knew that many fellows his age had not had sex as he had with Lenora, and he felt wiser and more experienced.

He had known that eventually they would break up. She'd never be an actress. She wasn't really bright and she took her future far too seriously. Sometimes she talked as if she were really a successful star. Many of his remarks and some of his best wit had gone over her head. She had pretended to understand him but she hadn't. Not only that, Alec knew that in a pinch she would always bend to her father's will. And he hadn't been at all sure that she was or ever could be a one-man woman. If she'd met some fellow who could have advanced her stage career, she'd most certainly have gone to bed with him. Alec did believe that she had liked sex with him and that he had really satisfied her. This had kept him pretty well set up and when he'd fall into the dumps, his assurance that he had really made Lenora like it with him was a prop to his own self-confidence.

Alec had attributed more importance to the Forum than was merited, and he had credited Wilbert Wilmer with more intelligence than the poor man had. Alec had thought of himself as the rising young man in an enter-

prise that would become as important on the South Side
as the Wild Onion was on the Near North Side. He had
imagined that the Forum would become a meeting place
for people who really were intelligent and superior. Not
only had he been enjoying himself and having a better
time than most fellows his own age, he had believed that
he was in the very center of something exciting and sig-
nificant. All of this had been conceited and perhaps more
naïve than he would have cared to admit to anyone. But
he had had a good time, untroubled and without the
friction that had marked the weeks which followed the
advent of George Raymond and Eddie Ryan upon the
Forum.

Each of them had, in their own way, been an unsettling
influence. George had become the source of strife and
rivalry. Not only was there the constantly recurring possi-
bility of fist fighting, which Alec thought was uncivilized
and worthy only of morons, but there had also been the
danger of arrest, and of jail. Even though George had
done it on a small scale, he had, nevertheless, introduced
bootlegging on the premises. Alec couldn't openly admit
to his objections to George's bootlegging because some
of the others would have thought that he was afraid. And
he was, just as Eddie Ryan had been. But young men
should not admit to fear; to be involved in risky under-
takings without admitting fear brought its own kind of
satisfaction. It meant that you had dared; or at least in
the eyes of others, you had dared. Alec believed that he
had shown his mettle. He believed that he had begun
to appear as bold and daring—pretty much the same as
George Raymond.

But the truth was that Alec thought that petty crime
was stupid. George Raymond's bootlegging was petty
crime, law-breaking for a mere twenty or thirty dollars on
a Saturday night. If George had been caught, arrested

with the goods on him in such a way as to involve him,
Alec was fairly certain that they would have had a good
chance of escaping jail. At least he believed that they
could have escaped jail. But his practical objections to
George's bootlegging were not based solely on a desire to
stay out of jail—Alec didn't want his name on a police
blotter. It could stand as a permanent black mark on his
record. He might want to return to law school, and maybe
one day he would want to enter politics. He didn't want
a police record to ruin his future. Too, there was his
mother; he didn't want to cause her pain and mortifica-
tion. As it was, he was hurting her enough, turning out
in such a way as to disappoint her, after all the hopes she
had had for him during those hard years when she had
worked as a servant. He knew that he well might cause
her more heartache in the future. When the day came
for him to marry, if he ever did, he was certain that he
would not be able to fall in love with a girl who was a
practicing Catholic and get married in the Church. And
if he married outside the Church, it would be a blow to
his mother, a hard blow. He still pretended to a faith in
which he did not believe in order not to wound her. Alec
thought that life had dealt cruelly with his mother and
that he should spare her any harsh blows if he could. He
did not love her, or at least, he wasn't certain that he loved
her. But he pitied her and did not want her to be hurt any
more, especially by him. His bond to her was one of memories of his boyhood, of her demeaning work to support and
educate him, of their days and years together. There was
little rapport between them. Sadness and silence still filled
their home. There was misunderstanding on the part of
both of them, but there was a closeness that was a habit
of closeness—they had had only each other for so many
years.

Now that he was a man, Alec could understand some

of the sorrow that was in his mother's character. He could understand the loneliness of all those years, the wound her pride had sustained when his father had deserted them, and the strength of character she had revealed. He could understand, too, why and how she had become so dependent on religion and almost fanatic in her faith. All those years seemed to be full of waste. He was not the son she had wanted him to become, and he could never be such a son. The repayment he gave her for those years had to be insincere, mere lip service offered so that she would not be wounded anew. All of her sacrifice, her prayer, her performance of duties, and her devotion to God would not bring her her expected reward in Heaven, because there was neither God nor Heaven. Because he knew this, Alec pitied her the more.

Alec wanted to be away from his mother because her presence kept him from being himself. He had to pretend for her. Every day that he stayed at home, he felt he had to compromise with his real self.

He wanted to leave home, and more than once he resolved to, only to postpone acting on his decision. He did not want to leave for a life of uncertainty and the kind of danger on which George Raymond seemed to thrive. And the danger to which he could become exposed by George also carried the risk that he would cause his mother too much added pain.

Eddie Ryan was an unsettling threat to Alec in a different manner. In action, Eddie often followed along with George—Eddie knew that George Raymond did not know the meaning of the word fear. Eddie pretended that he didn't either.

Eddie had no confidence in the impression that he made on others; he believed that he was disliked. His desperation was covered by an attitude of "I don't care," "the hell with the world," and with Max Stirner's *All*

Things Are Nothing to Me. But Eddie Ryan did care, and
he was determined to make others care. He was intellectually restless and dissatisfied; he felt the need to know
more. He believed that one must be consistent and one
must act on the basis of what one thought to be true.
He was not insensitive to the hurt he had caused at home
by announcing his loss of faith but he had felt that he
had had to do it—anything less would have been a compromise. Eddie repeatedly declared that one must burn
one's bridges behind one. Compromises could not be
made, because to compromise meant to retreat, to leave a
bridge unburned so that it could be recrossed in retreat.
And the bridges Eddie felt he must burn led not only to
all that he had rejected, but also to a past in which he believed he had been a failure. He had failed by not having
more courage; he had failed in not being successful with
girls, and he had failed in not learning more.

Sometimes Eddie made remarks which struck at Alec,
even though Eddie was not aware of this when he said
them. He felt that he had to take a chance with his life,
otherwise he couldn't be a writer. The desperation within
him, the recklessness which is not courage but a bitter
reaction to a feeling of being unloved or not loved enough,
helped create a confusion about Eddie's taking chances.
The real chances that he believed he must take were not
those that George Raymond took—a sock in the jaw or a
night in jail—the chance that Eddie had to take was that
of not being afraid to fail.

Alec had no such ambition or need and George Raymond only talked about the things he was going to do.

But often they felt themselves kindred spirits and would
call themselves "The Three Musketeers." There was, however, much that separated them. Thus they were, three
young men.

Chapter Eight

I

Eddie Ryan made the next break in his series of breaks. He said he was going to New York, burning more bridges, abandoning his job as he had his formal education, and his share of the family burdens. George agreed to go along. They decided that they would hitchhike.

One summer afternoon, shortly after they had decided to go to New York, George and Eddie, along with Alec, happened to be walking across the Washington Park ball field. There was a scrub game on Diamond Number One near the field house at the northern end of the field. They heard shouts, the crack of the bat, and saw men in motion, running with the plays. Off ahead, kids were playing. They looked very small in the distance and their cries sounded plaintive.

As they walked, Eddie's mind turned back to his boyhood years. He remembered himself in short pants, wearing the shirt of a gray baseball uniform with green letters across the front. He had caught fungo flies and imagined himself another Happy Felsch or Johnny Mostil, playing center field for the White Sox. He used to play in any game that he could get into, with kids or men. All his playing and practicing had been for a purpose, he had been preparing himself for the day when he would be a big-league star on the Chicago White Sox. Every time he'd felt thwarted, Eddie had resolved again to show them, to try twice as hard; and one day he would receive the cheers of thousands and the name of Eddie Ryan would be famous. He would have succeeded in showing them.

The three of them continued to walk through Washington Park.

Eddie turned to Alec:

"Why don't you come to New York with George and me?"

"Yes, Alec, why don't you join us? We can all go on to New York and explore a new territory. There'll be new activities, and new girls," George laughed. "We'll leave Chicago to the Babbitts."

"Sure, I'll come along. I don't want to go down on record as the one who broke up the Three Musketeers."

They decided that one of the three of them could get some kind of job to provide food. They might ship out to sea, go to Europe or even Asia on a freighter. They would see new places. The Babbitts could stay here, find safety in a nice little job with a nice little girl and grow as fat and dull as the little missus.

They walked on, talking.

A sense of Eddie's past was lingering in his mind. He thought of a phrase that he had read in one of Nietzsche's books—"the pathos of distance." He was burning more bridges now and nostalgia was like a monotonous, sorrowing song in him. Would he be lonely for the past that he was leaving, the sighs and the hopes of yesterday? He didn't have to go. But New York meant all of the experience he had not had. New York meant that his life would become new again.

They came to the driveway at the southern end of the

ball field. Far behind them now, faintly, they could hear the sound of a bat on a ball.

Alec was talking about how he would break the news to his mother.

"She won't understand," he said.

"I've broken in my mother and the gaffer. They aren't surprised now, no matter what I do," George said.

Eddie thought of his grandmother. Would she die while he was away? His leaving would hurt her.

"I don't know how I'll break the news," Alec went on, concerned. "My old man will be delighted—that s.o.b., if you'll pardon my affection for my father. I can hear him now and how he'll be going on to my mother—'You slaved and sacrificed and worked yourself to the bone for him. You stinted and saved and toiled. You went without and gave him the best of education—boarding school, no less, and what is your reward? Does he repay you for all you did for him? No, and with no more than a by-your-leave, he ups and goes, and where is your reward? Where is the money you spent to educate him? He's one of your clan—not mine. You'll never see the day when you'll get back a penny of all you spent for him. That's how you raised him and spoiled him.' My old man will go on until he gets his full measure of enjoyment. And then, he'll put on his hat and coat, go out and get boiled, boozing and playing poker with his cronies. And my mother will just sit there and not say a word—she'll probably say the rosary with her beads, big black beads. I can remember them since I was a little kid. I'm going through with this; but it does hit me. This will come as a real blow to my mother."

George and Eddie exchanged meaningful glances. They both believed that Alec would back out. He wasn't "one of them," a phrase which had acquired added meaning in the last few months. They were both convinced that Alec was

tied to his home and to his mother and they considered
this a weakness in him. He wouldn't take a chance and
wield the knife to cut the bonds. He wouldn't burn his
bridges behind him. He valued safety more than George
Raymond and Eddie Ryan did.

They couldn't understand Alec and his feeling for his
mother. They could break their bonds. George was bored
with the Slow-Down Club, the Forum, and since he didn't
want to take a job and settle down in Chicago, he would
try New York. His home situation was different from
Alec's. He never stayed long at any one thing.

And Eddie was going because he had to, despite his
guilt about ending his contribution to the support of his
mother and the help he gave her for the education of his
youngest brother and sister. He was still giving half of
his salary to his mother. But he had to go. He was not
going merely to find material for his writing, as he had
told them at home. He had already begun turning on his
own past, his family and his neighborhood as the subject
for some of his intended writings. He wasn't going just
for new experiences even though he did need them; he
wasn't going because New York was the publishing center
of America where all the magazines were that he hoped
to write for.

II

But Alec had to live his own life, just as George and
Eddie had to live theirs, locked in their own skins.

Crossing the driveway, Eddie said that he'd treat for sodas in the refectory. They were hot and thirsty from their
walk.

While they were eating ice-cream sodas, Eddie remarked
to Alec:

"You know, I first met George in this park. It was down a little bit farther, near the 58th Street entrance."

"Yes, and no one witnessing that meeting could have predicted that we'd become the friends we are today," George said.

Eddie grinned. They always enjoyed hearing themselves talked about.

"It was about ten years ago, I guess," George said. "We were still punks in short pants."

"It was the fall of 1919," Eddie said.

"One thing that Eddie has in his favor as a writer, Alec, is his memory."

"He always surprises me. He catches things you wouldn't think he'd get. Maybe he will become a writer at that, a Chicago Dreiser or Anderson or Ben Hecht," Alec said.

"We almost had a fight on our first meeting," George said.

"That sounds like an episode in the life of George Raymond," Alec joked.

They had finished their sodas and pushed their glasses away from them. The refectory was noisy. There were quite a few kids in it, and many of them were little. They screamed, shouted, whined, and a couple of them cried. Some were with their mothers. Many of the mothers were getting fat. Eddie thought about his own mother, and now so many women got fat after they had children and how all of the wonderful mystery of girls was smothered. Girls that you wanted to fondle and pet, kiss and love, girls who gave you the illusion that they were linked with the stars and the moon, the sun, sky, spring, and all the natural beauty of the world, scarcely seemed to belong to the same sex as fat worried mothers. Eddie watched one stout mother lose her temper, her wide face contorted as she yelled at a girl of about five who had spilled part of an

ice-cream soda on her clean blue dress. He read the disillusionment of love into the scene. As he watched them,
he wondered, as he often had lately, if he might fail as a
writer if he were to marry.

"So, what did happen when you two guys met?" Alec
asked.

"Oh," George exclaimed, laughing, "I was playing touch
football with some of the kids who lived around 57th
Street. We had recently moved into this neighborhood
from 53rd Street and Prairie Avenue. A snotty, curly haired
kid and another kid . . ."

"One of the Goldman kids," Eddie said. "His old man
owned a grocery store on 58th Street. Herbie was his
name."

"We asked them to get off the field—the part of the
grass where we were playing," George continued. "The
snotty kid in the glasses wouldn't move. I rushed over to
him and sounded off. I was ready to fight. He seemed
undaunted. He told me the park was for the public and
he'd damn well walk anywhere he wanted to, nobody was
stopping him."

"Sounds like Eddie in one of his obstreperous moods,"
Alec said. "And, Eddie, I've known you long enough to
know that when you do get obstreperous, there's no one
who can be a more unpleasant s.o.b. than you."

Eddie grinned. He didn't know if what Alec said was
true or not; but he liked the idea of its being true, at
least at times.

"It looked as though we'd definitely tangle, and I remember thinking, 'This snotty little four-eyed punk will be
duck soup.' Then Eddie spotted my kid brother, Charles."

"He went to St. Michael's school. He was in the sixth
grade, a new kid, and I was in the eighth. I often walked
home with him along Indiana Avenue," Eddie said.

"So Eddie said, 'Come on, Charles, let's clean this bunch up and chase them the hell out of Washington Park.'"

George had added the "chase them the hell out of Washington Park" to the story.

"You started young, annoying the human race, didn't you, Eddie?" Alec joked.

"I felt cocky that afternoon. It was a gray sunless day and I didn't have anything to do. I was just walking in the park, looking for some kind of excitement," Eddie said.

"Didn't you worry about wasting your time, or your friends wasting your time in those days?" Alec kidded.

"At all events, we didn't have a scrap. Charles said that he knew Eddie and that he was all right. Then he told Eddie that I was his older brother. And that's the story of how George Raymond and Eddie Ryan met," George said.

"The first time I saw Eddie wasn't in the Kent Hotel basement," Alec said.

"Where was it? When?"

"Another time when he was being snotty," Alec said genially. "It was when I was in boarding school at St. Hilary's. Do you remember the football game when your high school, St. Basil's, came down and played us, Eddie?"

"Yes, we got the hell beaten out of us. We lost 35–7. It was a warm, sunny Saturday afternoon in November, more like summer than autumn," Eddie said.

This casual reminiscing brought back more of the past to Eddie. The present moment, the three of them in the refectory, seemed almost unreal to him. Eddie could not fully believe that they were planning to leave Chicago within a short time. Eddie felt that he was a stranger to his own past.

Alec was talking. He was telling about the afternoon of the football game. He had been standing near the dressing room when Eddie Ryan had come out after the interval between halves. Eddie had passed Alec, whom he neither knew nor noticed, to go out on the football field. He had turned to some of his teammates and said:

"Let's go out and get these bastards."

"They got me pretty much," Eddie said, laughing. "Toward the end of the game I had to be taken out. I was groggy."

"I wasn't the only one who heard you talk about getting the bastards," Alec said.

"They kept coming at me at my end, and you had some big guys in your backfield," Eddie said.

"Yes, they were big and tough," Alec said. "They plastered the hell out of almost every team that came to play us."

The game was vivid in Eddie's memory. He remembered the bright sunshine and the mildness of the afternoon.

Eddie had played well that afternoon, turning the plays in when the offense came around his end, and breaking up the interference. But from the very beginning, it was evident that Eddie and his teammates were outclassed. St. Hilary's was a better team and much heavier, too. Their big fullbacks tore and slashed through the lines. When the St. Basil fellows had the ball, they were stopped dead. Their line was rolled aside. Eddie remembered when three of the St. Hilary backfield men came at him, running low and hard, followed by their right halfback who was carrying the ball. They flung their bodies at him; Eddie hit them off with his hands and sidestepped and dodged to keep on his feet and not allow the ball carrier to get around him. But they were fighting a losing game with bigger fellows ramming and battering at them. St. Hilary kept driving into the St. Basil line. The players would unscramble and get back into position. The St. Hilary quarterback would bark out the signals, his voice cocky and snappy.

At half-time, the St. Basil players dragged themselves off the field, a tired bunch with many bruises. The score was 21–0.

Alec had overheard Eddie burst out in frustration as he was returning to the field for the second half. Eddie was going out to fight on, for no glory, no victory. He and his teammates were going back to be battered, bruised, and beaten up and down the field. All they could do was uphold their morale and keep their pride. Eddie hoped he could become one of the heroes of defeat; but the game was grueling.

In the second half, Eddie caught two forward passes for short gains. He went up between two of the St. Hilary backs and took a pass with one hand. He kept his feet and turned in the play when they came at his end. Then as the third quarter was about to end, Eddie was hit by two backs at once and went down with a thud. He got up slowly, shaking his head; he had been jarred.

The sun had gone down. They played with the shadows falling over the field. The air was gray. The afternoon was dying. Eddie was hit again. He beat off interference, and then, they came at him for the third time. He went down, falling hard. When Eddie got to his feet, slowly, he was groggy. The next play went off tackle on the opposite side of the line. Eddie watched it in a daze. Then he was taken out of the game.

Remembering the game while he sat in the refectory with George and Alec, Eddie thought how unimportant it was. The game seemed so meaningless in retrospect. His childhood, his adolescence seemed as meaningless as that football game. He thought of his life as one of dreams-unfulfilled, abandoned and lost. All of his efforts had been

like those he'd made on that football field. His dreams had
been vast, but his successes had been little ones.

Now he had a new dream. He was going to New York.
Soon.

III

"What are we going to do about the goddamned Slow-
Down Club now? Drop it?" Alec asked.

"We've slowed down the Slow-Down Club," George said.
"I'd like to finish the business of slowing it down and
wrecking it."

"Is it worth our time, George?"

"No, not unless it amuses us. I have two items on my
agenda to attend to and I'll have to attend to them ex-
peditiously—is that correct? One is Nora. On Sunday night,
I'm going to allow her to have possession of the body that
Riggs wrote about in his letter. And then, I'll settle with
Bill Pfeister."

"What the hell's the use of fighting with that moron,
George?"

"What's the use? He's insulted the name of Raymond.
He's been asking for me to tee off on him and he's going
to get what he's asking for. That's all of the remaining
interest I have in the Slow-Down Club. We got our use
out of it."

"I'm ready to forget the whole goddamned affair," Alec
said.

"I am too; but I'm going to manage it so that Pfeister
doesn't forget me."

"It's getting late. It's after five," Alec said.

"What's time? It's something to waste," George said.

"Yes, if the wasting is enjoyable. But I did say I'd be
home for supper tonight. What are you two bums going
to be doing later?"

"Oh, I don't know. Why don't you come on over to the apartment?"

"Maybe I will; I'll see you there," Alec said.

After Alec had gone, George and Eddie went to a restaurant on Garfield Boulevard and ate. George asked Eddie why he had asked Alec to come along with them to New York. Eddie was surprised. He had imagined that George would have welcomed Alec as added company. But George said he didn't think it was a good idea for Alec to go along with them. Three would be too many for traveling, it would be harder to thumb rides. And Alec didn't have any money; he'd be in the way.

"Hell, I thought you liked Alec."

"I do. But you and I've been friends longer and we have more in common. Alec doesn't want to leave home and go bumming the way you and I do. He doesn't want to take his chances."

Eddie was a little nonplused although he could see that it would be better for the two of them to go to New York without a third.

"I'll handle him so he'll give up the idea without feeling that he's backing out," George said. "He'll actually be glad not to go. He's not ready to make the break from home."

Eddie was relieved. He hadn't thought of the added problems of three people traveling instead of two. And there'd be more problems after they got to New York. They'd have to have two rooms instead of one. It would be harder to ship out, too, if they decided to. And there'd be more problems in deciding if there were three to decide.

IV

At the next meeting of the Slow-Down Club, George Raymond and Alec McGonigle were expelled. Eddie Ryan was kicked out for good measure.

George sent a challenge to fight to Bill Pfeister and Pfeister accepted. George changed his plans and decided to seduce Nora on the next Saturday night, instead of Sunday.

All this seemed anticlimactic to Eddie since they were planning to leave for New York soon. But there was an atmosphere of excitement at the apartment on Drexel Boulevard. There were rumors that Pfeister's friends planned to gang up on George and not give him a chance to fight Pfeister fair.

Alec and Eddie wished that the planned grand finale could be avoided. They didn't see the sense of a fight and did not want it turned into a free-for-all. Although he was sore about being thrown out of his Slow-Down Club, Alec had given up on it in his own mind. With his interest gone, he believed that the less done about the whole affair, the better.

George Raymond, however, was enjoying his role. He had become the sole issue of contention. At the Kent Hotel, efforts were still being made to persuade Nora to stop seeing him, but all these had failed. George was certain of a conquest; he already considered himself a victor. Pfeister would get the remains of the Slow-Down Club, and he, George Raymond, would get Pfeister's girl and her virginity. And then, to add insult to injury, he was going to beat up Pfeister. He had no doubts on the outcome of the fight.

One day, Old John Mason showed up at the apartment on Drexel Boulevard with his suitcase in his hand. He had been thrown out of the little basement room in the Kent Hotel. He was broke. Old John didn't know why he'd been thrown out except he was friendly with George and Alec. And that old faker, Conrad Jackson, who claimed that he'd been an actor, didn't like him. George offered to let Old John stay at the apartment until they were evicted. They owed rent and expected to be kicked out at any moment, but Old John was welcome to stay there until that did happen.

At the Kent Hotel and at the Drexel Boulevard apartment, everyone was keyed up. Something was bound to happen at any minute. Wilbert Wilmer was afraid that George and Alec would descend on the basement with a gang and wreck his Forum. He thought of going to the police for protection. Conrad Jackson convinced him not to, claiming that the bark of young puppies was much worse than their bite. And now that they were eliminated, he believed that a real honest-to-goodness Slow-Down Club could be organized, and he had the plan for doing this. He would take charge of things himself until the young people could manage their own club. He'd allow his beautiful daughter, Lenora, to serve as an example, and he'd arrange for suitable publicity.

Wilbert Wilmer didn't know what he wanted and he was afraid of any more Slow-Down Clubs. His Forum was almost wrecked as it was; and while he was rid of George Raymond and Alec McGonigle, or at least he hoped he was, Wilbert was not fully comfortable about Bill Pfeister and his friends. He'd been glad to have Pfeister around when he had felt threatened by Raymond and Alec; but now he was afraid that Pfeister and his friends would start acting as if the Forum belonged to them. And they looked like tough customers to him. Pfeister kept talking about the beating he was going to give Raymond and of what would happen to any of his friends who butted in. There was too much talk of fighting, for Wilbert. He was afraid that it would take place in his basement. Pfeister and his friends weren't the type he wanted as the regulars who would hang around his Forum. They would keep away the kind of people he wanted to attract. Wilbert sometimes wished that he had never started the Forum. It had brought him troubles, squabbles, ill will, and fighting. Why damn it to Hell, his experiences were almost sufficient to destroy his faith in human nature. The only comfort he had was that he had learned lessons that he would be able to apply when the time came for him to found a colony in the Ozark Mountains. And when that time came, and he would actually be making plans and picking the people for the colony, he would know enough not to pick anyone like George Raymond. Yes, God Almighty, his troubles at the Forum all began on that Sunday night when that fellow had first set foot into his place. He wished he could go to the Ozark Mountains immediately and live in a colony where there wouldn't be anything going on like what had been happening in his Forum during the last couple of months.

Riggs was slithering around the basement with an air of hurt martyrdom. The unfair and vile slander had victimized him; and all because he had acted out of a kindly and poetic spirit. George's rejection of him had condemned him to a loneliness which he believed would be lifelong and eternal. Not only had Riggs been spurned and scornfully sentenced to loneliness but his pure feelings, all that he had written to George Raymond in one of his noblest moments, had been spattered with mud. His letter had been exhibited—shown to one and all, copied on a typewriter and passed about. He had only tried to do good for George Raymond and he had been repaid with harm and evil. George Raymond, who could have been so fair and noble— George Raymond had been the cause of his suffering, the ultimate disillusionment. But it was not revenge he sought. No, not revenge. In his soul he wept for the youth who could have been so god-like and was lost. The evil done to Riggs could not go unavenged. If the fair promise of George Raymond's youth were lost, then George Raymond was as nothing and could be destroyed. Poor Oscar Wilde was right:

For each man kills the thing he loves

Riggs almost enjoyed a physical sense of pain when he thought of the coming fight between George Raymond and Bill Pfeister. He would stare at Pfeister in a new way, he must be as strong as a bull, much stronger than George. George would get a merciless beating at the hands of a brute like Pfeister. It could only be madness or the machinations of McGonigle that had led George to issue such an insane challenge.

For each man kills the thing he loves

In what strange ways this was done. There was a deliciousness of irony in the fact that Pfeister would be the agent, symbolically killing the thing that he, Riggs, loved.

But it was all low and of the gutter. The two of them would punch and pound each other, claw and kick and do, he didn't know what, all because of that stupid girl who had the soul, instincts, and organs of an alley cat; and who, through some accident of circumstances, had reached the age of eighteen with her virginity undefiled.

Perhaps, though, after George Raymond was beaten up he would come to his senses, Riggs thought. Then the youth might realize how he had betrayed all that was best in himself in his betrayal of Riggs. Only then would poor Riggs take George Raymond and help him to be what he could.

Pfeister would have liked to knock Riggs over almost as much as he would Raymond. Riggs was a freak and a queer. Raymond should have been in love with the freak and kept his lousy paws off girls like Nora Lewis. If it had not been for Raymond, he and Nora would still be in love and he'd be feeling hunky-dory. He was losing Nora; maybe he had already lost her. This hurt him in a way that he couldn't admit to anyone, not even to his best

buddy. He had been humiliated in public, in front of all
his pals. But he still wanted her. He loved her. She was
the only girl he had ever loved. He didn't see how he could
ever love another girl. But how could he take her back, even
if he could win her back? How could he do it and face his
friends? No man should allow a girl to do what Nora was
doing to him; and once you did let a girl treat you like
that and get away with it, you lost the respect of the girl
herself and you didn't seem like a man to her. Even your
pals would be disappointed in you although they probably
wouldn't say so to your face. Any guy who let a woman
turn him down for another guy and then would try to get
her back, and would have her, just wasn't respected. He
knew all this, but he wanted Nora. There was something
deep inside him that cried out for her. Maybe she had already let Raymond jump 'er. If she hadn't already, he was
goddamned afraid she was going to and nobody would be
able to stop her. He shouldn't have waited so long to fight
Raymond. He should've hauled off on Raymond the first
time the heel had given Nora the eye.

What a fool he'd been! Christ, he couldn't wait to get
his hands on Raymond. He kept thinking of his snotty
puss. He'd see himself smacking it, slugging it, and bash-
ing it until not even Raymond's own mother would recognize her son's puss.

Nora had refused Bill a date for Saturday night or Sunday night. She'd told him that she was going to go out
with her girl chum, Evelyn. She didn't want to go out with
Bill, or even see him any more. He acted like he had
rights over her and she was furious about his jealousy of
George. He had no right. She didn't want Bill Pfeister
following her around, or questioning her or sticking his
nose into her business and treating her like she was a
little girl to be protected. She was a woman now, a young
woman, and it was George Raymond who had made her

that, not Bill Pfeister. Nora's thoughts all were a form
of whistling in the dark. She was afraid of what she was
going to do, and she was not at all sure but what Bill and
some of the others at the Kent Hotel were right in their
warnings. Maybe it was bad, a very foolish thing that she
was going to do. Maybe after she did it, George wouldn't
love her or respect her. But somebody like Bill couldn't
understand that she had to do it, she couldn't say "no."
She couldn't not let George do anything he wanted with
her. She couldn't do anything else but go to George Raymond and let him take her and have her, and hurt her,
too, if that was the way it was.

She was mixed up. She wanted it done and over with.
She was glad it was going to be George Raymond. Glad,
glad, because she felt she had been waiting for him all of
her life, and only him, to make her a woman. Maybe it
would be wonderful. It was wonderful when he kissed her.

She was too mixed up to think straight. She was afraid
that when George saw her without any clothes on, he'd be
disappointed and not think her body was beautiful; or that
she wouldn't know what to do and how she should do it,
and she'd do something wrong and spoil it and disappoint
him. She wished she could stop thinking about it and just
do it. Do it, and find out what it felt like and not be so
mixed up.

Chapter Nine

I

Nora worked a half day on Saturday. After she got home, she was so nervous she didn't know what to do with herself. It was such a beautiful afternoon. She wished that George had asked her to come in the afternoon instead of at night. She wished he would take her walking in the park and that he would sit on a bench with her and put his arm around her, and then take her rowing, and talk to her, and put his head in her lap while she sat on the grass and ran her fingers through his hair. Then they would go slowly to his apartment and she would feel so full of love for him that it would be poetic and beautiful, like a story or a moving picture. She wished it would happen that way.

"Nora, have you something on your mind?" her mother asked her.

Mrs. Lewis was a big stout woman with a ruddy complexion, and her kindliness of heart showed in her face.

"Oh, no, Mother, I was just thinking."

"Tell me, Nora, I'm your mother. Is there something on your mind?"

Nora wanted to rush over to her mother, put her head

in her lap, and tell her and ask her if it was bad. Nora was afraid.

"I was just thinking, Mom, you know, sort of dreaming."

Mrs. Lewis looked understandingly at her daughter. Nora was afraid that she had given herself away and that her mother would guess that something was wrong.

"It's a fellow, isn't it, Nora?" Mrs. Lewis asked, her voice full of sympathy.

"Well, Mom, I sort of, I don't know. Maybe I'm falling in love," Nora said shyly, with an apologetic smile on her face.

"It's the new fellow you met, isn't it? What's his name?"

"George Raymond," Nora said quickly, glad that she had a chance to say his name.

"Is he decent and does he work like the other fellow you went out with, Bill Pfeister?"

"Oh yes, Mom. He's so good looking, he's dark and has curly hair, naturally curly hair, and he's handsome, Mom, he's awful nice."

"Why don't you bring him home and let your father and I meet him?"

"That's what I'm going to do, ask him to come to supper, maybe some night next week."

"You know any young man you're interested in is always welcome here."

"Yes, I was going to tell you I was planning to ask him to come to supper."

"And you think you're in love, Nora, dear?"

Nora dropped her eyes. She was ashamed. What would her mother say if she found out? And her father? Her brother, Joey?

"Well, Mom, he's different. I feel, you know, Mom, I'm a young woman now. You were young, Mom, you know how a girl can feel."

Mrs. Lewis shook her head slowly. A light of memory and nostalgia seemed to shine in her gray eyes.

"Nora, you're still a girl," Mrs. Lewis said, her voice firm, but kind. "What kind of work does this young man do? Raymond, you say his name is?"

"Oh, he's a salesman," Nora said quickly, remembering that George had told her of good selling jobs he had held.

"What does he sell?"

"Advertising, direct-by-mail advertising, I think."

"Is he talking to you about marriage, or engagement?"

"Oh, Mom, I hadn't thought of that, and, well, no—he treats me nice, like a gentleman, and, oh you know, I'm dreaming."

"Does he get fresh with you?"

Nora looked away. Her heart was beating fast. She was afraid she was giving herself away. She didn't want to lie to her mother.

"I let him kiss me, Mom. I like him. I think maybe I love him, Mom."

"Nora, child, is he trying to take liberties with you?"

"Mom, I'm growing up. I'm working and helping support myself. I let him kiss me. I can't talk about things that are private."

"You well can and you well should with me. Who else can a girl talk to but her mother?"

"Yes, Mom, I know. I know I can and should."

"Well, Nora, what is it? What's on your mind?"

Nora couldn't answer immediately. She wanted to tell her mother everything, how she felt she had to go to George tonight, and let him, and how she was all mixed up. She wanted her mother to know, maybe save her.

"It's nothing like that—it's romantic, Mom. He makes me feel romantic."

"Nora, every girl comes to the time that she feels like you do. I did."

"You did, Mom? About Pa?"

"About a lot more fellows than your father. He didn't just come along and sweep me off my feet. He had to win me. A girl can be swept off her feet by the first fellow who comes down the pike. She can think he's the only fellow but no fellow is the only pebble on the beach. Tell me, Nora, does this young man try to take liberties with you?"

"I'm kind of ashamed to talk about something like that, Mom," Nora said, with strain in her voice.

"You can't be ashamed to talk to me. There are certain things in nature. You know what a woman is, I've told you. I've told you what men want of a woman. You know it. Some fellows have to try to get fresh and take liberties. They can't be any different nowadays from what they've always been."

"But if I love him, Mom?"

"If you love him, and allow yourself to be cheapened, will he love you? Will any fellow love a girl who lets herself be cheapened? You can't let a fellow go too far, not for your own good."

"Mom, I couldn't do that, I couldn't. I don't know what it's like. I'd be afraid. I don't know what that's like, and what it feels like—Mom, I never . . ."

Nora was full of shame. She felt that it must be a dirty thing. She was ashamed of her mother, and her father. They had done it. If they hadn't she wouldn't be here. But she wanted her mother to tell her about it, what it was like, how it felt the first time.

"A girl must protect herself. You have to know when to stop."

"But I do."

"A man won't respect a woman who's damaged goods. It's what a man's after, and it's the most precious thing you have."

Nora wanted to run up to her room, close the door and hide her face in the pillows on her bed.

"There's nothing wrong in a girl being kissed and petted if you really like and think you love a young man, and you want to. It's in you. Love is a woman's life. But if you don't know when to stop a young fellow, then Nora, you can ruin your life."

"Yes, Mom."

"The first time, Nora, hurts a woman. It's no joy. The first time has to be love, and it has to be on your marriage bed."

"Yes, Mom."

"You're a good girl. Don't let any young man think you're the kind of girl who gives herself away or makes a fool of herself over a fellow. Every girl, every woman has to protect herself."

"Yes, Mom."

"Nora, tell me the truth," her mother said, looking straight at her daughter and speaking with the firmness and authority with which she dominated the Lewis home.

"I haven't, Mom—never."

"This young fellow, this young man isn't asking you— is that what he's trying to do?"

"No, it's me. I'm afraid I might be in love with him more than maybe he loves me."

Nora was tormented because she was lying to her mother. But she could do it. She could lie. She had to because she had to go to George tonight. She had no power over herself.

"Don't let him know it, Nora. If he's the young man who will turn out to be the one you love, he'll let you know. He'll try to win your heart. That's something every girl should know without even being told."

"That's what's worrying me, Mom. I do know. But he's different. I feel—well, I feel he wouldn't love me."

"Why? What's wrong with you that a fellow wouldn't want to love you?"

"Oh, nothing—nothing like that—I'm not damaged goods—but I'm not too well educated, or beautiful; and I feel so dumb sometimes when he talks, and I'm afraid I'm not romantic enough."

"Stop talking such nonsense. You're a good decent girl and you've been brought up decent. You'll find a nice young man some day who'll appreciate you. If you don't value yourself, Nora, no one else will. Remember that."

"Yes, that's right, I guess. It's just that he's so different, Mom."

"I want to meet him and I want your father to meet him. How come he's never called for you?"

"He's brought me home, to the door here."

"But he doesn't call for you?"

"He wants to, but you see, I go to the club and he lives near there. I just didn't want him to come all of the way over here on two streetcars, and go all of the way back."

"If he wants you, he'll come. You're making a mistake right there. You should make him call for you, Nora, it's wrong not to."

"You think I should?"

"I never went out to meet your father. He came and got me. He knew that if he didn't, there were others that would."

"Yes, maybe I should have him call. He must like me, because he and Bill Pfeister, I was afraid they were going to fight over me."

"If a man will fight for a woman, he'll want her."

"He would, Mom?"

"You invite him here."

"I will."

"Now you stop worrying and dreaming. I've tried to

bring you up a sensible girl, use your sense. Take a nap so you'll look fresh and at your best tonight."

Nora rushed to her mother, sank her head in her mother's lap, and sobbed.

Mrs. Lewis stroked her daughter's head, and gently told her not to cry. Nora felt secure and protected with her head in her mother's lap. Her mother was stroking her hair and talking so soft to her, like she was still little, almost a baby.

She knew she was going to do wrong. She wanted her mother to understand. She couldn't tell her mother. She couldn't help herself. She wished she was still a little girl.

Gradually, Nora stopped sobbing.

"Nora, look me in the eye," Mrs. Lewis said, holding her daughter's cheeks between her big, roughened hands, and looking down at her sad, tear-stained face. "Tell me, are you in trouble?"

"No, Mom. No. It's just that—nothing like this ever happened to me. It's . . . I'm afraid. Maybe I'm in love. I don't know."

"You remember what I've told you. Don't show your feelings. Don't wear your heart on your sleeve. You're too young to know your heart. You come to me. You can always come to me."

"I will. I feel better now. I just had to cry, that's all."

"You go up and take a nap, Nora. And bring that young man here—invite him tomorrow evening."

"I'll try."

"You invite him. If he won't come, he's not worth your wasting tears on him. You be careful. Tonight, don't let him kiss you. Make him come after you and then you'll know how he feels about you. Understand?"

"Yes, Mom."

She had lied again.

"I just had to have a cry, Mom."

"If you have to cry, you come to me. Now take a nap and follow my advice. You'll do well by yourself."

"Yes, Mom, I guess I had to get the silliness out of my head."

Nora went to her room, undressed, and looked at herself naked in the dresser mirror. She didn't think her body was so much. Her hips were a little wide, and her breasts kind of small, and she didn't like the dark hair down there. It looked, well, not pretty at all. And it caused her all of this trouble and made her lie to her mother.

She felt ashamed.

It would hurt, the first time, her mother had said. She should be hurt, she deserved to be hurt.

Nora got under the covers and felt the clean white sheets against her skin. She liked that.

It was too late now. She had to do it. She closed her eyes and thought about George. She saw his face, his lips, in her mind. She remembered how he had kissed her. She began to feel hot and she wanted to, she wanted him to hurt her and do anything he wanted to with her. She couldn't stand it if she didn't let him.

Nora felt almost sick with desire. She told herself that she was George's, and her resignation and surrender calmed her down. She fell asleep.

II

She woke up feeling that she had done something terrible. She got out of bed, feeling sluggish and dull. The sun was still shining. She must still have a lot of time before she was due at George's.

She shouldn't go. She could go downstairs and confess to her mother. But she was going. And she had to be clean and look her best.

Nora spent about a half hour in the bathtub. The warm water soothed her and made her sensuous. Her body felt good. She felt her breasts; they were soft. She wanted George to kiss them. She was making herself clean for him. She wanted him to think she was beautiful. If she could make him feel happy, no matter how much he hurt her, he would love her. And maybe then, he wouldn't go to New York. She didn't want him to go. She wanted him for herself. She was in love with him; and she was in love like a woman, not like a silly girl.

Nora had bought new stockings and underthings. She felt the silk next to her skin and thought that he would find her underclothes clean and new, when he took her clothes off. She brushed her hair, polished her nails, and perfumed herself. She wore her red silk dress because it made her look older and sexier.

When Nora was ready to go, she tried to get out quickly because she didn't want her family, especially her mother, to notice how dressed up she was.

"Hey, Sis, you look like a vamp," Joey said as she came down the stairs. He gaped at her with admiration and surprise.

"Do I look pretty?"

"Pretty? You look like you'll set the joint on fire. Where you going?"

"You're teasing me."

"I mean it this time, Sis. I'd go for you myself if you wasn't my sister."

Her father, a big, fat bald-headed man, frowned.

"Holy Cow!"

"I just felt like dressing up, Pop," she said.

"Where did you buy that dress?"

"At the Fair."

"Are you going to a dance?"

"I'm going to the Slow-Down Club. I've told you about it, Pop."

"Slow-Down Club? In that dress?"

"Don't you like it, Pop?"

"It's too loud, it's cheap. You ought to go upstairs and take it off."

Nora was frightened. Suppose they didn't let her wear this dress? Suppose they wouldn't let her go?

"Pop, styles are different."

"Listen, you be home early tonight. Be home by midnight."

"It's Saturday night. I'll be escorted home."

"By the Fire Department, Sis," her brother laughed.

"Look at that getup, Sally," her father said to Mrs. Lewis as his wife joined them near the front door.

"Let me have a look at you, Nora," Mrs. Lewis said.

Nora was shaky.

"You look mighty pretty, Nora; but you don't look like yourself in that dress. If I were a young man, I'd like you better in a dress that wasn't so bold."

"Oh, Mom, I wanted to dress up, my real best."

"You mind what I told you this afternoon, young lady," Mrs. Lewis said.

"I will, Mom."

She wanted to get out, she had to.

"Don't be out too late," her father said.

"Don't break too many hearts, Sis."

"Mind your P's and Q's tonight," her mother said.

III

Nora walked rapidly to 35th Street. She hurried, she was afraid that they'd call her back. They didn't. When she neared the corner, she slowed down. A couple of neighbors

stared at her with startled curious eyes. Tim Clark, a friend
of Joey's, gave her a pop-eyed stare.

Waiting for the streetcar, Nora felt bold in her red
dress. She was full of excitement. She felt like a character
in a book. She was a woman now, going to her lover. She
was a new Nora Lewis.

She trembled when she rang the bell of the Drexel
Boulevard apartment. She couldn't hear a sound inside.
She waited for several long seconds. Then she heard someone. The door opened and George stood in front of her
with his hair mussed, his white shirt opened, exposing his
chest.

"Come, my sweet. I've been waiting for you," he said
in that voice of his which she knew she couldn't resist.

He led her in by the hand and closed the door.

The apartment was straightened up and cleaned a bit.
The In-A-Door bed was down in the center of the room.
The sight of it frightened her. She tightened up inside.
Suddenly, George seemed like a stranger. She couldn't
speak.

He embraced her. She closed her eyes. She couldn't
respond to his kisses. She was helpless, without will, and
waiting for a stroke of pain to pierce her.

She started to cry.

"Take me fast or I'll die," she said as she sobbed.

"No, my sweet, don't be frightened. Nora, Nora, prepare
for the most beautiful moment of your life," he whispered
into her ear.

The sound of his voice soothed her. He talked to her
and recited snatches of poetry for about twenty minutes.
Then, while holding her in his arms and kissing her, he
said:

"Now, Nora, I want you to know fulfillment. I'm ready
to offer myself for your fulfillment."

"Fulfill me," she said, not knowing what she was saying.

Nothing in the world existed for her but her own self, tormented with desires. And only George who held her could end her torment. There was neither past nor future. They would be close together forever in the darkened room and the desperate wildness in her would last forever.

Chapter Ten

I

The next day, Eddie Ryan dropped by the apartment. George was grinning when Eddie arrived.

"Raymond's technique was never better. Last night was my real *chef-d'oeuvre*," he boasted, mispronouncing the French phrase.

His brother, Charles, Ken Gilmore, and Phil Dumont were listening to him.

"Cut it out, George," Charles barked. "I can't stand so much crap, even from my brother. A screw is a screw."

"That is true but not profound. Everything is equal to itself, even a lay. Any man can lay; but some do it better than others."

"I wouldn't want a virgin," Charles said. "She'd be too hard to get rid of. And the mess."

"I'll take on anything, virgins, jail bait. I'll take my chances about getting rid of them," Ken said.

"You guys bullshit about pussy as if you were surprised to get any of it," Phil said. "What the hell do you think pussy is for?"

"That's a profound question," Ken said. "I'm going to

refer it to the Department of Profundity and when I get the answer, I'll tell you. What is pussy for?"

"Bill Pfeister and the hypocrites of the Slow-Down Club failed to protect the virtue of Nora Lewis and save her from ruin," George said. "And tomorrow night, I'll settle my last score with that thick-headed moron."

"Hell, you've laid the guy's girl," Phil Dumont said. "Ain't that enough? What do you want to beat him up for?"

"He's got it coming to him," George said. "I know how I'll fight him. I'll dance around him and keep my left in his face. I'll cut him up until he's open and I can lay a right on him. He's one sonofabitch I want to lay out cold. This fight is a grudge. That moron has blown his horn once too often about me. Tomorrow night, one of us is going to be stretched out cold."

"If that's your pleasure, George," Ken Gilmore said. "As for me, I can think of easier and safer ways of having a jolly evening."

"It will be a pleasure to beat what little brains that sonofabitch has out of his thick skull."

"He looks tough, George. We might have to chip in to help," Charles said.

"I don't want anybody getting into this—unless Pfeister's friends pile in. Otherwise, it's him and me. Pfeister and Raymond, to a finish."

George meant what he was saying. He liked to fight, but usually his fights were not premeditated. He'd lose his temper and in a split second, challenge anyone who had angered him. If the challenge were not accepted, he might calm down and shake hands with the fellow he'd been raving to punch a few minutes earlier. He might even become buddies with the fellow.

It was different with Pfeister. George seemed to have a genuine hatred of him.

"Some day, George, you're going to get into a scrap with a guy that's better than you," Charles said.

"Let that guy come along," George said. "It won't be Pfeister. Hell, it took practically an army of Irish punks to throw me off the freight car that time, remember?"

II

They had really been a tough gang, George thought. Some had come from around Garfield Boulevard and Wentworth Avenue, and a couple of them were from Halsted Street. They had trapped him alone on top of a freight car across from White City at 63rd and South Park. They had overpowered him and thrown him off the car. He had landed on his head, and had gone out like a light. It had been a mean, brutal fight and he had had to be carried to a hospital. He had suffered a concussion and had had to stay in the hospital for several days. For weeks afterward, he had had headaches and dizzy spells.

George Raymond often spoke of this experience. For years he would say how, when he had hit the ground head-first, it had been as bad as being struck on the base of his skull with a billy that had a lead filling. The moment his head smashed onto the ground, he didn't see stars but a quick flash of light. The pain was blinding and shattering —he felt like his brain was being crushed by a steam roller.

This had happened the instant he had hit the hardened dirt. At most, it was a matter of two or three seconds. Then Mrs. Raymond's son, George, had gone out like the proverbial light of all proverbial lights. He remembered pitching over the side of the freight car, a regular freight car painted a dull red and marked *Rock Island Railroad*. He hurtled through the air, and it had seemed that he was a long time falling. It wasn't unpleasant, falling through the air. He remembered thinking that he could break his fall, and then jump up, grab rocks or anything in sight that would be useful for his defense for a dirty attack. Then he had hit, head first. He couldn't turn himself or twist his body in midair and fall forward. He had been thrown off too suddenly, and the distance of his fall had been too short. He had experienced the most sickening and nauseating pain of his short, sweet, and happy life. He was all head, a stunned and aching head. And then, the lights had gone out.

Once released from the hospital, George Raymond had wanted nothing more than to organize a party and go over around 63rd Street and Halsted, and Garfield and Wentworth too, but he had been in no condition to play fi-fee-fo-fum with those Irish who could not fight him fair, not even at six-to-one odds. By the time he had fully recovered, his desire for revenge had been dulled by time.

But he remembered a couple of the faces of that gang of bastards and he kept an eye peeled for them. When and if he saw any of those faces, he knew he would attend to them so that their mothers wouldn't know them until some plastic surgeons and beauticians had performed miracles.

George Raymond had been about eighteen when he had been thrown off the freight car.

III

Alec and Myrtle walked in. "They didn't have thirty people last night for the dance at the Forum," Alec said.

"That's good news," George said.

"Of all the screwy things you ever got into, George," Charles said, "this was the screwiest."

"It served its purpose."

"The Slow-Down Club," Eddie said. "Virgins deflowered, every guy in the place trying to make a girl, you selling your washtub gin, and Riggs."

"We haven't sounded off on Riggs in three or four days. That's not being fair to him; we should give him some attention," George said.

"All I have to say about him is that he's slimy," Alec said.

"Riggs, the eagle, who would fly with me to a mountain," George laughed.

"You got to admit, George, you conquer them all. Your sex appeal has no limits," Charles said.

"Riggs is such a worm that no one would ever take the trouble to step on him," George said.

"You're unusually quiet today, Ryan," Ken Gilmore said.

"I was thinking about New York," said Eddie.

"It's going to be lonesome when you two guys go away," Alec said. "And quiet. There won't be any excitement."

Eddie looked at George Raymond—he must have talked to Alec and taken him "off the hook" as he had planned to.

"I feel sorry for little Old New York. You two supermen going there," Charles said.

"Write me a post card from there. Let me know if the waitresses there are any better than the hash slingers of Chicago," Ken said.

"When Eddie and I get out of here and settled in New York, I'll be happy. I'll read and write. We can take long walks and chew the fat, discuss profound philosophical questions, and argue about who the best writer is, Dreiser or James Branch Cabell," George said.

"What, and no wenches?" joked Ken Gilmore.

"I'm beginning to feel *ennui* about women," George said.

This produced hooting laughter.

"I mean some of the things I say," George said. "I'm

ready for a quiet and uncomplicated life, studying, reading, thinking, making some notes, maybe writing a little. That'll satisfy me."

"How about you, Eddie?" asked Charles.

"That's all Eddie wants, that and once in a while to go on a bender and blow off steam," George said.

Eddie grinned. He did want a quiet life, but he also felt the need for experience and for adventure. He thought of how much more experience George had had than he; and how he was often the witness, the main audience, for George in many of his experiences. It would be different in New York, he would have experiences and his personality would change.

"Before you come back, Eddie, maybe you'll write the great American novel," Ken Gilmore said.

"There's a better chance of Eddie doing it than me," George said.

"If you do, put us all in it."

"Don't put me in it," Charles said.

"I don't know whether or not I'd want to be put in a book by Eddie," George said. "He knows me too well."

Eddie knew that he might put some of them, or all of them, in a book. He wanted to put everything in books. It seemed strange to be sitting and talking with them and to think about putting them in stories or novels. How might he do this? When?

"I know this guy, Ryan," Charles said, "and I don't put it past him to put us all in a book."

"I have to learn how to write better, first," Eddie said.

"Well, I'll be just fine right here in Chicago," Ken Gilmore said. "There are always broads to pick up, and I've got my old jalopy. That's excitement enough for a night unless something more exciting happens."

"I might go back to law school nights and get my degree," Alec said.

"That's not a bad idea. Sooner or later I'll need you to keep me out of the hoosegow," George said.

"Clarence Darrow might not succeed in that," Ken said.

"I see that I have an excellent reputation," George laughed.

"If you two guys get thrown into jail in New York," said Charles, "I'll write you a post card."

As Eddie listened, he found himself sad about leaving. They had had more fun than he had realized and suddenly he felt close to everyone present. Eddie wondered if some day they'd all look back on these past few months as a remembrance of fun. These months were part of their youth and their rebellion.

Soon everybody left the apartment but George, Alec and Eddie. They sat, talking idly, and mostly about the planned departure for New York. George and Eddie intended to leave within the next week or two.

"You guys don't know when you'll come back to Chicago?" Alec asked.

"No," George answered.

"It could be a long time," Eddie said.

"Or even never," George added.

"I'll miss you bastards. You'll have to write," Alec said.

"Eddie's the letter writer. He's the most faithful letter writer I know," George said.

"I'm not too good at it myself, but I'll write," Alec said.

"You'll have to keep us informed of what happens to everybody and what sequels we leave behind," George said.

"Listen, I'm not going to keep in touch with every goddamn person we've collided with in the last few months, and most certainly, I'm not going to follow up the wails and heartbreaks of all the girls you've left behind."

"There aren't many, Alec. Nora might take a little time. She wishes I weren't going."

"Last night was the night, wasn't it?"

"Yes it was."

"Well, I suppose I should ask—did you succeed?"

"Of course I did."

"I suppose that calls for congratulations. When you seduce a virgin, that's a special accomplishment."

"It's more of a favor to them. Somebody has to start them down the primrose path to Hell," George said.

"And so you did Nora that favor."

"Yes I did. She might have been a virgin for a long time to come but for me."

"I suppose I should ask—how was she?"

"She could be a nice morsel if I were going to be around long enough to enjoy the nibbling. When she came in here, she was like ice—she was afraid. I had to work on her until I got her aroused. I delayed the fatal entry until I had her so aroused that she didn't know she was hurt."

"I don't want any virgins," Alec said.

"Nora was rather touching. She's winsome and there's a pathos about her. She's hungry for romance. She's had an ordinary life, and her mind is commonplace. She became a heroine in a farce and Pfeister and I are going to have a fist fight because of her—partly because of her. She's a sweet kid."

"She impresses me as being pleasant. We all have to outgrow our notions about romance. I had romantic feelings, I think I told you about the girl who lived near here, Teresa Donlan."

"Yes, you told me, Alec."

"Girls like sex as much as we do. Puritanism and Victorianism are, I guess, responsible for notions that they don't like it and are always the victims," Alec said.

"It's a game, love and romance are lies," George said.

"What do you say, Eddie?" Alec asked.

"Hormones," Eddie answered.

They all laughed.

"Do you mean to go through with this fight with Pfeister, George?" Alec asked.

"I challenged him. I want to fight the smug moron."

"Well, there's nothing I can say then. I was hoping I could talk you out of it."

"You aren't afraid he's going to take me, Alec, I hope?"

"Hell, no. I imagine you can beat him if you don't break your hands on his head. It's as hard as wood. But I don't see the sense of it. It's not going to prove anything. You know you're smart and he's dumb."

"It'll prove that he has to eat all of the goddamned things he said about me—calling me yellow and a four-flusher."

"Since you feel that way, I can't argue you out of it."

"Not even God and the two of you could," George said.

IV

Nora was coming to see George that afternoon, so Alec and Eddie went out to eat and take a walk.

"What do you think about this fight, Eddie?" Alec asked.

"I wish that George hadn't challenged Pfeister. I agree with you—it is a senseless fight but George is dead set on it and Pfeister seems to feel the same way. I'm sure that George will clean up the guy."

"Do you think that Pfeister's friends will pitch in?"

"I don't know," Eddie said.

This worried both of them. There was nothing they could do but wait and see what happened. Neither of them wanted to get in a gang fight but if Pfeister's friends jumped in, they'd have to do the same for their friend George.

"You know, Eddie, I'm sorry everything is ending and you two are clearing out," Alec said.

Eddie felt sad at that moment.

"I don't mean the Forum and the Slow-Down Club. Hell if we'd gone on getting worked up about that, we would have proven that we had holes in our heads. But I've enjoyed knowing you and George, our walks and talks, and, yes, the times we got drunk together. I'll miss you guys."

"I'll miss you, too, Alec."

"I discussed my going along with the two of you with George. He sees my point. You're dead set and determined to be a writer. And George, he might want to write but he has no fixed purpose. It would be fun, going with you both; but it makes more sense for me to go back to law school and complete my course. I'll have to make a living all my life and I don't want to end up like Old John Mason or Wilbert."

"I agree with you, Alec."

"I'm glad you do, Eddie."

But Eddie still thought that Alec was afraid. He wouldn't take his chances. Eddie was taking his.

"I hope you both have a hell of a swell time, and I'll be eager to get news of your adventures."

"I'll write, Alec."

"You'll both be resourceful enough to take care of your-selves. And you ought to get the material you need for writing."

"I hope so."

"It's interesting how much my life has changed, and how other people have, since you and George busted into the Forum that Sunday night, looking for trouble."

"We weren't looking for trouble."

"The hell you weren't."

"At least we weren't in search of contentment."

"That's certain. I, of course, have gained a lot from

knowing you both. It's helped me to grow up more. That's why I decided to go back to school."

Eddie wondered what would happen to the three of them. Which of them would die first? What if he were to die? Young and Unfulfilled? How would George and Alec talk about him?

"I feel sorry for that kid, Nora Lewis," Alec said.

"She's in love with George."

"He's an attractive guy with girls. She's probably never met anyone like him. She goes to bed with him, loses her virginity, and off he goes. She might take it hard, and I do feel sorry for her even though virginity is strictly overrated."

"I wonder how she felt today?"

"What do you mean, Eddie?"

"I wonder how she felt after last night."

"Now, the writer in you is at work. I'll bet that some day I'll read a story about somebody like Nora Lewis."

Eddie was thinking about writing a story based on George and Nora. There was something wistful about her. After George left, she'd be sad. Could he write a story about a girl like Nora? He knew so little about girls.

"Oh, hell, I'm not going to get sentimental about her. She'll get over it. And everybody has to learn how to protect themselves in this damned world," Alec said.

"Men have died from time to time, and worms have eaten them, but not for love," Eddie quoted.

"What's that?" Alec asked.

"It's from one of Shakespeare's plays," Eddie said.

"It's true. When you're a kid—God, you can tear your heart out because you think that some girl named Teresa Donlan or a rose by another name doesn't love you. And in a couple of years, you're laughing about it. Lots of girls have lost their virginity and survived."

"I don't know that I'm capable of falling in love," Eddie said, and at the moment, he believed himself.

"You're not above human nature. Who are you kidding, Eddie?"

"I'm not talking about sex. What I mean is that I don't have illusions."

"That's one of the things that the three of us have in common. We don't have illusions. Other than the illusion that we're Nietzschean supermen."

"I don't agree with George on Nietzsche's idea of the superman," Eddie said.

"You two are the ones who read Nietzsche. I'll have to."

"You ought to, Alec. He helps clear your head."

"I think my head's pretty clear," Alec said.

"You can stiffen your mind on Nietzsche."

They sat on a bench on Drexel Boulevard. Automobiles swished by. Eddie watched people passing. Some sat on benches. They seemed relaxed and at ease, the way so many people are on Sunday. A married couple sat across from them. He was fat, gray with a big, stupid face and heavy jowls. She was turning gray but looked younger than her husband. They both looked sad. She talked to him but he stared straight ahead with dull eyes, paying little attention to her. It seemed to Eddie that feeling had died in both of them. This struck him as both sad and horrible.

This, he thought, was the way most people ended.

The sun went down. The air was gray. They sat for some time. Alec talked about his boyhood. Eddie thought that Alec's had been worse than his own. Both Alec and he had carried inferiority complexes out of their boyhood. This is how they differed from George. Eddie saw his life as a struggle to get over his inferiority complex. This is why George had drawn him. This was also why Alec was attracted to George.

"He's had all of the time he needs with Nora. I guess we can go back now," Alec said.

They rose and went back to the apartment.

V

Nora was still at the apartment when Eddie and Alec
returned. She was wearing a print dress that had been
washed many times. She smiled sadly. George was smoking
a cigarette. He was poised and quite at ease.

Nora made some coffee and they all sat around the
table. It was raining. They listened to the rain. Nora did
not have much to say and her presence put a strain on
Alec and Eddie. George didn't want her to think that he
had told them.

Eddie Ryan left the apartment at the same time that
Nora did. It was a few minutes after nine. The rain had
stopped but the sidewalks were still wet. The air was fresh
with a damp smell in it.

"I like the rain," Nora said.

"Yes, it's nice after a summer rain like this," Eddie said.

"It washes everything clean," she said. "It kind of washes
the world clean."

After a lapse she went on:

"It makes me feel like I'm a little new, like things that
happened, didn't happen. But that doesn't mean much,
does it? It sounds a little silly, doesn't it?"

"No."

"It was sort of a feeling I have about the rain, that's all."

She got a Cottage Grove Avenue streetcar. Just before
Eddie helped her get on, she asked him, appealingly:

"Eddie, please take care of George in New York."

There were tears in her eyes as she turned away from
him and stepped onto the platform of the streetcar.

Chapter Eleven

I

George Raymond was supremely confident about his fight with Bill Pfeister; but both Alec and Eddie were nervous. So was Charles Raymond. They left the Drexel Boulevard apartment with him. George and Pfeister had agreed to meet in the southeast corner of the Washington Park ball field at nine-fifteen on a Monday night. By that time it would be dark and all those who were playing ball after supper would have gone home.

George didn't talk about the fight. He spoke of Nora.

"She touches me," he said. "It's too bad, but she'll get over it. I explained to her that I've got to follow my destiny and I can't be tied down in one place."

"What is your destiny?" asked Charles.

"I don't know. Yes, I do. My destiny is my whim. In a world that is full of hypocrisy, why shouldn't I make my whim the law of my life?"

Nobody answered him. They were thinking of the fight.

"Going to New York is not a mere act of whim. I can be more quiet there. I can think more. I explained all this to Nora. She took it bravely and didn't cry when I explained that we had but only met, when we must part.

But it is better to leave something beautiful in memory than to destroy it by falsehoods. I explained to her that everything ends, all love dies and all lovers die. All that life would allow us, I explained, was a flaming moment of beauty. That was a treasure that we both could preserve in our memories. She's a brave kid, I was really touched. I did do one thing for her; I saved her from Pfeister. Oh, yes, I'm on my way to fight with him now. Here's our streetcar."

They boarded a southbound Cottage Grove Avenue car and took a short ride from 47th Street to 55th Street.

"If any other sonofabitch butts in, Eddie, you and Charles and whatever friends I've got will have to come in swinging. But you watch and give a signal. Don't unless they try to gang up on me," George said on the sidewalk by the park entrance.

"Yes," Eddie said, but he was nervous as hell and hoped for the best.

George walked ahead of them, alone, whistling jauntily. They followed a few feet behind him. There was a crowd of about thirty-five or forty fellows in the park. Pfeister was already on hand and waiting. Ken Gilmore and Philly Benton and a couple of other friends of George and Eddie were standing on the edge of the crowd. Most of those present were friends of Pfeister's.

George's group was on the verge of getting jittery, except for George himself.

"I'm sorry if I'm late. I was unavoidably . . ."

"Never mind the bullshit. I'm here to fight you, Raymond," Bill Pfeister said.

". . . detained," George finished his sentence in his most arrogant manner.

It was a clear night. The moonlight was bright, the park was light enough to make the fighting easier for George and Pfeister. Eddie looked around. Many of those present were strangers to him. They seemed like shadows, that had suddenly become real people. Some of them were husky.

"Frisk him, see if he's got anything on him," one fellow said in a surly voice.

George stepped back as the fellow moved toward him.

"I came here to fight him, clean and fair to a finish. After I finish with him, I'll accommodate anybody else who wants to fight."

"Quit talkin'. I been waitin' for you. I didn't think you'd have the guts to come," Bill Pfeister said.

"We'll strip to the waist," George said coolly.

He took his coat off and held it out. Charles took it. Then he removed his tie and white shirt. Eddie Ryan took them.

Bill Pfeister pulled off his shirt and flung it on the ground.

"No dirty work," a big fellow shouted at Eddie Ryan.

Eddie was convinced that they'd be ganged up on. He looked around to see how many of their friends were there, and where.

The crowd widened out and formed a half circle.

George Raymond stood alone, stripped to the waist, with the moonlight on his back. He was well built, with big shoulders. Bill Pfeister was a few inches shorter but he was solidly built and heavier. He looked at George who stood waiting with his arms at his sides.

"Hey, you, get the hell back," a friend of Pfeister's shouted at Eddie.

Eddie was standing near George. The big fellow that had yelled started toward him and Eddie thought he was going to start a fight. But he didn't, he merely called out for everyone to give the two fighters room.

Bill Pfeister hunched up and moved slowly toward George. George watched him and when Pfeister was about three feet away from him, George went quickly into a de-

fensive posture with his left fist cocked and his right held
in close to his chest. He balanced himself on his toes.
Bill Pfeister lunged. George's left snapped out, traveled
only a short distance, and the thud of his fist against
Pfeister's face was heard.

"Get in close, Bill," someone yelled.

"The left, the left, George," Charles Raymond called.

George was shifting and swaying in front of Bill Pfeister,
who had been surprised by George's short left jab and the
power it packed.

Shifting, dancing to his left, George again caught
Pfeister with a hard jab.

"Cut him up, George," Eddie yelled.

"Never mind your lip. Keep back and give 'em room,"
a friend of Pfeister's shouted at him.

Pfeister moved in. George caught him again with a left
and backed away.

"Hit him once, Bill, and he'll stop that fancy dancing,"
someone called.

George kept moving in front of Bill Pfeister, shifting to
the right, to the left, circling and throwing in jab after jab.
They could hear the smack of his left fist against Pfeister's
face again and again. Pfeister was slow and fought flat-
footed, coming in with his head low and his face unpro-
tected, as he lunged with lefts and rights. For about the
first five minutes of the fight, Bill Pfeister did not hit
George Raymond, and he took jab after jab in the face.
Some of George's left jabs only traveled a couple of feet
but they were hard punches. Pfeister's nose was bleeding
and someone yelled that he had a broken nose. There was
a swelling over one eye. Blood dripped down his chin and
his bare, hairy chest. George's fists were smeared with
Pfeister's blood. Pfeister looked beaten already.

"You got him licked, George," Charles yelled.

"Who's the prognosticator?" one of Pfeister's friends yelled.

Pfeister looked inhuman in the moonlight. His face and chest were smeared with blood and the blood was still flowing from his nose. Some of it had splattered on George's chest.

George was still fresh and fast, fighting on his toes, dancing, shifting, moving in to hit; backing away, while Bill Pfeister helplessly kept lunging forward. The sound of George's fist smashing into Pfeister's face was almost sickening.

Pfeister finally caught George with a powerful lunging right above the eyes. George reeled backward, knocked off balance for a second. Pfeister's friends roared. But George regained his balance and stopped Pfeister with a left and a hard right. When George's right landed on Pfeister's bloody and battered face, Eddie Ryan winced.

The fight went on.

George's fist slid when it collided with Pfeister's blood-soaked face. Ten minutes passed, fifteen. Pfeister kept coming in, lurching, and George jabbed and pounded him. They were both splattered with blood. The pace of the fight slowed. Bill Pfeister moved wearily but still threw powerful punches, sometimes getting George on the arms or chest and occasionally on the face. George was getting tired from hitting Pfeister. He was no longer fighting on his toes and was fighting to save his strength.

They looked weird in the moonlight. The spectacle became gruesome. Bill Pfeister wouldn't quit. He could scarcely see. His face was battered into pulp. He was coated with his own blood and more kept flowing from his nose, his lips, and a cut over his right eye. George met him with arm-weary punches. He was covered with Pfeister's blood. He was now fighting flat-footed and sev-

eral times he did not follow up with punches when he had
openings.

They fought on. Their long black shadows moved over
the dark grass, an elongated shifting shadow picture of the
fight. The crowd was no longer noisy. For moments at a
time, everyone watched in silence. Now and then, someone would sigh at the thud of George's fists hitting
Pfeister's swollen, bloody, and pulpy caricature of a face.
Pfeister caught George with a few more blows, and they
hurt. Once, George kept backing away for about a minute until he recovered from the shock of a wild, hooking
right which had caught him on the jaw.

Suddenly, George stopped punching with his left hand,
changed his position, and fought with his right fist forward. He jabbed with his right, and used his left only to
block punches. His left hand was hurt and he could not
punch with it. When he punched, he would try to put
every bit of his extra force into the blows. He was hurt
and tired, and he wanted to make Pfeister quit.

Fellows in the crowd started yelling to stop it. Pfeister
was almost blinded with his own blood. He was gasping
and wheezing. He lunged at George more and more wearily.
George was breathing heavily and forced himself to keep
smashing at Pfeister's unrecognizable face with his tired
right arm.

They had been fighting for about thirty minutes.
Pfeister stood, almost blinded, punching empty air while
George stepped back. George then moved forward and
threw another right into Pfeister's raw face.

Ten or fifteen fellows grunted at the sound of the blow.
Almost everyone yelled at once.

"Enough!"

"Stop it!"

Several of Pfeister's friends stepped up to Pfeister, turned
him around and led him away from George. George walked

toward Eddie Ryan. Alec and Charles rushed to him.
George was breathing heavily and trying, with his right
hand, to pull a handkerchief from his back trouser pocket.

"Here," Charles said, handing him a handkerchief.

George put it on his bleeding left hand.

"I must have broken a knuckle. My left fist is split open,
look at it," he said.

"How are you, George?" Eddie asked.

"I'm all right. My goddamned hand hurts. I broke it on
his face."

"We'd better get the hell out of here fast, before those
bastards pounce on us," Alec said. "They're in a nasty
mood and there are a helluva lot more of them than us."

Several of the gang around Pfeister were looking in their
direction.

Eddie helped George put on his shirt but he kept his
eyes fixed on Pfeister's friends who were gathered around
Pfeister about twenty-five yards from where he and George
stood. A couple of lights flashed and went out, fellows were
lighting cigarettes. There was a mumble of conversation
from the other crowd.

"Let's go. George had better see a doctor about that
hand," Charles said.

He draped George's coat over his shoulders. They
walked off in the opposite direction from Pfeister's crowd.
The crowd did not call out after them.

George Raymond and Bill Pfeister had fought their
grudge fight and were now walking away from each other,
in opposite directions, with their friends. They had not
shaken hands or said one word to each other.

"Somebody light me a coffin nail," George said.

Alec lit a cigarette and put it in George's mouth.

"His own mother won't know him. I hit him with my
left until I broke my hand on his face," George said.

"Don't talk, you must be worn out," Charles said.

"I'm in good shape—except for my goddamned hand. Christ, it hurts!"

George winced.

"He hardly hit me. I have a bump over my right eye. I know I broke his nose and split his lip. Did you see his face? It looks like hamburger."

"You won, George," Charles said.

"Of course I won. I got to get this hand looked at right away. I think I'll need stitches in it."

"There's a small hospital at 49th Street and Cottage. I was taken there the night I had my stomach pumped when I almost died of bootleg liquor," Eddie Ryan said.

"Have we got enough dough?" George asked.

"We can all chip in," Eddie said.

They hurried on, and left Washington Park at 51st and Cottage Grove. Alec and Eddie took George into the small hospital. The others waited outside.

They had to wait for about fifteen minutes in a small, dreary waiting room. Then a fat, sleepy-eyed doctor showed up. He took George into the emergency room.

About forty-five minutes later, George came out with a strained smile on his tired face. His left hand was bandaged. He had broken a knuckle and had split his hand. Three stitches had been needed to sew it up.

The next day, Bill Pfeister swore out a warrant against George Raymond for assault and battery. George moved out of the Drexel Boulevard apartment and went back home with his parents on the North Side.

II

Old John Mason and Charles stayed on in the apartment. The first night after George left, Myrtle had stayed there with them but she didn't want to stay there the second night.

Eddie Ryan took her in a cab to a hotel over a store near the Garfield Boulevard El station. The hunched clerk didn't question them when they walked up the stairs to the second-floor hotel. He gave them a room. Eddie paid him five dollars, put Myrtle in her room, gave her a dollar, and told her that he'd see her the next day. Eddie left without even trying to make her.

Although Alec and George had shared her, Myrtle had refused to go further than to neck with Eddie.

"Alec wouldn't like it," she had told him although they both knew that Alec wouldn't have cared.

But Eddie had accepted Myrtle and gotten to like her. He had talked to her about books, read her a couple of stories of Guy de Maupassant in translation, and had loaned her books to read.

The hunched clerk was surprised to see Eddie leaving and refunded him two dollars and a half.

The next day, Alec and George had a conference about what to do about Myrtle. They decided that she should return to the apartment. George couldn't go there because the police kept visiting it with the warrant, and Alec had to go home early that night. They asked Eddie Ryan to take Myrtle back to the apartment.

"You can lay her," Alec said.

Alec and George had told Myrtle to let him. Even though they all joked about how she was the sweetheart of the Marines, and had gone to bed with so many men that she could hardly be excited any more, they liked her. Myrtle was lazy and sloppy and could sit for hours listening to highfalutin talk that didn't interest her.

III

Eddie Ryan recalled an incident when they had first met Myrtle. George and Alec were already laying her and Eddie wanted to.

Alec had come up to him one day and said:

"Eddie, George and I don't have any objections if you lay Myrtle. But she doesn't want to. She likes you but she doesn't want to go to bed with you."

Eddie had said nothing but he had been hurt.

"We're friends, the Three Musketeers," Alec had said.

"That's all right, Alec, I waste too much time as it is, I should be doing more writing."

Eddie was hurt, but he didn't feel any anger against Myrtle. She was "Sweetheart of the Marines" but she didn't want to sleep with him. Was there something wrong with him?

One night she did get in bed with Eddie and they had laid on the bed in the dark, French-kissing. Then she had said:

"No, I can't, no—please, don't."

It was because of this and what Alec had said that Eddie had not tried to stay with her the night before, even though he had paid for her room.

Eddie was surprised when Alec suggested that he take Myrtle back to the Drexel Boulevard apartment and lay her, if he wanted to. Alec and George must have arranged this—they were giving her away as something of a discard but they were friends, close ones, Eddie thought.

Eddie liked Myrtle; she was easy to be with. Eddie felt no need to talk every minute and he knew she liked him even if she had refused him. He had looked and hoped, and except for an awkward, not completed experience over two years ago, Eddie had only been with a few prostitutes. Almost all of these experiences remained in his memory as disquieting ugly events.

Eddie was glad to be able to go with Myrtle and to know that he would not again be refused. Instead, he would be able to have it with her and to sleep all night with a woman.

He took Myrtle back to the apartment. Twilight was about to seep over the city. They rode in a cab, not talking. Eddie was shy, but not tense or unsure. The cab shot into Washington Park. On his left, Eddie saw the big ball field. Scattered about were the small dots of white shirts.

He looked at Myrtle. She struck him as plain. She was wearing a print dress and there was a dull red in the pattern. Her legs were stretched out and her shoes were dusty and scratched. They looked large and wide.

Perhaps he should say something to her but he had nothing to say. His strongest feeling was sympathy. In a few years, what would she be? Maybe she would marry. Myrtle had no trouble in being liked by fellows. Her placidity, her acceptance of whatever situation she was in, and her ability to be quiet—these were all traits that could help her. Then, too, Myrtle could get a job as a waitress and have good times.

What would happen to her?

"Maybe I'll look for a job, in a restaurant. Restaurants always need waitresses. They come and go like the wind," she said as though she had read his mind.

"You ought to be able to do that, Myrtle. It might be easy if you go to an employment agency."

"They make you pay them for the job."

"But it can save you a lot of tramping around and looking."

"Alec says I can stay at his house a week or two."

Eddie Ryan was surprised. Alec's mother was religious,

almost fanatically so. What would Mrs. McGonigle think
if Alec brought Myrtle home? She might well think that
her only son had brought home a whore. She would be
jealous of any girl in whom Alec was interested. And
Myrtle with her easy, sloppy ways—to bring her home for
a couple of weeks could only kindle all of the jealousy in
Mrs. McGonigle.

It must have been George's idea, Eddie thought. It had
all of what George would term a "subtle irony."

Eddie paid the driver at 47th Street and Cottage Grove
Avenue. Myrtle waited outside with her battered suitcase
while Eddie went inside the drugstore to buy rubbers. He
didn't want Myrtle to become pregnant and even though
she said she couldn't after an abortion, he didn't want to
take any chances.

They walked slowly on 47th Street, and Eddie carried
her suitcase. It was beginning to get dark. The street was
noisy; quite a few people were out.

"We had some good parties and lots of fun at this
place, didn't we, Eddie?"

"Yes, we did," he answered.

A slender, dark-eyed girl with a short, tight-fitting blue
dress passed. Underneath her dress, she seemed to be all
soft and yielding flesh. Eddie wished that she were Myrtle
or that Myrtle's figure were like that girl's. But a bird in
hand, he quickly thought.

He felt adventurous. He'd heard much talk about the
difference between having an experienced girl and a whore
who got rid of you as fast as she could. He remembered
how exciting it had been to kiss Myrtle in the dark bedroom.

"That suitcase ain't too heavy, is it, Eddie?"

"No, Myrtle."

The suitcase was light; Myrtle had few belongings.

The apartment had been put in some order by Charles. He and Old John were sitting at a card table, having sandwiches and coffee. They were surprised to see Eddie and Myrtle.

"I thought you were the cops again, trying to serve George that warrant," Charles said.

"My grandmother's first cousin is the desk sergeant at the station. I spoke to him," Eddie said.

"Does that mean we'll all be arrested?" Charles joked. "Sit down, have some coffee. And, Myrtle, this palatial residence of the Raymonds hasn't been the same without you."

"Hello," said Old John Mason.

"We came back because I might as well stay here as long as I can instead of in a hotel. It's lonesome and there's nothing to do in a hotel," Myrtle said as Eddie Ryan set her suitcase down.

"There's always something to do here," Charles said. "I'll go further, there's always something to do whenever a Raymond is around."

"Where are George and Alec?" Old John asked.

"They ain't comin' tonight," Myrtle answered.

Charles' eyes grew keen with anticipation of pleasure. Eddie would be going home soon and John Mason was an old man, probably incapable of doing it. Myrtle had fallen into his lap. She was better than nothing. Sleeping with her was better than sleeping alone. He'd be able to chalk up one more, one more name of a girl in the short list of girls he'd made, a list pitifully small when compared with his brother George's.

Eddie Ryan quickly grasped what was on Charles' mind, but he didn't feel worried. Charles was George's kid brother and Eddie had absorbed much of George's attitude about him.

Eddie was amused watching how Charles looked at Myrtle.

They had coffee and talked. Myrtle said little. She was taken care of for the night, that was enough for her. And even though she had been with so many men that all novelty was gone and she rarely lost herself in strong passion, she liked it. She liked sleeping with a fellow better than she liked sleeping alone. In the same way, she liked a good breakfast and a cup of coffee more than not having breakfast.

"George is a smart young fellow and the world will know it, once he settles down," John Mason said.

"Yes, he's my best friend," Eddie said, but he wished Old John would say something complimentary about him and his future.

"He has to outgrow this business about Nietzsche," Old John went on.

"Nietzsche is someone to learn from, not to outgrow," Eddie said.

Charles looked at them, bored. Then he fixed his eyes on Myrtle. She was having coffee and toast and appeared to be quite content.

"Supermen? Who is a superman? You boys are foolish if you think you are," Old John said.

"Supermen who don't work and go around talking big. What can they do that the rest of us can't?" Charles asked in a sudden outburst of bitterness against his brother.

"Where Nietzsche isn't right, not completely so, is in his idea of the will to power. Most people are not motivated by a will to power but by a wish for security," Eddie said.

"What's wrong with that?" asked Charles.

"The hell with security," Eddie said.

His statement had no effect; he turned to John Mason.

"John, socialism might be inevitable, but it won't save mankind. Mankind can't be saved."

"As long as men go in chains under the slavery of capitalism, there'll be injustice in the world. When the workers break their chains, then all your talk, Eddie, will sound like air, and 'much ado about nothing'."

John Mason talking like this was pathetic, Eddie thought. Here he was, on his uppers. Any day the landlord would toss him, Charles, and now Myrtle out of the apartment. John had been living as he was in recent months, and failure exuded from him. He spoke more like a broken-down actor than an old Socialist.

But Eddie was not in a mood for talk as he usually was; he was marking time until he and Myrtle would occupy the big In-A-Door bed.

Myrtle left the table to go to the bathroom and the three of them lapsed into silence.

"Eddie, can we have a conference?" Charles asked. This was the phrase that George and Alec always used.

"Why not?"

Charles and Eddie went to a corner. To hide his embarrassment, Charles was overly casual as he asked:

"Have you got any rubbers?"

Eddie handed him two condoms, thinking how he was playing a trick on him.

"Thanks, Eddie, you always were a good friend."

Charles was confident.

Myrtle came out of the bathroom in a long nightgown.

"I'm sleepy and I don't want my clothes on," she said.

"I'm sleepy too. We've been going at a fast pace and everyone needs his sleep," Charles said.

They got up from the table. The dirty dishes were left on it. Several ashtrays were filled with cigarette butts, some of them stained with lipstick.

Myrtle in her nightgown affected the atmosphere.

Charles kept looking at her. She sat with her legs opened widely and her cotton nightgown curled up, exposing her thighs. Although she was plump, and her figure was too filled out, she had thin and shapely legs.

Charles was visibly affected. His eyes were fixed on her and at what she exposed. Once he mopped his brow.

Eddie was enjoying this situation—it was new and unusual for him.

Old John Mason sat in his starched shirt and feigned dignity; but he was far from unmindful of Myrtle, and the youth and sexuality which seemed to him to be bursting through her long cotton nightgown.

Old John Mason was about sixty-two and a failure in life. He had nothing. When the landlord threw them all out of the apartment, he would have no place to live. He had been living from hand to mouth and on handouts in the small Bohemian world for months. Occasionally, he went to Bughouse Square by the Newberry Library on the Near North Side and made a soapbox speech, taking up a collection of a few dollars.

The girls he saw were young enough to have been his daughters or even his granddaughters. They were free and easy, unconventional. They kissed passionately in front of him and sat in nightgowns with their legs open, carelessly revealing themselves, just as Myrtle was doing. The young fellows spoke lightly and casually of these girls. New girls came and went and usually George or some other young fellow would make them, and Old John would hear all about the conquest. He could not approach the girls himself, nor could he hope that he would ever be accepted by one of them. No one thought of Old John as a man with sexual needs. He was an old man, presumably past his prime. But Old John wanted girls. In their presence his years, his old age was a sadness that he bore. Sometimes he would lash out and condemn the girls for their immorality; but he wanted one of them, and badly. He looked

at them day after day and faced up to the blunt and un-
changeable fact that he was an old man and that never
again could he do as a young man did with girls.

Myrtle, in her nightgown, sitting with her legs spread
widely, was causing him to sweat. Sitting in his prepos-
terous dignity, Old John kept looking at her out of the
corner of his eye. He said little, and smoked a five-cent
cigar, filling the room with its smoke.

Charles sat watching Myrtle.

"I don't know why, but I'm sleepy tonight," he said,
looking at Eddie Ryan.

At just this moment, Myrtle yawned.

"You're not seeing George and Alec tonight, Eddie?"
Charles asked.

"No—I saw them."

"Do you work tomorrow?"

"It's my day off," Eddie said. He saw the disappointment on Charles' face.

"I'm sleepy," Myrtle finally said.

"Let's turn in," Eddie then said.

"Aren't you going home, Eddie?" Charles asked.

"No I'm staying here tonight," Eddie answered, looking
at Myrtle.

Charles became furious but he controlled his fury.

Eddie pulled down the big In-A-Door bed and turned
out the lights. Myrtle kissed him on the cheek.

This was the first time that Eddie Ryan had felt physical passion with the loss of breath, the excitement, the
tension, the release, and the relief.

IV

Ten days later, George Raymond and Eddie Ryan set
out for New York. On the Lincoln Highway, Eddie Ryan
saw fireflies at night for the first time in his life.